Leaves & Love

by

Rachel Cooper

The Blue Mountain Series, Book One

Cover Art by *The Wild Rose Press, Inc.*

The Wild Rose Press, Inc.
PO Box 708
Adams Basin, NY 14410-0708
Visit us at www.thewildrosepress.com

Publishing History
First Edition, 2024
Trade Paperback ISBN 978-1-5092-5651-8
Digital ISBN 978-1-5092-5652-5

The Blue Mountain Series, Book One
Published in the United States of America

Dedication

To partners who bring coffee or tea to their loved ones every morning. To Chris.

Chapter One

Jaime closed her laptop and considered ripping off all the motivational stickers. The peeling golf ball could stay. Even the Virginia sticker about lovers. Neither her favorite hobby, nor her home state deserved her frustration. It was the education themed ones that had to go. Goodbye to the cartoon apple and ruler. Goodbye to the calligraphy-style quote about teaching changing the world. Because despite loving it, teaching hadn't changed one thing about Jaime's world. Or the number of zeros attached to her student loans.

Administration had promised that the summer teaching positions were given away at random via a lottery to keep things fair. Yet, the same teachers that got them last year landed them again this year. And though Jaime had set money aside from each paycheck for the vacation months, it wasn't enough. It didn't matter that she made a decent salary, decent was all it was. And it was markedly less decent when put alongside all those red figures from not only her bachelor's degree but her masters too. Throw inflation into the mix and the fact that she was largely responsible for buying her own supplies—that she couldn't stand to see children left out during the optional ice cream on Fridays—and her savings was in rough shape.

After searching for anything beyond fast food and live-in camps, Jaime had gotten nothing but a headache and a slew of application receipt notifications. Her bangs, a bad decision two years ago that she was still trying to outgrow, draped her vision in brown. Pushing them back, she searched her couch cushions and end table for an extra bobby pin and secured her hair into a half-up do. Sitting here, reminded of the haircut she needed and the coffee she craved, was doing her no good. She needed a win. Or, at least, a pick-me-up.

"Alright then," she told herself. "Time to get up."

With no better storage space, she slid the computer underneath the couch, stood, stretched, and grabbed her purse before heading out of the apartment. A walk would help clear the screen induced brain fog.

Dogs barked from behind closed doors along the inner hall of the building, and she half-considered trekking to the library to print out dog-walking and house-sitting service offerings. Odd jobs like those were unlikely to pay the rent. However, they *might* keep her golfing the entire holiday, covering greens fees and new balls so she could use her time off to play, spending her time having fun like her students. She wished she was golfing now. In the elevator, she lined up her feet as if she were teeing off and waited for the ding.

Outside, it felt more like the end of summer than the beginning. Settled in a valley below the Blue Mountains, Roam usually escaped the worst of the heat. But lately, the humidity had been oppressive, the temperatures record-setting. The tendrils of Jaime's bangs that had already escaped the bobby pins curled. She blew upward, hoping to force her hair back and avoid the sheen of sweat before she made it down the block.

There was a coffee stand a half mile away. That would be her goal.

Jaime walked on. Houses and small apartment complexes giving way to the brick and stone buildings of downtown. She couldn't afford to live on the trendier side, where business was booming, and outdoorsy tourists stopped after a day of mountain biking and hiking. Looking for relief after too long in the sun sampling wine at any of the new wineries that bordered town. Or golfing at one of the local, premier resorts if they were wealthy. On this side of the literal train tracks, many of the faded, fifties era department store signs still hung above windows. But the doors were shut tight, and the insides empty except for maybe a cardboard box. None of these places were hiring.

Even if they were, Jaime couldn't imagine herself selling perfume from behind a counter. Or peddling milkshakes on roller skates like was popular when this area was in its heyday. Teaching was all that Jaime wanted to do. No, it wasn't the career paths her parents dreamed of—becoming a doctor, vet, lawyer, scientist (the list could go on and on)—but it was what *she* wanted. Her mother and father associated power with a paycheck. She associated it with the confidence she felt around a group of kids where, for once, she was one-hundred percent sure of herself. She knew exactly what she was doing. There, she led without ever having to second guess herself. She thrived in a classroom.

The growing sense of knowing herself—setting aside the frustration from earlier and acknowledging how much she did love teaching—doubled Jaime's pace. Without realizing it, she'd gone nearly a mile and a half. Stopping to get her bearings, she noticed a red brick corner shop with black doors and window trim, and a very small—so small that it was honestly a miracle she

3

even spotted it—*Help Wanted* sign. It was more like a *Help Wanted* sticky note, shoved into the side of the window like one of those scavenger-hunts that museums hosted to try and encourage kids to stay longer than one minute at each display.

Brass lettering above the door read "Plant Life". Whoever owned this place must have a degree in marketing from the days when it was imperative that brands sell not just a product, but a lifestyle. And although Jaime felt more than a little snarky about the place, from its modern farmhouse styling right down to its standoffish, snooty name, the idea of watering plants all day long sounded rejuvenating. Like the break that the summer holiday was intended to be. And she'd never have to worry about leaving work smelling like greasy fries.

Jaime took a deep breath and opened the door. The faint tinkling of a bell made her jump, and feeling foolish, she pinched the skin of her wrist as she adjusted to the light of the room. It wasn't that it was darker than outside. No, it was almost painfully bright. As if this shop somehow magnified and concentrated the sun with its interior, painted-white brick walls, gleaming glass vases and plant-holding orbs. The many, many leaves, like miniature mirrors, added a shimmer like a heat wave.

The air was humid with a rich smell that was too good to be described as soil, and yet, that was the closest that Jaime could come to placing the scent. The light from the windows hit the painted concrete floors in patches that were so geometric they looked like a dizzying display of freshly painted road markings. And, once adjusted to the light, everywhere there was green.

Leaves that were long, short, frayed, and bulbous cluttered every surface. This shop was a sensory wonderland, and Jaime wished there was a kid inside too, just so she could encourage them to take their pointer finger and run it along the fuzzy plant directly in front of her. She'd direct them to compare the feel of it to one of the larger, waxier looking ones.

"Can I help you?" A woman with cropped, short hair and chunky, red glasses that looked like they cost more than Jaime's car, repositioned herself on a stool and put both hands on the counter that partitioned a small area at the back of the room.

"Actually—" Jaime suddenly felt embarrassed. This wasn't the garden section of a hardware store; this was a plant *boutique*. One that apparently did well enough to afford the people who worked here designer eyewear. Why would they want a teacher whose left eye had been twitching since March and whose idea of fancy was business casual from a clearance rack at the mall?

"Are you here about the job?"

"Yes," Jaime answered before she could think twice.

"Perfect." The woman hopped down, scooted around the wooden counter where a small tablet card-reader sat above a matching white cash register, stacks of fliers and handouts beside, and headed directly to the front window.

Jaime swallowed when the woman plucked the *Help Wanted* sign from the bottom pane, not even sparing a second glance for the leftover tape on the otherwise perfectly clean windows. Not sure whether Jaime was supposed to start pleading her case or wait, she cupped her neck and dabbed at one of the floor's sunspots with her toes. "I feel I should say, I'm not well versed in plants." She straightened. "I don't live the *plant life* per say."

"Good lord, honey. None of us do." The woman threw the index-card-sign into the trash. "And you'll learn soon enough. I didn't know anything about plants, either. All people ever want is ferns anyhow—force the Boston on them—snake plants, and occasionally an orchid until they see the price. It's not hard."

"All of that went over my head." An odd combination of tension, and yet, ease warred inside Jaime. She really didn't know much of anything beyond the fourth-grade science requirements for understanding plant growth, and she couldn't pick out a snake plant if her life depended on it. But this woman felt like a seasoned teacher, one who had been around the block so many times that she no longer remembered what round she was on. There was safety in competence that others (especially children) sensed innately. Here was a woman who knew how to handle people even when they were fragile.

The woman clucked her tongue. "Don't you worry. You'll learn. Let's start with our names before we worry about all the different names for these things, though. I'm Helen."

"Jaime. Jaime Krause. Nice to meet you, Helen."

"When can you start?"

"Immediately." Jaime followed Helen who headed behind the dark, wooden counter and started opening and closing drawers in the rows of cupboards that lined the back wall. The color of their wood matched the checkout counter, all of it tasteful and likely, very expensive. That spark of apprehension flamed inside of Jaime once again, making her unsure of what to do with her hands while she waited.

"Good—" Helen looked over the top of her glasses as she thumbed through papers inside one of the drawers. "Here we are." Without looking away from what she was doing, she jerked the paper in her hand toward Jaime, shaking it until Jaime took it. Then Helen continued to thumb through the drawer some more, muttering to herself.

It was a job application. Jaime hadn't filled out a hard copy version since she was a teenager trying to get hired as a summer day-camp counselor in the mountains. Now, despite Roam's quaintness, everything was electronic. On the first page was the standard laundry list of questions. No, Jaime had never been convicted of a crime. Yes, she was a US citizen and was legally allowed to work in the state of Virginia. A state for lovers but not for teachers with a boatload of student debt.

Jaime continued to check the necessary boxes. She paused when she got to the bottom of the work history.

"What should I put if I haven't stopped working at my last job?" she asked Helen, feeling a pang of dread. This was going to be the part where Helen put the *Help Wanted* sign back in the window.

No one wanted to go through the effort of hiring only to find out that it was for two months' employment. Well, some places did, but Jaime didn't want to have to move a few hours to the beach nor end up at a resort for seasonal work. She wanted to keep her apartment and her life here—and ultimately, her real job.

"This will be a second job for you, then?"

Jaime shook her head. "No, I'm a teacher. I need a job for the summer—but just for the summer."

"So, we'd have you until—"

"Mid-August," Jaime said, hoping that Helen couldn't hear the desperation in her voice. She wanted this job; she wanted to work with Helen.

Helen looked Jaime over slowly. "What grade do you teach?"

"Fourth."

"I don't know how they recruit people to teach. What with the overcrowding in classrooms. All the behavior problems. And now the gun issues. I could never do it."

"Teaching is what I love." More than anything else in the world. Jaime didn't say that part out loud though. Helen's words had been dangerously close to her parents' when it came to being anything that wasn't the doctor they'd wanted her to become. Just like her sister. And there were only so many times that she could stand to hear that she hadn't lived up to the expectations that Gretchen had set. That what she wanted for herself wasn't right—wasn't enough.

"Finish filling out that paperwork and just leave the quit date blank."

"Okay." Jaime continued writing, signing everything Helen handed her.

Helen squinted at the application. "He probably won't look closely enough to even notice." She handed Jaime a W2 form.

"Excuse me?" Jaime wondered if there was some sort of finance person or office manager that might chastise Helen and call Jaime a bad hire decision.

"Just my son." Helen waved her hand as if that should have explained everything.

Jaime fought the urge to raise her eyebrows and waited.

"This shop is my son's," Helen said. "I'm only filling in here and there until he finds some real help. But he's been saying no to every single applicant and I'm tired of being free labor. I know you're around for just a few weeks, but I'm going to Greece next month and I'm not going to miss it on Ryan's account. You seem wonderful. I think you'll be a good addition to this place. And, at the very least, you'll allow me to make it to the Mediterranean." Helen took off her glasses and cleaned them with the hem of her shirt. "Olives and wine," she added dreamily.

"Oh." Jaime didn't know Helen, not really, but it still felt as though some of the immediate win of this job was slipping away. The fragile purchase of the best possible summer gig a little shakier without this wonderful woman to latch onto. Helen had never said, *this is my shop and I work here all the time. I'm so excited to spend the summer with you.* Jaime had assumed it anyhow.

"Ryan can be a bit of a control freak, and he comes across curmudgeonly—" Helen replaced her glasses, leaned in, and tapped a finger to her nose. "But beneath all that, he's the nicest man you'll ever meet."

Jaime nodded tightly. "Okay." She believed Helen. If this was his mother, how could he not be a nice person? No matter what, it was only two months. She could handle a difficult personality in a place as beautiful as this, knowing that she'd be back in the classroom in two months. She could already smell the dry-erase markers.

"But, Jaime dear?"

"Yes?"

"Don't tell Ryan that you're a teacher. Tell him— tell him you just got done with college and you're trying

9

to find yourself or something. He'll love that."

"Really?" Jaime had written teacher on her application's background history section. The end date glaringly empty. Her ears grew hot as she considered lying all summer long.

"No, don't actually say that. I was joking. I don't know. I guess you could tell him that you're a teacher. Though maybe... maybe suggest the standardized testing killed your passion or something. If you're a bad liar, and I hope you're not, keep it simple and insinuate that you're done with teaching."

"I'm not sure I can manage that all summer," Jaime said, her voice wavering. She was fighting the rising feeling of buyer's remorse, the one that always set in once seated in the car and staring at the receipt instead of the book, the dress, or the extra splurge at the grocery store. Five-dollars for a chocolate bar was a bit crazy— beautiful packaging or no.

"All I'm trying to say is, don't tell him that you're leaving. Make him think that you're here to stay, because if he finds out you're temporary, I don't think I'll be able to convince him to keep you through August." Helen leaned in and looked at Jaime over her glasses. "And I'm going to Corfu, Jaime."

"You're telling me to lie, then."

"Let's call it avoiding the truth."

Jaime nodded but her throat felt knotted, the sensation migrating down into her chest.

"What's his name again?"

"Ryan," Helen said. "And here. Here's a list of our current stock. I recommend researching at least a few of the bestsellers over the weekend. I'm not saying there will be a test, but knowing Ryan, there may be. You'll have to wait on him for any extra info on duties. When I'm here, all he expects is that I open the doors and help the customers check-out. Even then, half the time I end up needing to call him with questions, and he comes rushing back."

Well, Jaime would start with learning the plants, then. She glanced at the list. Every single one of these suckers would have its own flashcard by the end of the night. This job was for two months. And if she needed to treat each day like one giant, never-ending exam, then she would. She wasn't going to get screwed out of another summer job like she had with the summer teaching positions. She was grabbing hold of Plant Life and hanging on.

***

The next morning, Jaime was determined to be the first one in the shop. She turned off the podcast she'd only half listened to since running out of the apartment, and inched the car forward, ready to step on the gas as soon as the light turned green. If she got there an hour early and spritzed all the humidity-loving plants—like Helen's ferns and orchids—maybe she'd be able to convince *Ryan* that she deserved this job.

There were three parking spots behind the building that looked better suited to motorcycles than cars. Dumpsters crowded the street so that it was impossible to swing into a spot and get within the lines first try. Jaime muttered and reversed, already missing the teacher's parking section with its SUV and mini-van minded spots. Once she was well within the lines, she turned the key and sat. Hesitant to get out after rushing through morning traffic, her butt sank further into the well-worn fabric seat. She took a deep breath. This was simply another sort of student teaching experience, one where she was not only learning, but also doing.

She wouldn't lie to keep this job—just, keep certain things to herself. The urge to text her best friends, Bree and Talia, was strong. Instead, Jaime swallowed hard and got out of the car.

The back door was gray, dinged metal, inset in the red brick and shaded by the row of maples and dogwood trees that lined the other side of the fence bordering the small parking strip. The door looked the type to squeak and squeal, necessitating a shoulder to open. So it was a surprise when Jaime inserted the key Helen had given her and turning it, the heavy door opened easily and silently into a small hallway with two more gray doors on one side and a large wooden one on the other. Jaime knew from having been in the shop yesterday that the lone door at her far right led to the storefront.

Always good to know where the bathrooms were, she opened the second gray door directly across from the entry into the shopfront. A clean, white tiled bathroom, with soap that she recognized from the natural food store aisles but could never afford herself. That was that.

Jaime walked back out and put her hand on the handle of the last door, the one closest to the exit. She pushed down. No give. The handle resisted any attempt to raise or lower it, signaling that whatever was inside was something important enough to keep locked during non-business hours. She let go and stepped back.

Another deep breath and she approached the shop door on the opposite wall. It was just her here. She had time to get herself together and maybe squeeze in a few more minutes of research on her phone. Shuffle through the flash cards she'd made last night and stowed in her purse. More importantly, she had time to get her story straight in case Ryan had given her application the attention Helen swore he wouldn't.

With all the confidence she could muster, Jaime opened the door, pushing hard. It swung only a third of the way, then slammed into something. Something soft and yet hard enough to create a heavy *thwack*.

"Jesus Christ," exclaimed a deep, masculine voice. Movement on the opposite side made the door swing open another couple of inches.

Jaime quickly pulled it back to closed and held her breath, eyes wide, immediately taken back to that time she was out golfing with her dad and a man got hit in the head by a stray ball. Even half a mile away, they'd heard the *whump* of his body hitting grass. What if she'd gotten this person with the metal handle? If a small ball could cause a concussion, couldn't a doorknob? Jaime shook herself—this wasn't the green. This was just a door. Nobody was hurt. At worst, startled. She gently eased the door open again, going slow this time, her neck growing splotchy and threatening to spread the color to her cheeks.

Now, nothing blocked her path. A sliver of light shone through the crack in the doorway. Jaime nudged some more. "I am so, so sorry," she said, squeezing through the small opening. "Are you okay?"

A man leaned against the counter, rubbing his hip. Even if their meeting had been totally random—crossing each other on the street or bumping into one another in a coffee shop—Jaime still would have done a double take. He looked like he'd just stepped off the plane from the Pacific Northwest, with a flannel on, his hair longer than was currently the style, and a short beard that bordered on scruffy. He had none of the usual East Coast identifiers: short shorts (which Jaime really did appreciate), boat shoes, and sunglasses on a string around the neck.

"Well, at the very least, I guess you'll be good for security detail. Don't do that to customers, though, please." His forehead scrunched and small lines appeared to the side of his eyes, but he didn't smile.

Jaime sucked in her cheeks, embarrassment making her want to run out of Plant Life and never come back. Instead, she stood her ground, knowing she'd be texting all of this story to Bree soon, and promising herself an extra pail of balls tonight for her bravery. "Of course not. And again, I'm so sorry. Are you sure you're okay?"

"I'm fine." He looked away.

"Do you think you'll need something for the pain? I have—"

"You want to hold up fingers and force me to count those, too?" Now, he was smiling. Congratulating himself on the brilliance of his snark, no doubt.

Jaime bristled. She bought name brand and had kindly offered this man some of her very expensive, often necessary medication. Headache pills were to teachers what cigarettes were to long haul truckers. Too frequently needed, and often in short supply. This guy could cut the attitude. All she'd done was bump him with a door, there was no need to make a big deal out of it.

"I—Well—" He straightened. "Bad joke, I guess. I'm Ryan, by the way."

"I gathered." Jaime kept her voice tight. Guarded. "I'm Jaime. Your mother hired me yesterday."

"So I heard."

"Have you had time to review my application and

paperwork?" She hoped that this question sounded normal, and not like a prompt to investigate.

"Mom told me you're a teacher?"

Jaime hesitated; she traced her pointer finger with her thumb. "Well, yes."

"Do you know anything about caring for plants?"

"Why else would I be here?" Oh, the lies were really piling up now. Jaime was going to have to climb her self-made mountain of deceit every day.

Ryan narrowed his eyes—espresso dark, but lighter just around his pupils.

Jaime swallowed. "I know that ferns and orchids love humidity. They need moist soil—but not too moist or it'll encourage rot."

He crossed his arms and settled against the counter again.

She ignored his forearms, the corded muscles that tightened as he pulled them in, closer to his chest. The tightly woven, thin bracelets on his right wrist—a perfect conversation starter with any woman. "And I know that snake plants—a particular favorite at this shop—need very little watering, even less in the winter—"

"So, Mom gave you our inventory and told you to memorize her favorites, did she?" The forehead lines deepened, and the barest tug of his lips changed the way the light reflected off his beard.

"Well—" Jaime blushed, wishing she'd thought to study the plants on the list with names she couldn't pronounce. *Alocasia* had been up at the top and sounded like a spell straight out of *Harry Potter*. She wouldn't even know where to begin with taking care of it, let alone finding it in here.

"Look. You're probably a great person. But this

shop isn't just some fad for me. I'm certainly benefitting from the trendiness of houseplants—it got me out of the wedding floral market—but this is my business, my life, we're talking about. I can't have this place watched over by someone who's only here because of the same whim that brings in most of the customers. I need someone who is as committed as me."

Based on the lumberjack, forest man outfit, that person would be hard to find in Virginia. Jaime thought about making a joke that she'd come in flannel with dirt pre-caked under her fingernails tomorrow. She didn't.

"So, if this is your idea of an early-life crisis—using my shop as therapy to escape the horror of a room packed full of small children who can't spell or subtract—then you're in the wrong place and I'm sorry, but I don't have any use for you here."

Jaime corrected her posture, straightening like she was lining up her club to the ball, envisioning the angle of her swing, and bit down on the words that wanted to spill out. A wall built up around that most important part of herself.

People made fun of her for being a bubbly personality that couldn't do anything more than make fun bulletin boards about the merits of the ocean (ignoring all the plastic, the more pessimistic ones might add). Jaime wasn't going to let this man join in on the mockery and derision. Just because she didn't argue her side every time she disagreed with someone didn't mean she didn't think for herself. Just because she was never first to speak-up didn't mean that she didn't have something to say. It simply took her longer than others. Others who typically couldn't stop talking long enough to make room for those who wouldn't butt in or risk speaking over them. This was why Jaime taught; the order of a classroom was known. Her voice mattered and there, she was finally given the space to use it.

Ryan waited and Jaime found that same space—the time to find her own words—now. She swallowed. "I'm the hardest worker you'll ever meet. I'm dedicated and a fast learner. What I don't pick up right away, I'll come back to in my spare time. I need this job. And your mom made it clear you need me."

Helen had to get to Greece. And Jaime *had* to pay her rent.

"What's your availability?"

"All day, every day." But only for two months. Her ears grew hotter just thinking the unsaid words.

"Even on the weekends?" Ryan jutted his chin forward, raising his eyebrows.

Holding that expression, Helen's features shone through all the masculinity of his beard and square facial planes. He looked the same way she had when she'd peered at Jaime over the top of her glasses.

Jaime folded her own arms and tried to look equally intimidating. An impossible task when she only reached his shoulders. Maybe chin on tiptoes. She narrowed her eyes. "Especially, the weekends." With no papers to grade and no lesson plans to prep, her first weekend off from school had felt empty. And lonely.

Ryan cleared his throat into his fist, looking straight into Jaime's eyes and making her fidget. "Consider this a trial week," he said. "You're not for sure hired until I say so, and I have the rest of the week to decide. Sound fair?"

Keeping her mouth shut had gotten her this far, so Jaime didn't add that she'd already signed a W2 and documentation that guaranteed she was definitely hired. Though, that did make it possible for him to fire her. She nodded. "Got it. What do you want me to do first?"

Chapter Two

"So, how's it going?" Helen handed Jaime a latte and settled into one of the chairs behind the counter.

"It's only been three days," Jaime said, pulling one of the two stools to the customer side of the counter and sitting down. Helen had been in and out of the shop all three of those days, and Jaime had the sneaking suspicion that she'd been there to try and discourage Ryan from firing her. Though, for all his big talk on her first day, he'd been largely absent or, when he was around, silent. Watering, transplanting, and trimming, all with his earbuds in. The quiet felt luxurious the first day, odd the second, and then stifling.

The group messages with Bree and Talia had kept her going. Usually, Jaime was the quietest member. But for days, the thread had been filled with her blue bubbled texts, desperate for Bree and Talia to keep her company while she waited around for a customer to distract her. By day two, Bree had announced that she was suddenly as excited for school to resume as Jamie. The anecdotes about students were apparently a lot more entertaining than the barrage of newly acquired fun facts about plants.

Today, when Helen reached out to ask for her coffee order, Jaime had launched herself at her phone, desperate for human contact. She'd asked for a latte despite usually avoiding caffeine after mid-morning. It was worth the risk of extra anxiety.

"Well, you've made it three days longer than any of Ryan's other hires." Helen saluted Jaime. "Many customers?"

Jaime shook her head as both women glanced around the empty store. There was no wind to rustle the leaves inside—the steady drip from the plants' morning rinse long finished. Silence and the slow rotation of the industrial ceiling fans answered the question for Helen.

"Is it always like this?" Jaime asked.

"It comes in waves. Foot traffic here isn't what keeps this place afloat. The commercial jobs, plants for office spaces and such, keep the lights on. I honestly think Ryan pays for the retail space exclusively for the excuse to own his own private, little Zen Garden."

"I guess I never thought about all the plants that I see in corners of office suites and hotels and stuff."

"Oh, yeah. There's been a lot of buzz about how healthy exposure to greenery is. Especially for mental health." Helen blew the foam on her latte. "Corporations are jumping on that bandwagon as part of their *Caring-For-People* initiatives. One of Ryan's best clients is a consultant who helps companies optimize workplace performance. She always starts by increasing the amount of available natural light and then filling the buildings with plants."

"I should put some in my classroom."

Helen set down her coffee. "Did you tell Ryan about teaching this fall?"

"No."

"Good."

Jaime tightened her hands on the white paper to-go cup, feeling that the dishonesty was anything but good. The two women sat in silence another minute.

"People are a lot like plants, you know." Helen hopped off her stool and walked over to the front of the shop, stopping to turn several decorative pots holding a combination of succulents so that they faced the light from a different direction. "The television, and now our phones, are constantly trying to tell us that we need so much stuff. You can't be happy unless your car has three different reverse cameras, or your bathroom a mirror with lights that go all the way around it, unless you eat food that comes from a place with a certain logo. Yada, yada, yada. But all we really need is light, nutrients, and a place to settle." She turned and returned to the counter where Jaime still sat.

"Don't forget water," Jaime said, smiling.

Helen clapped. "See? What did I tell you? You'll be a horticulturist in no time."

"Horticulture usually refers to a more industrialized approach than ours, Mom." Ryan walked through the back door, the upper half of his body and face obscured by a large cardboard box with several plastic water collection plates balanced on top. Even with most of him hidden, Jaime would have been able to sense that it was him. Something about Ryan drew her attention. Like a stranger's face so familiar it demanded placing. Every look necessitating a double take.

"Whatever." Helen waved her hand above her head. "Hello to you too, by the way. I was simply saying that Jaime here is a quick study. I knew I chose a goodie."

Setting the coffee aside, Jaime stood, needing to do something to dispel her awkwardness. "Can I help with that?"

"No." Ryan dropped the box at the end of the counter, repositioned the water trays atop the lid and gave his mom a quick pat on the shoulder. She grabbed his hand and squeezed it.

"How'd it go?" Helen asked, her voice completely different from how she'd been speaking just moments ago. Now, it held a note of urgency, and also, sadness.

Jaime looked out the window, as if she'd spotted a potential customer, trying to give mother and son some privacy. Ryan had walked out of the shop at ten, telling Jaime to keep the place from burning down. When she asked where he was headed, he'd simply said, "Out."

"I guess how you'd expect," Ryan said.

Helen pressed, "It's official, then?"

Jaime had no idea what they were talking about. She put her hands in her pockets, and, feeling useless, followed the same path Helen had taken to the front of the store, turning a few more of the window plants. Mimicking Helen's earlier efforts to keep the plants from getting lopsided in their pursuit of sun.

Ryan sighed and Jaime turned round, trying to get a read on the man who for the last three days, had barely said hello and goodbye to her. She flushed when he shifted and his eyes met hers. Hoping he hadn't looked up and thought she was staring. It was one of those unlucky timing things. She looked, he looked.

He cleared his throat. "You'll find out as soon as I leave the room, I'm sure, so I might as well tell you myself. My divorce was finalized today. That's what Mom's talking about."

"Divorced?" Jaime croaked the word, shocked, and unable to think of anything except to say it again. She hadn't known he'd been married, much less divorced.

"Congratulations." Helen clapped her hands and half-ran, half-walked the few paces he'd put between them back to Ryan. She grabbed him round the middle, pulling him into a hug. The top of her short, graying hair stuck up above his shoulder, his shirt dimpling as she squeezed.

"It's not something to celebrate," he said.

"It absolutely is. You now have the chance to move on with your life and can stop moping around here forever. Should I get in touch with Elise? Maybe drinks tonight?"

"No." The word was a hoarse, throaty exclamation.

"The consultant," Helen said, peeping at Jaime from around Ryan and winking. "She's been sweet on Ryan forever. But *Mr.-Stick-in-the-Mud* wouldn't do anything about it until he was legally single. Right?"

He extricated himself from his mother's half hug and walked to the counter. "Have there been any customers today?"

"Doesn't matter that they've been separated for nearly two years—"

"Stop," Ryan said. "Please, Mom. Just stop."

"Well, would you let me take you out?" Helen's glasses flashed as she swiveled, facing Jaime. "Or better yet, the three of us could go. Like regular coworkers."

"I'm free to go out for drinks tonight," Jaime offered. She was definitely inserting herself right into the middle of what was obviously a contentious issue. But she'd felt so silly for dumbly repeating the word divorce, that she wanted to say, *do*, something—anything to relieve the growing hyperawareness and self-consciousness she felt around Ryan.

"It's settled then," Helen said. "We'll close early and go out for at least one drink to toast your new beginning."

"It's an end. That's all it is." Ryan grabbed his earbuds case from the cubby beside the till. "I have to load a delivery. If you need me, I'll be in the back. We can close at five today, no earlier."

A young woman wearing an army green romper and gladiator sandals walked into the shop. "Hello."

"Do you need any help?" Jaime asked her.

"Just looking"

Helen elbowed Jaime. "Thank you."

"Thank you for what?" Jaime asked.

"For being that extra little push Ryan needed to get out tonight."

Jaime swallowed. "I didn't mean to get in the middle of things."

"I'm happy you did. The boy's just reacting badly because he's terrified of becoming his father, who walked out on us when Ryan was only eight. It was an impressionable age. Then the idiot did the same thing to his next wife when Ryan was fifteen. Now, Ry's so bent on being the man his father wasn't that he's turning himself to stone. Any assistance I can get, chipping away at that armor, I'll gladly take."

"I'm sorry," Jaime said, positioning herself so that the customer would know she was welcome to come chat. To Helen, Jaime said, "Sorry not just for Ryan, but for you, too."

The customer waved her hand. "Do you know what these are, here?"

Jaime could have kissed the woman for choosing the plant that she'd forced Ryan to explain to her this morning. "That's a Peace Lily," she said, in her classroom voice—confident and breezy. "That whole table is full of them because they're very popular. And for good reason. Easy to care for, they're not only beautiful, but also great for purifying the air in whatever room you place it."

"And these?"

"I—" Jaime faltered. It looked kind of like the Peace Lily.

"That one's *anthurium*, dear," Helen said. She gave Jaime's shoulder a squeeze. "It's a little more temperamental than the *spathipyllum*—better bang for your buck with the other. Unless you've got cats. They're toxic for felines."

The woman picked up one of the Peace Lilies. "No cats." She smiled. "You sold me with easy-to-care-for," she told Jaime. After she paid and walked out of the shop, the door caught and didn't close all the way. Jaime walked to it and pushed until it clicked shut, the bells tinkling like applause.

"I told you on that first day that you came in, Ryan can come across like a grump. But he's been through a lot. His brother is much older than him and left home for college shortly after his father walked out. Then, with his dad's next divorce, he lost his second family too. Now, the woman he married. He's struggling to make sense of it."

"I think anybody would." Jaime thought of her own two parents and her older sister. She had her complaints, but they'd always been there for her. Though, maybe not Gretchen anymore. Not after last Christmas. Since then, her parents' words had more bite too, the risk of a fight a lot more pressing each visit. Even so, Jaime still saw them weekly. And after dinner every Thursday, they always told her they loved her when she went to leave.

"Yes, but most will eventually get with the program

and go with the flow. Being a rock in the ocean doesn't stop the waves from coming. It just wears the rock down to nothing."

"Ryan is the rock in this scenario?"

"Darling, Ryan is the entire cliffside."

He walked into the shop, nodding at the two women. "You need something?" he asked, pulling one of his earbuds out.

"No," Jaime said too quickly. She crossed her arms and looked out the window.

"Give the ferns one last spray, please?"

"Of course." Jaime went to fetch the misting wand and Helen followed Ryan into the back of the shop again.

Jaime misted water over the fringed leaves, admiring the complexity of the greens present in each frond. Watching the water bead, collecting until the weight became too much and it spilled down into the dark soil, she couldn't help but feel like she was about to become one of the crashing waves Helen had lamented. A seemingly dedicated worker who was actually only using this small business to bide her time until she could get back to the classroom. Another person who would simply let Ryan down.

****

After they closed the shop, Ryan double checking that Jaime had locked up, and nodding to her when it was clear she had, they got into their separate cars to drive to the restaurant Helen had chosen for their outing. The place surprised Jaime.

It wasn't the price point, nor the menu that made Jaime pause, but the atmosphere. She'd imagined Helen as the type of woman to always go for cushioned seats, with yellow, kind lighting. The sort of bar-restaurant combo that would have a host who wore a bowtie. This restaurant was all modern, industrial chic, with large wood-plank booths and metal chairs and barstools.

Their group arrived early enough that crowds weren't an issue but other days, driving through this part of downtown to get back home, Jaime had seen lines out the door. Especially on the weekends. Bree had added it to their list of places to check out on one of their bi-weekly dates.

Helen ordered a sangria and Ryan asked for a cider—another surprise, considering everything about him always seemed so hard edged. The fruity drink spoke against the clichéd stoicism that Jaime couldn't help but associate with her boss. Straight whiskey, downed in a single gulp, would have been her guess. Jaime chewed on the edge of her thumb, reading the menu and trying not to get too fixated on the prices. "I'll have the hazy IPA on tap, please?" She handed the paper drinks menu to the waiter.

"Anything to eat for y'all?" the man asked, shuffling the menu to sit beneath his small notepad, pen poised. His accent was too drawling to be Virginian, and Jaime wondered which further south state he'd come from.

"Would you be alright with just sharing starters, Jaime?" Helen looked over the rim of her glasses to make eye contact. Obviously uninterested in the waiter's home of origin. Maintaining the eye contact, she nudged Ryan who sat beside her. "Yes, no? It's still fairly early."

Ryan nodded. "You choose." He put the menu to the side, his brown eyes seeming to take in the room before fixing on a bedraggled, viney sort of plant, hanging limply off the side of the hostess's podium.

Another waiter lifted a shade on one of the front

windows opposite their table in preparation for evening, and the late evening summer sun streamed through the glass, turning Ryan's eyes to caramel.

Jaime sucked in her cheeks and looked away, squinting into the bright light eking through the borders of the still shaded windows. She began to say that appetizers sounded fine but was distracted by her phone buzzing inside her purse. It was either a phone call, or texts from her mother. Her mother liked to send messages in quick beats. As if hitting enter was so much fun that she simply had to do it as much as possible— every thought entitled to its own text. Her communication always a barraging cascade of nonstop ideas and questions.

"Excuse me for a second," Jaime said, bending over to root through her bag. It *was* her mother. "Oh." The word slipped out as she read.

"Yes?" Ryan asked, eyebrows raised.

"Nothing, sorry." Jaime hit send on her response and threw the phone back into her purse. "I'd forgotten that I'm supposed to have dinner with my parents tonight. I won't be able to stay long, is all."

"Sticking with starters is perfect, then." Helen finished telling the waiter their order and folded her hands on the table.

"Thank you," Jaime said, smiling at the waiter as he rounded up the rest of the menus.

"They live in town, then, your parents?" Helen asked.

Jaime nodded. "Mmhmm. We have dinner every Thursday, but last week, Mom had said she'd needed to cancel tonight's. I'd already marked it off my calendar by the time she changed her mind. And I've just been too scattered to remember much beyond what the difference between a bulb and seed plant is."

"You've both been making lots of changes," Helen responded, tapping the table with her middle finger. "A new job for you—" She leaned toward Ryan. "And a new lease on life for you."

"Not a good alias for divorce."

"Sure, it is. It was for me."

"Oh really?" Ryan leaned back in his chair, linking his fingers behind his head. "Where'd you go on that journey?"

"Well, mister, I maintained a career that I loved—"

"You were already a lawyer. We're talking a new lease on life, remember? What's something that you did drastically different after your divorce?"

A lawyer and a business owner. Two more people in her life that had jobs Jaime's mother would be proud to share with friends and family. Jaime watched Helen and Ryan bicker as if she was a bystander in a game of Ping-Pong, the kind of match where the two opponents considered it a professional sport, and not simply a pastime for bored teenagers or drunk adults in an unfinished basement. As their bickering went on, the edge to their voices started to make her palms sweat. She'd never been able to understand people who argued as if it were no different from any other conversation.

"I'd say single parenting was a big enough change for me." Helen was smiling but her tone was terse, her posture rigid.

Kids did that when forced to defend their answers in school too. Having raised their hands, sure of what they had to say, they never appreciated an immediate negation of their response. A slow, steady, guiding approach was always better. Jaime cleared her throat. "So, it's always been just the two of you? You never remarried, Helen?"

"Did she even date?" Ryan made a face as if to insinuate that Helen's love life was meant to be a big secret.

Jaime's throat tightened. "I'm sorry, I—"

"Don't worry, Jaime. Ryan is just being a pill. I *have* dated."

"Dated, or dating?" Ryan wouldn't let up.

"You know the answer to that."

"Jaime doesn't." Ryan's eyes locked with Jaime's at the mention of her name. The intensity that he brought to each word made her ears heat. Coming out for drinks was one thing. Getting in the middle of this? Jaime repositioned in her chair, unsure what to say.

Helen angled herself toward Ryan in the seat beside her and gave him a stern look, the kind that said, *the principal's office is next, buddy*, then shifted to face Jaime across the table again. "I'm dating a wonderful man who I've been seeing for many years now. His name is Gerald."

"Ask me if I've met him," Ryan said to Jaime. From the way his eyes traveled the length of her face, she wondered if he felt the same draw to linger with each look that she did. His gaze shifted before progressing any lower.

Helen put her hands up, not giving Jaime the chance to respond. "You haven't met him because I wasn't about to do to you what your father did. When I decide the time is right, you'll meet him."

"It's been years, Mom."

"Your father's second wife lasted years, too. You had a stepmom and a sister for years. Do you see them now? You made it very clear at the time that you couldn't handle anymore loss. With everything going on with Ashley, I've got good reason to delay an introduction."

Ashley must have been Ryan's wife. Jaime tried to keep a perfectly neutral face though all of this felt more than a little over the top. Back at the shop, during Helen's speech regarding what sounded like abandonment issues, she'd chalked Helen's story up to the motherly protectiveness same as she'd experienced at every parent-teacher conference. There was always some reason for bad behavior that made none of it the kid's fault. But listening to them now—maybe Ryan *did* have some sort of complex. Jaime tried to imagine the man who looked like he belonged in an outdoor sportsmen magazine as the weak-hearted boy his mother seemed to think he was. Impossible. The two pictures simply wouldn't blend into one recognizable person. There was the fragile son, and then there was the version of Ryan sitting across from Jaime—a man who was quiet and yet, so masculine that he made every other guy in the restaurant look too young to sit on the bar side.

Their drinks arrived with an apology for the delay, breaking the silence that had settled over the table.

"Your food should be out any minute," the waiter added, lingering as if he too sensed the tension.

The following thanks were muted. Grumbled by Ryan. But enough that the waiter felt free to leave. Maintaining the former quiet, each took a minute to try a sip of their drinks. Jaime's beer was crisp with a citrusy tang that she always chose IPAs in search of.

"Is it good?" Ryan inclined his head toward her glass.

"Yes," Jaime said, licking her lips. "You want to

try?"

"No. Thank you though." He raised his own glass. "I'll stick with this."

"How is it?" Helen asked. Her voice was back to its usual pitch and cadence, all of the defensiveness and aggression gone.

"Delicious." Ryan gave Helen a one-armed side hug and kissed her cheek. "You didn't have to do this, but I appreciate it."

Nobody mentioned the toast that had been Helen's intention in coming out, but they all agreed that the place served excellent drinks, and good food too. Jaime was sad to have to stick to only one beer, but she needed to be at her parents' house within the hour, and it was likely that once there, she'd need at least one more drink to get through the rest of the night.

****

"You're working where?" Jaime's mother called out the question from the kitchen where she'd gone for the proper salad tongs. Ed had apparently put the wrong ones on the table when he'd set out the napkins and utensils.

"At a plant boutique downtown. Plant Life," Jaime said. She balled up her napkin in her lap and wished that she'd had time to pick up a six pack so that she could have a drink without having to resort to wine. And there wouldn't be time to go to the driving range after this, which was what she really needed right now—to get into that headspace where it was just her, the club, and the ball. There, time slowed, and she was able to focus, leaning into what she was good at. Instead of being forced to juggle what different people wanted and expected. Dramas from the past.

"What made you take that job?" Jaime's dad

continued to root through the serving bowl of spaghetti, searching out meatballs while Zofia was distracted.

"Destiny," Jaime said, smiling and waiting for the mockery that was sure to follow.

"I thought that teaching was your *destiny*," Zofia said, walking back into the room. "That's why you forewent a livable wage and the chance at ever retiring."

"Please, Mom, don't do this right now." Jaime sighed and put the balled-up napkin back on the table. "It's been less than half an hour."

"How can I not mention it, when every summer it's going to be some new minimum wage, no-prospects temp-gig? You're taking a job that belongs to a teenager just so that you can continue to work far below your paygrade and ability the other nine months of the year."

"It's my choice."

"Well, it takes away *my* choice regarding retirement, because I know you're going to have to rely on me forever. Or worse, your sister." Zofia looked to the family picture on the wall of her parents on their wedding day. As if to imply that all their hard work, their move to the States from Poland, was all in vain thanks to their granddaughter's unwillingness to make the most of the opportunity. She picked her fork back up. "What happens if you ever have a medical emergency and end up owing twenty thousand out of pocket? It happens all the time. All the time."

"We've been over this. The state retirement plan available to teachers is great. And I have health insurance." Nobody was going to delay their retirement for Jaime. Especially not Gretchen who Jaime would never ask for anything but forgiveness. Even that rankled though, because there was nothing that truly demanded forgiveness. Jaime had done nothing wrong.

"I've seen the health insurance you have—the deductible is as much as our mortgage."

"Well, then why don't you just come over and fix me up when something happens, huh? You can retire and become my personal on-call nurse." Jaime's neck was hot, the heat traveling to her tell-tale ears. They were her barometer for conflict. Argument incoming? Hot ears. Always. Jaime grabbed her napkin, kneading at its edges.

"Ladies—"

"Don't you start, Ed." Zofia slammed the tongs onto the table beside the salad. Jaime's dad shoved an entire meatball into his mouth and began chewing methodically, staring at the plate in front of him.

"Can we please just eat?" Jaime felt exhausted. Between the drama with Ryan's divorce and the at-least-once-a-month family discussion about her life choices— it just had to be this dinner when it came back up—she was tired. Weary of the ritualistic fight.

"I'm just worried that you're going to end up living paycheck-to-paycheck. That you'll regret this later when you want to help put your own kids through school, or when something happens, and you need to rely on savings. Teaching is all well and good, but unless you marry—"

"Enough," Ed said. "Enough, Zofia. She's heard it before. You know I agree with you." He cut his gaze over to Jaime. "But this approach isn't helping. Jaime, you know we want the best for you, always have, and when you decide you're ready for a change, we'll support you every step of the way. You know that I've still got connections to the college. And with your masters already finished, you could always get into

34

administration."

Even the word made Jaime feel nauseous. Administration—never, ever. "Thank you. Really. If that day ever comes—" (It never would) "—I will absolutely let you know."

"That's all I ask." Her dad twisted spaghetti onto his fork.

"Tell us about the new job, then," Zofia said, gesturing for the serving bowl.

Jaime pointed between the salad and the pasta. "Which?"

"Spaghetti please." Her mom held both hands out and Jaime handed it over. "Do you work with a lot of people? Are they nice? Do you make more than minimum wage?"

Jaime rolled her eyes. "The last question was the only one you really care about, right?"

"No. I want to know everything you care to tell."

"I make one penny above minimum wage. Each one will go directly into a fast-growing retirement plan, I swear. And I work with one person, Ryan."

"He sounds handsome," Zofia said. Then, "Where'd all the meatballs go? Seriously, Ed, did you eat every single one?"

"There were maybe four in the entire bowl. How's a man to survive on one meatball?" He sang the last bit. "Living like the Great Depression's back on. I swear."

Jaime traced the lower edge of her plate with her thumb. "Why'd you say he sounds handsome? Because he's a man and I work with him?"

"Ryan from the plant boutique." Her mother leaned across the table and grabbed a meatball from Ed's plate amidst his protests. "He just does. Is he?"

Yes. "No. And don't get any ideas. He literally got divorced today. And apparently, he's got some hot shot corporate lady already on his heels. No sugar daddy for me." Jaime put her hand to her forehead and pretended to faint from the disappointment.

"Stop it. If you're not going to make any money for yourself, you'll have to marry into it."

"Yeah, and some pothead plant hippie is your best bet." Ed snorted.

"I don't think he's that kind of guy," Jaime protested, though she didn't add that he wore a lot of plaid and always had on some sort of twiney-braided bracelet—possibly even hemp, the horror!

"Trust me," Ed said, cutting a meatball in half and giving another to Zofia with a mean mugging, squinty-eyed look. "If he works in a plant nursery, he's that kind of guy."

"Too bad." Zofia sighed. "There's always Jonathan, dear. I know he'd love to see you. As soon as you say the word, I'll drop a hint to Beth and she'll have him on the doorstep, flowers in hand, faster than you can blink. An anesthesiologist," she murmured dreamily.

"Watch out, Dad," Jaime said, raising her eyebrows and making a thin-lipped, nervous face.

"She used to talk about me like that before I retired too, you know."

"Back in the good old days." Zofia laughed. She pretended to lunge for another meatball from his plate.

They avoided the subject of Gretchen, managing to skirt even the usual comparisons between the two sisters: the successful and the not. The one who had supposedly been sabotaged by the other, apparently, all because of a jealousy that Jaime didn't feel. She didn't want

Gretchen's life as a surgeon, and the rest of Gretchen's life—especially Brody—held just as little interest beyond well wishes and Jaime's hope that Gretchen really was happy.

After dinner, when it was time for Jaime to leave, her mother followed her to the door. "Jaime dear, I'm serious about Jonathan. He got called into the ER the other day at work and he asked me about you. He managed to sneak in a question about whether you were still single."

"What did you tell him?"

"The truth. And then I gave him your new number."

"You didn't."

"I absolutely did. And when he calls, if he hasn't already, promise me you'll give him a chance."

"Mom—"

"I won't say anything else about the job. All I'm asking is that you give him a chance. Please?"

"I'll think about it."

"I love you, baby."

"I love you, too." Jaime walked out of the house and got into her car. After turning the ignition, but before she shifted out of Park, she double checked her phone to make sure that Jonathan hadn't messaged or reached out. Nothing yet. She took three deep breaths. If he called, she was allowed to say *No*. If he messaged, she was strong enough to stand up for herself. He was her ex. He didn't control her. And neither did her mother.

Chapter Three

There was an odd, hushed tone to working on the weekend that Jaime had forgotten since her last job in retail a couple years ago. Fewer drivers on the road meant an easier commute without the normal cacophony of honking, buzzing music, or phone calls audible from the inside of passing cars. The lack of traffic meant gray squirrels scampering across the street with abandon. Even the odd deer showing up on the side of the road before the day fully set in and forced them to take cover. The quiet, peripheral movement gave the morning a special feeling that made Jaime slightly self-conscious as she walked into the shop.

The world felt alert and focused on her.

Ryan was on the phone and gave the barest hint of a nod as Jaime stepped through the back shop door. She dropped her bag behind the counter, giving him as much space as she could without looking like a jerk, and went straight for the hose. The length of it was looped neatly around a winding rack and Jaime gave the line a few tugs and headed for the tropic-variety plants. The ferns were always her first stop.

Maybe because it was one of the few names she'd already known before starting—though she couldn't begin to identify the many different varieties Ryan had—or maybe just because it made her feel like she really was immersed in some sort of jungle—but they were her favorites. She savored the first minutes of the day misting them and checking the soil. They were the only plants that Ryan allowed her to water from the top. Everything else had to be watered from the bottom to avoid rot or disease.

After the watering was finished, she'd check the shelves and any pots for dust, then prepare to man the phone and counter. She wasn't yet trusted to help with any plant care beyond simple tasks. Ryan handled everything else, still spending most of his days in the back, out of sight.

Whoever had called this morning was either placing a very large order, or already had, and was now struggling to take care of everything they'd bought. With a look of concentration, his jaw set and his hand flexing in and out of a fist, Ryan answered question after question, using Latin names that made it difficult for Jaime to track the conversation. With half an ear, she ran a finger along the sides of the ceramic succulent containers, checking to make sure that their rock bases looked neat.

In the week that Jaime had worked, the cacti seemed to be the most popular plants with customers, but she didn't understand the appeal. There were other plants, like the snake plant, and even a rubber tree, that could resist a black thumb without the potential for harm should any child or pet accidentally bump the plant or touch it, drawn in by the deceptively fuzzy look of many of the small prickles.

Ryan sighed as he hung up. "I'm going to move the *ravenea* to the front, and then I need to work on the inventory plan for buying next week." He continued looking down at the phone. "Do you need anything before I get busy?"

"Is there something you want me doing?" Jaime asked, making her way to the back wall to begin respooling the hose. The shop was due to open in five minutes.

"Helping customers, and I'd be grateful if you could take over the phone. Unless there's a lot of questions, then come find me."

It wasn't a surprising answer. Jaime didn't know much about the plants, though she did think that she was catching on quickly. That didn't mean it didn't sting, suddenly being the weakest link at work. People came to her for help at school, for ideas about how to handle difficult behavioral issues as well as for the best book recommendations. Summer jobs in the past had been an exercise in patience, not knowledge.

"Of course." Jaime swallowed her pride and went for the broom on the hook just beyond the hose.

Turning back round, she nearly ran into Ryan as he hefted a huge palm-looking plant onto the dolly. She waited, taking one step back to give him more space. As he finagled the pot into the perfect center of the dolly's shelf, Jaime took a moment to look at the table that was closest to the counter.

"What's this one?" she asked, pointing to a broad, circular leaved plant with white splotchy dots on the top side and a reddish bottom. Like the peek-a-boo-red under-heel of the plant world.

"Which?" Ryan set the palm back down, and without his usual groans and grumbles, squeezed past the leafy fronds to join her at the table.

"This one," Jaime said, pointing to the plant so beautiful, so unique, it didn't look real. It belonged in the

40

world of the Lorax, or some other Seuss book.

Ryan smiled. "*Begonia corallina*, or the angel wing begonia. It's one of the cane varieties versus the waxy. Popular—but I like it."

Jaime lifted the pot and inspected it. "I don't know how I missed this before."

"We were out, I brought this one in from the back room. They go fast."

"I can see why."

"You want it?"

She clutched the base of the small white pot. "For real?"

"I wouldn't have said it if I wasn't serious."

She didn't dare tempt fate by further questioning the display of heart that Helen swore he had. "I'd love to have it."

"Check the price tag and I'll ring you up."

Jaime nearly dropped the plant. "I—" Her cheeks heated, and her pulse became heavy in her throat. Of course, he wasn't just giving her one of his beloved plants.

"I'm kidding." Ryan grinned. "It's obviously yours."

She narrowed her eyes, distrusting.

"I promise. Besides, plants belong with people who will love them. This one will be lucky to go home with you."

"You're a jerk, you know that?" Jaime's face still felt hot, but she brought the plant closer to her, guarding it from any further jokes that would make her question whether she understood him. Ryan was infuriating.

"So I've been told," he said.

"Not by me," a woman's voice called from the front

of the shop, accompanied by the tinkling of the doorbell.

Jaime hadn't realized the door was open. She figured that it would stay locked until the minute that the open hours began—like every other self-respecting establishment that both depended on customers, and yet, loathed them.

"Elise," Ryan said, brushing his hands on his jeans and stepping round the palm once again. But this time, to get to the woman just beyond Jaime's vision.

The woman, Elise apparently, had a voice that sounded confident, regal even. Like she was used to dealing with people and certain that whatever she wanted would happen. Jaime walked up to the dolly and grabbed the handle. The last thing she needed was to disrupt the sudden overture Ryan seemed to be making by dumping one of his plants by accident. She applied some pressure to the handle without the intention of hiking the tree up or moving it. Still, the little force she used did nothing to move it by even a fraction. The thing had to be a hundred pounds. Trying to force away the image of Ryan's arms as he strained to move the palm initially, she peeked past the fronds.

The woman's smile was focused on Ryan, her red lipstick appearing to be the only makeup she wore. So, either she'd taken Vogue's Parisienne beauty tips to heart or, was very sneaky with her blush and eye makeup. Jaime hoped it was the latter and that her foundation was simply expensive and therefore invisible, because no one should be allowed to be this gorgeous unless they were a movie star. The woman wore a chambray button down effortlessly tucked into a pair of green belted chino shorts with designer sandals. Sunglasses far out of Jaime's price range pushed up atop her long honey-colored hair. Elise pushed a wavy tendril behind her ear and then reached out for Ryan's arm, nudging him.

"You said you'd have some figures for me by the end of the week," she said, letting the hand drop, though not after a significant stall on his forearm.

His voice was nonchalant. "I emailed them yesterday evening."

"You encouraged me not to check my email when I was off work."

Jaime could smell her perfume—light and floral—it was as perfect as the rest of the woman. The woman that Helen had mentioned, the corporate one that kept this place afloat. The woman that Helen wanted Ryan to date.

Ryan lifted one of the dangling stems from a String of Pearl plant, inspecting the underside. "I think everyone's personal time should be protected."

"What about yours?"

"It's different for me. This is what I—"

"Ahem." Jaime cleared her throat. Interrupting felt rude, but she also didn't want to get caught watching them. And she needed them to remember she was still here. And maybe, a part of her didn't like this beautiful woman's claim over Ryan. "Did you want me to move these?" she asked, making her voice small to compensate for the interruption.

"No." Ryan started toward her "Don't. You might hurt yourself. They're heavy as—" He looked from Jaime to the movie star.

"As?" The woman's smile widened.

"There's a schoolteacher working here now—language matters." Ryan jerked his head in Jaime's direction. "Jaime, meet Elise, our best customer. Elise, meet Jaime, the new hire."

Jaime walked out from around the plants toward the two.

"So, this is your summer school gig, then?" Elise asked, extending her hand.

Jaime's breath caught in her chest as she met Elise's grasp; the movement suddenly mechanical and forced. A minute passed. Their handshake outlasting normal time limits and becoming awkward. Elise raised her eyebrows and Jaime swallowed. Could she bring herself to say the full-out lie versus skirting the issue? Could Ryan see that she'd stopped breathing and that her answer was quickly becoming overdue? "It was time for a change." Jaime's voice squeaked as she spoke.

"If you start to miss it, you should begin organizing classes here." Elise squeezed her hand, quick and tight, then dropped it. "I keep trying to tell Ryan that he's missing a huge opportunity, not hosting workshops." She assessed Jaime as if she were the final say on all hires and business decisions. "Or better yet, weekend wine nights."

Jaime managed a watery smile. "That would be good."

"Don't feel pressured. Classes are not on the agenda for this place anytime soon," Ryan said.

"Well, when she starts to miss it—"

"Relentless." Ryan shook his head. "I'll rescue you, Jaime. Can you move that cart with the herbs outside? Leave them right by the window."

Rescue was a tricky word. Although Jaime was relieved to be given an out from the conversation, her heart remained heavy as she waved. A quick, queenly wrist wag of a goodbye at Ryan's soon-to-be-girlfriend.

A woman who could be in partnership and not lose herself to whatever he wanted because she was confident. Because Elise likely didn't live her life low-key anxious all the time. Probably never felt afraid to stand up for the things that she wanted, be it her job or anything else. All while smelling like a combination of flowers and champagne. Jaime resisted the urge to pull the top of her own shirt up to assess the state of her body odor and whether her cheap men's deodorant (it always worked better) was still doing its job. She wasn't the type to sparkle unless she was doing what she loved, and that was still a few months, and many lies, away.

Her phone buzzed in her pocket as she stepped out the shop door. She didn't even have to look to know who it was. Still early, it had already been that kind of day. Of course, he would choose to message on a Saturday morning.

The text was long enough that she couldn't read its entirety from the notification. Jaime put her phone back down and went on with her day, trying to ignore Ryan and Elise as much as she tried to ignore the dread that Jonathan's text had filled her with. She'd have to respond to him soon. If she didn't, he'd read into her silence.

Ryan walked into the back of the shop and came back out with a box. Balanced under one arm, he opened the shop door with the other, ushering Elise out to her car.

Jaime couldn't understand the spike of irritation she felt when they left the shop together. Who Ryan was interested in was none of her business. Yet, she couldn't help but want to shout, *not her. Not her!* When Ryan returned, she busied herself, avoiding looking at him for fear of those feelings expressing themselves on her face.

Ryan wasn't supposed to be anything to her. Just a temporary boss. Worse, a temporary boss who didn't know he was temporary.

Jaime took care of all her chores until there wasn't anything left to do but settle herself behind the counter to eat lunch. She pulled her phone back out. Nobody but Jonathan had texted. Opening his thread, the panel of blue highlighted words was still overwhelming. She saw it like a great heavy block. A weight that would take time to fully address. Just in case her read receipts were on, she clicked to mark it unread again and exited the window. When she picked up her sandwich, half the bread had gone soggy from the jelly. Jaime grimaced and took a bite.

"Isn't peanut butter banned in most schools?" Ryan banged the door behind him as he walked back into the shop front from the side, hall door.

She slid her phone away from her, darkening the screen. "I never brought it to school," she said. She shrugged, refusing to let Ryan get to her. "It's the most affordable protein option there is."

He stopped. "Do you need a pay advance?"

Jaime's cheeks colored. Yes. "No."

He pulled himself fully upright and brought a hand to the back of his neck before blowing out a breath. "I don't know how to say this without being accused of being a jerk again." He gave Jaime a pointed look. "Please just say if Friday's paycheck needs to come now."

She sucked in her still hot cheeks and bit down on the fleshy insides, considering. Her account wasn't in the red, yet the green was such a minuscule number that it was constantly on her mind, a fly buzzing her every few seconds as she tried to go about her day. But Ryan had treated her like she was that same annoying fly all of last week. She wasn't going to let that dynamic continue if she could help it.

He cleared his throat. "Nobody should have to eat peanut butter every day. It's an insult to what lunches could be."

This was the in for a joke that she had needed. They needed to lighten the air, something to diffuse the tension she felt whenever he was near. It was the way that he looked at her. The way that she couldn't help but watch him. She waved the sandwich around. "You're not allergic are you?" Jaime smiled and took another bite. Deciding to enjoy it until it was off limits again when the teachers went back to school for prep work on the fifteenth of August. The first day of school only a week after that. So, she had until then. For peanut butter. And for this job.

Ryan grabbed his throat. "Sorry," he said with a garbled voice. "It's hard to talk through the swelling."

Jaime picked up a pen from the counter and threw it at him. "Too far. Too far."

He gagged, staggering backward.

She maintained eye contact, chewing aggressively.

"Tell my mother that the shop's hers." Ryan mock stumbled into the back door.

"Not on your actual life," Jaime said. She picked the sandwich back up. "From the way she puts it, that'd be worse than the news that you were gone."

"Well, then you better start actually learning how to take care of my plants, because if you kill even a single one, I'll haunt you forever."

Jaime set her food down and swallowed a sip of

water. "Two things. The whole 'you dying thing' is fun, but *do* you have a first-aid kit or AED in here? Secondly, I have been trying to learn about all your leafy babies. What would you like to know about the horticultural array in front of you?"

"The first aid kit is in the cabinet just below you in the clear plastic tub. I check it and restock it once a quarter—mostly because it's only ever me who needs it." Ryan held up his hands and inspected them.

Jaime noticed for the first time several faint scars, and a large one running in a zigzag down his left pointer finger. "No AED?"

He shrugged. "I should probably get one, but no. There's no federal requirement that we have one, and Virginia only forces gyms and anywhere there're adults exercising to have one." He walked past the counter to the window. "If Grandpa ever keels over in here, you call 9-1-1, and if I'm around, I'll run to the bank across the way—they'll have one. I assume you've got First Aid and CPR training because of the school-thing, yeah?"

The school-thing. As if it were some sort of cardigan she shrugged in and out of like no big deal. "Yeah," Jaime said, her voice cooled and her interest in saving the customers considerably smaller. "I do."

"That's good." Ryan rubbed the back of his head, mussing his hair as he looked around the shop. "Well—"

"Well." Jaime picked up the apple that she'd brought and bit down hard, not minding that the crunch of it was going to make whatever he had to say harder to hear.

"If you need me, I'll be in the back. Monday afternoons are usually my ordering days—it'll be nice to do it without any interruptions today. Unless you need something."

"I won't." Jaime took another bite.

"Well, if you do."

She swallowed. "I'll be fine. We've only had a handful of customers this morning, anyhow. And the mornings are usually busier, it seems."

"True." He stalled.

Jaime put down the half-eaten apple. It wobbled precariously on the counter. "Do *you* need something?"

He hesitated, lingering another minute. "No. Guess not." Then headed for the back door. "Find me if you need me. You'll know where I am."

Jaime waited for the click and then looked to the door. Ryan was a hard man to peg. After last week, she'd have described him as the sort of person who had maybe two friends and a partner whom he talked to and let loose with, leaving everyone else with the RBF and gruff voice that basically said, *I'm an introvert who grew up rich enough to never have to learn to talk to people.* But there was an undercurrent of kindness that sometimes surfaced, making the dickish tendencies seem secondary to something else. Like the kid who was bullying not because they enjoyed it, but because it made the bullying they received at home somehow more bearable.

And at some point this week, things had shifted. It was now her who was keeping their conversations standoffish and stilted. Jaime snapped the cover of her glass container into place. The last couple days at work, Ryan seemed eager to try to talk. Not so much the bully anymore, but the shy kid who decided to be friends by occasionally pulling out a new piece of artwork to show off, edging it further into Jaime's vision without saying anything. Ryan had been doing the same but with plants. *Have you looked into the care instructions for a peacock calathea? It's here because it can't tolerate direct sun from the windows.*

She slipped her lunch bag back into the corner that she'd claimed as her de facto cubby and closed the cabinet door that hid her purse and other belongings. After a second of sitting alone with her breath, she bent over and opened the door again, rifling through her bag until she found the crumpled package of peppermint gum.

A customer walked in who looked so much like Jonathan that Jaime stood bolt upright behind the counter, practically jumping and nearly shouting that she would get to his text message, she'd simply been busy. Not to be angry with her, she'd been busy at work. Please don't shout.

But it wasn't Jonathan.

The man *could* have been his twin, though. The same brown hair, darker than her own, cleft chin, and thin, runner's legs. Good thing her usual hesitance had saved her from embarrassing herself with the misplaced apology. The speech Jonathan would have wanted to explain why she'd ignored him.

"Hello," she said instead, a beat too late, edging herself back onto the stool as conspicuously as possible. She probably looked ridiculous to this guy, jumping up at the tinkling of a bell like some historical maid.

"Hey," he said, giving her a once over that made Jaime want to bring her knees to her chest. His eyes fanned over her body slow, without any of the social propriety that should make him try to hide his interest. Or his gall.

"Can I help you?" she asked in her most authoritative, this-isn't-my-first-day-of-school voice.

"Yeah." He grabbed his lower lip, twisting it between his thumb and index finger, looking around the shop. "My girlfriend is into plants. I just need something that's not going to get too big and won't die in the next few weeks. But I need it to be pretty. Not the usual leafy green shit."

Not the usual leafy green shit; got it. Jaime slid back off the stool and pinched the top of her shirt, pulling it upward so that even the hint of cleavage would be out of the question. As she surveyed the room, she suddenly felt defensive for the plants. They were living, breathing organisms, and none of them deserved to go home with a guy that didn't mind assaulting a woman with his eyeballs while also shopping for his girlfriend. Which one did she like the least?

Jaime stopped in front of the orchids but didn't allow her gaze to settle—she didn't want the douchebag customer to think she had paused here, contemplating whether these would make a great gift. Before she started to point him toward the succulents, still her least favorite, she caught sight of her body posture in the reflection of the window. Arms folded and rigid like Ryan's often were. The realization of why Ryan was so standoffish, why he acted like he didn't actually want a successful business, flooded through Jaime. He came into work every day with the mission of taking care of these plants: protection being part of that. And last week, she'd been one of the people he was protecting them from.

She breezed past the orchids. "Follow me," she said, heading straight for the table full of stickers and pointies. "Succulents are all—" (she let the *all* drag on her tongue)

"—the rage. Your girlfriend would love one of these." Jaime pointed at a cactus then held up one of the largest of the air plant glass orbs, filled with green tentacle-like plants, perched atop crushed rock, ornamented by smooth stones.

The guy reached out, checked the price, then put his hand atop Jaime's, applying pressure to guide the glass sphere back to the table. "How much are the smaller ones?"

As Jaime pulled away, his touch turned to a grasp, closing around her wrist.

She twisted. Breaking the contact. Bringing her hand to her chest and holding it there. "The smaller ones are cheaper." Jaime was a smooth-things-over and avoidance-oriented person until the last minute. And then, when peace wasn't an available option, ignoring the problem an unaffordable risk, she became a fighter. She could feel the anger clenching that cord deep inside herself now. But snapping that cord into action wasn't allowed in customer service. This was a business after all, not the playground. Nor did Jaime want this to progress to that point. She picked up one of the fist-sized teardrop air plant holders. "Fifteen for these."

The man held his hand out for it. Trying to force Jaime to come closer. "It's cute—" He edged forward. "Like you. You work here alone?"

"No." Jaime glanced to the back. "My coworker should be out any minute. If you have any questions, he'd be glad to answer them." Heavy emphasis on the *he* of her coworker. It shouldn't be necessary, but Jaime wasn't above using Ryan's maleness to force this guy to back off. "Or do you just want to go with this one?" She held the air plant higher, as if to help the man see it better.

She didn't move, refusing that still outstretched hand.

The light bounced off its curved edge and created a prism on the floor.

"Sure, I'll take it. But it's for my sister. I don't know why I do that. Lying about a girlfriend—I guess I just wanted to impress you."

"No need." Jaime took a step back, toward the cash register, where she could put the counter between her and this guy.

"Don't be like that. I'm just trying to make nice," he said, following as she got closer to her barrier goal. "Aren't customers allowed to be friendly?"

Once she made it behind the counter, she felt safe again. "I have a boyfriend." The lie was easy enough, but it spurred her to look toward the hall door to see if Ryan might have heard. The look was a mistake.

The man moved quickly. When Jaime turned around, he was right in her face, pushing her into the till and forcing her to lean back. His breath smelled of stale smoke and department store cologne. This close, Jaime could see that he had gingivitis. He barricaded her against the counter, craning his neck as if to peer down Jaime's top. She felt paralyzed, every cell in her body screaming *danger! Danger!*

A grin. Nasty and presumptive. "He can't be that great, leaving you here alone all day, where—"

"He doesn't." Ryan's voice splintered the air. An ax cutting through this awful moment. The customer jumping back like kindling being hacked from a log. Jaime sagged.

"Oh." The man suddenly had interest in everything except Jaime's chest. His eyes roamed the back area behind the counter like he'd somehow woken up from a momentary fugue on the wrong side of the customer and staff member divide. He shuffled backward apologetically, his demeanor signaling that his uncomfortable closeness to Jaime had simply been part of the same terrible accident that had landed him in the employees-only zone.

Jaime crossed her arms over her chest, both to hide her trembling and to shore up any cracks in her defenses, surprised as she'd been by the way he'd rushed her. She made her eyes bore into the man; her glare so intense that he'd feel it even if he was now only staring at his toes.

"It's time for you to leave," Ryan said.

He put himself between her and the customer then strode forward, forcing the guy to stumble. The man tripped as Ryan continued to pressure him toward the exit. Bearing down, an avalanche of palpable anger. In his scramble to leave, the man fumbled the door, knocking into the glass.

Once he was upright, and one foot out the door, Ryan grabbed his arm, fingers digging into the flimsy, classic rock tee shirt sleeve. "You're not welcome back ever again. I have your face on camera, and I'll be circulating the image around to all the local businesses. They'll know to watch out for you."

The door slammed and Ryan breathed out hard. Engaged the lock which *thunked* into place. The most comforting sound Jaime had ever heard.

"Are you okay?" Ryan's features were tight. Her adrenaline screamed that Jaime should run from him too. From those narrowed eyes. The line going between his eyebrows. Stark and angry. Reasons to get away. Or fight if necessary.

She needed to get her anxiety under control.

"Nothing happened," Jaime said. Yet her voice shook, belying the words. "Not really."

"That wasn't nothing. It was far from nothing."

She took a deep breath. "If it had gone any further, I would have done something about it. This isn't the first time I've dealt with something like this." Nor would it be the last unless society dramatically reordered its expectations and allowances overnight.

Ryan closed his eyes, his lips thinning. "I'm sorry to hear that."

"I'm okay," Jaime reiterated. Still, the encounter played at her nerves like the jittery feeling of too much caffeine. She hadn't realized how vulnerable she could become in such a short space of time. Alone in a service position.

"I'll stay out here for the rest of the day." Ryan double-checked the lock on the door. "And I'll make sure I'm in the front with you more often from here on out. If you need—want—to leave early today, you should." He winced. "This is me trying to say that I think you should. That I don't think that was nothing."

"I'm okay." Jaime concentrated on keeping the tears at bay. The ebb of adrenaline felt hormonal. An involuntary switchboard of emotions all turning the dials to crying. Crying would only prove Ryan right.

Right about the fact that although nothing had technically happened, her body was busy registering the memory as trauma.

Ryan tested the door one more time, then walked over to where Jaime was still braced against the counter, the till still at her back. Hand outheld, he said, "You look like you need to sit down. C'mon, I'll walk you."

Jaime's own hand trembled in his as she let him

guide her the few steps. His grip firm but gentle, the callouses on his palm a whisper against her skin. "Do we need that first aid kit?" he asked. "Or the doctor?"

"No, really. I'm fine."

Ryan took a step back and knelt down, looking up at her. "You're not going to pass out on me are you? You look really pale."

Jaime shook her head. "I think—" She closed her eyes, pressing them with the heels of her palms. "I think I'd like a minute alone, if that's okay."

"I'll grab some catalogs from the back and then I'll be right back out."

Jaime opened her eyes when no sounds of movement occurred. Ryan still crouched a foot away. The comedown of it all unmoored her, and she felt as if she was floating despite being planted firmly on the stool behind the cash register. "I'm good," she said grabbing either side of her seat. "I promise."

"I'll be right back."

Promises aside, there was enough residual panic to remain hyper-focused, the shop's colors and lights overwhelming, every sound sharper. The quick clip of Ryan's footsteps walking down the back hallway, the drip of the hanging plants, the murmur of the air conditioning and the flap of loose papers on the back counter. Jaime reached for her phone. A habit that reinstated some normalcy.

The notification for Jonathan's unread text still glared red, and she tried to ignore it as she messaged Bree about what had happened. There was no immediate response. Work must be busy, but her best friend was the only person Jaime really wanted to talk to right now. She waited an extra minute, then clicked into the only text there was to read.

Jonathan wrote that he'd been reviewing a lot of his life choices lately, and the decision to let Jaime get away had been chief among them. Could they meet for dinner?

Jaime set the phone back down and chewed the edge of her thumbnail, her shakiness making her bump her nail against the groove of her teeth. Ineffective against the tides of her anxiety. She could almost hear the plants exhaling.

"Well," she asked them, needing to speak if only to hear something beyond the suggestive silence, the wait for whatever was coming for her next. "What should I do? Should I give him a second chance?"

"If you're talking about the asshole from earlier, then absolutely not." Ryan set a cup of tea down in front of her. Catalogs rested snugly beneath his arm, cinching his shirt around the bulge of his bicep. "I hope you like mint. It's all I have." He looked to the door again. "One more trip to the back. Then I'll be up here to stay." He ducked once more into the hallway.

Steam unfurled from the blue clay mug, the smell of peppermint spicing the air. The sound of Ryan shuffling things combined comfortingly with the click of the fans, circling like clock arms. Jaime breathed in the steam and looked at her phone. Saying yes to Jonathan would make her mother happy, and in this moment, what he'd asked for felt like an opportunity that sounded a lot like safety. Stability. A way to avoid the internal churn and sense of danger that was making her want to dive face first into the tea in front of her.

Jaime sent her reply—one word for his many.

Chapter Four

Jaime had gone back and forth on her decision about agreeing to meet up with Jonathan. Ultimately though, they'd set a time and place and she'd said little more than, *sounds good*. Maybe it was the desire to make her mother happy, because her mother's disappointment was as hurtful as it was frustrating. Or maybe it was that Jaime sometimes did want partnership. Companionship. Not just after moments like what had happened at the shop. No, long before that day, Jaime had been lonely. Eating dinner by herself most evenings, reaching for her phone for any conversation. The need for a television simply because she craved another voice. Friday nights were especially quiet. Most school weeks, that was a blessing, and yet. And yet.

She checked herself in the mirror by the front door and smoothed her eyebrows with her thumbs. It was only lunch, so, possibly, not a *real* date. Jaime hadn't committed herself to anything absolute. And neither had Jonathan expressly labeled their lunch. Maybe he would let her lead, now that she'd proven she could live on her own. That she was independent. This meeting could potentially be as simple as a couple friends meeting up after a long time apart. Jaime grabbed her keys and then stepped out the door.

The drive to the restaurant was faster than she'd hoped, Sunday's traffic minimal. Where she'd intended to arrive exactly on time, she managed to pull into the parking lot five minutes early. Would Jonathan read that as excitement? Was she excited?

She and Jonathan had begun dating during their junior year of high school. When they left for college, both initially majoring in biology to pursue medicine, Jaime was sure that they would graduate still a couple, maybe enduring long distance during med school or residency, marry several years later, and then have children when the time was right. Growing old with an album full of photos that complemented their picture-perfect prom portrait.

It was when she was just before graduate school that she'd ruined things. Dates had begun to have a claustrophobic quality that all Jaime's friends laughed off when she described it. Except Bree. Bree had been the one to wait as Jaime explained how she found herself zoning out when Jonathan talked and daydreaming about living on her own—and in her darkest moments, with someone else. How despite the sudden reversal of postgraduate plans, pursuing a masters in education instead of med school, her life had still begun to feel more like a movie that she was being forced to watch than her own lived experience. One where her clothes were up for debate, her expressions and tone of voice something to be commented on and corrected, and where she would be given her lines if she strayed too far from the plot.

When Mom had called Jaime at the house she shared with Bree, Talia, and two other friends, Zofia had been giggly and tipsy from the prematurely popped champagne, eager to spill that Jonathan had asked Ed's permission to propose. At a point where Jaime was supposed to be beside herself with joy, she only felt dread. It was already as though her life was characterized by the marriage—by Jonathan—instead of her own dreams and actions. The very next day, after keeping both Bree and Talia up for most of the night, she broke it off before Jonathan could ask the question. For herself, and for him.

That's when the issue of Jaime's switch to teaching became an issue at all. It was the easier stand-in for her mom's disappointment over never sharing grandchildren with one of her best friends. A best friend who'd everybody assumed would be Jaime's mother-in-law.

Teaching was now her mother's favorite punching bag for the rage of missing out on the wedding that she'd already started planning. It was easier to direct all the frustration to the questions and ridicule that would come to redefine Jaime's relationship with her family. Not only had she surprised everyone by switching career tracks without asking permission, but she'd also closed the door on marrying a future doctor. And without him, how would Jaime afford the life her grandparents had envisioned for them all when they'd fled to the country of opportunity? Live in the style of house that her mother deemed appropriate? Afford the family vacations alongside the student loans and cost of living? Without Jonathan, dependent only on the career of her choice, Jaime couldn't.

She checked the time on her phone and got out of the car, heavy with the memories of the days after the breakup and the continued fallout. She knew that her mom and his were still close, despite the drama, but she didn't know if they still considered each other best friends. Mentions of Jonathan or his family had become off-limits.

Thankfully, she saw him before he saw her through the window. Jonathan had chosen a table at the very front of the restaurant. She approached from the opposite side that he faced and took slower steps, trying to measure up the man he'd become these last six years before he noticed her outside. He kept his hair shorter now, the sides practically buzzed as seemed to be the style for all men lately. No facial hair, which accentuated the changes in his face after another backward glance once she'd passed him by. He'd filled out, with more defined cheeks and a few extra lines that took him from the boy she'd known to the man he'd become. Jonathan had always garnered extra looks, but now, if he were to subject himself to online dating, every swipe would be to the right. It didn't seem possible that he was still single.

His looks aren't everything, Jaime told herself. Remember what it was like, being with him. *Remember who you had to become.* Someone else entirely, his version of her. She grabbed the handle of the main door and pulled.

As soon as she was inside, Jonathan rose from his seat and waved, beckoning her over to the table. His impish smile was identical to the one from her memories, and though Jaime was glad for the familiarity of it, the sameness made all the hurt that she'd caused sting once again. Shame mixed with happiness as she accepted the hug that he offered in greeting.

"Hi," Jaime said into his shoulder, suddenly shy. He smelled like heavy cologne. Citrus notes piercing the back of her sinuses, making her nose tickle.

"Hello, you." Jonathan stepped back and held his

arms to the side of her, fingertips brushing the tops of her hands. "You look amazing."

"I could say the same to you," she responded. Because it was true.

They sat down and Jaime startled when she noticed the iced tea already waiting at her place.

"I remembered." Jonathan smiled.

"How kind," she said, working to find the return-smile that was expected. The tea was iced, not hot, but it still provoked the memory of the cup of peppermint she'd been served last. And how differently she felt about the two offerings. One had been given with such tenderness that she'd nearly cried after the first sip. Looking at the sweating glass in front of her now, Jaime felt none of the same tenderness—this felt like control. She stirred the ice.

"Tell me about work," Jonathan said.

Jaime dropped her straw, surprised that he was interested. "Still teaching," she said.

"Grade?"

The unease triggered by the tea relaxed into the routine of old gestures and tone. Of talking about the things that were uniquely hers. Not chosen by anyone else. "Fourth grade. I started with middle-schoolers, but a few years of those hormones and I was ready for a break."

Jonathan grinned. "I bet. When we have kids come in for surgery, the preteens stink no matter how thoroughly the nurses scrub 'em down beforehand."

"They can't help it." Jaime uncrossed her legs and settled her purse on the back of her seat. Jonathan asked more about the children in her classes and laughed appreciatively when she talked about the year's most memorable behaviors. She'd forgotten all about the kid who had answered every single question on the spelling test with: *Spell check.*

Jonathan's stories made Jaime feel embarrassed about her complaining tone when she'd detailed one of her students disrupting class by overturning his desk, screaming, and ripping pages from the classroom books. His depictions of patient behavior made her kids look positively mild-mannered in comparison. And though he laughed, seeming to appreciate the hostile environment, Jaime felt herself becoming uneasy with how commonplace violence was in the hospital.

"That's awful," she said, breathing out through her nose.

"Yeah." Jonathan shrugged.

Conversation stalled, and as if on cue, the waiter dropped their sandwiches off.

"How's your family?" Jonathan asked after thanking the young woman.

Jaime swirled her tea with the red, plastic straw. "They're doing really well, actually. Dad is retired and Mom is still working—as you know." She looked up at Jonathan, hoping he'd answer the unasked questions. How long had he and her mother worked together? Did they see each other often? Did they talk at work? Did they talk about her? Did her mom visit his while he was at the house?

He picked up his sandwich. "I've heard your dad is loving retirement."

Jaime leaned back. That answered one of her questions. Apparently, Jonathan didn't have the same no-mention rules regarding her life. She folded a fry in half. "I think so. But he needs a hobby. I'm afraid he's not getting out enough. That's probably just me trying to find a reason to worry, though. And your parents? How are they?"

"They're great. Still just busy running the business you know. I think they'll be roofing till they drop." He took a bite, chewed, and swallowed. "Well, not actually roofing themselves, but you know, managing it all."

"And your brother?"

Jonathan's eyes lit up and Jaime was reminded of just how much he cared for his little brother. "Mark is in college. Can you believe it? He's at Notre Dame, studying poly-sci. Little brother wants to be a congressman."

"Wow." Jaime could almost feel her mother salivating at the notoriety of a politician in the family.

"Yeah." Jonathan shook his head, eyes crinkled from the force of maintaining a smile for so long. "Wants to try his hand at the change that no one else seems to be able to manage."

"If anyone can do it, it'd be him. He was so good at everything." Jaime could hardly imagine the little boy whom they had helped shuttle from debate club to swim meets and birthday parties standing behind one of the wooden podiums to address the nation on C-Span. This entire lunch felt like something out of a television show. Certainly not real life. Not her life.

"But I hear that you're a woman of many talents too." Jonathan leaned back in his chair.

Jaime's cheeks colored and she set her fork down. "Really?"

"Your mom said that you're working in a plant nursery now?"

"Not really a nursery, more like a boutique." She

picked up another fry, smashing this one.

"Do you like it as much as you like teaching? Seems like it would be a dream after all those runny noses and complaints about homework. I mean, you sound wrecked just talking about it. You obviously leave each day exhausted from all those kids."

Had Jaime truly only focused on the negatives about her job? She must have made her fourth graders sound like toddlers. She kicked herself for not making the aspects she loved the primary topic of conversation. Then picked at the crust on her sandwich, considering the positive things she could say about Plant Life so that jaded wasn't the overarching perception of her.

"I'm learning a lot. I knew that the plant world was diverse, but I had no idea just how many different species of plants there are. And I'm only learning houseplant varieties. It gives you an appreciation for how complex their world is—and the people who study it." Her thoughts strayed to Ryan, and how absorbed he'd been in pruning yesterday as he stayed in the front of the shop with her. His assessing gaze with every customer that walked through the door. Then, when they were alone, the time he'd taken to explain his process and method to Jaime. He hadn't laughed at any of her questions, even when she herself could hear how dumb they sounded. And he'd listened—really listened—when she'd talked to him about what she'd learned, and what she thought of it all.

"Come back," Jonathan said, leaning forward and waving a hand in front of Jaime's face.

She blushed, embarrassed that she'd been so zoned out. This was why Jonathan always accused her of consistently having her head in the clouds. "Sorry. I guess I got caught up in my thoughts."

"Maybe you're actually a botanist in hiding?"

Jaime shook her head. "No. Definitely not. Just an enthusiast for education in all its many forms."

"I've always been an enthusiast for you."

"Jonathan—"

He raised his hands in the air. "You don't have to respond to that."

Both stalled; Jaime pinching her crust into crumbs, Jonathan leaning forward and placing his head on his hands. When he straightened, he made such intense eye contact that Jaime felt like he was going to try for that long-delayed proposal right now. Her stomach tightened.

"Jaime, I'm not trying to make you uncomfortable, I just never managed to forget about you. About us. And it took me a long time, but I can now appreciate that you were right to end things when you did. We both had a lot of growing to do, and we needed the space to do it. But I've never stopped thinking about you. And if you'll let me—I'd like a second chance at us."

Jaime's heart had gone from steady to galloping, the tick of her pulse a metronome where the vein met the surface of the skin on her wrist. Tick, tick, tick. She thought about their high school days, their college, and then graduate days. The horrible months after the breakup. She thought about Jonathan and the ways he seemed different—and the same. His family, hers. And then out of nowhere, she thought of Ryan too. The kindness of that tea he'd brought her, a small act of comfort that she'd needed in that moment. Jaime looked up at Jonathan. "Can you give me some time to think about it?"

"Of course." He twisted the large metal watch on his

wrist. "All the time in the world." He tapped the faceplate on the watch. "Well, not *all* the time. By eighty I may have finally given up."

Jaime forced the necessary laugh.

"But maybe not." Jonathan reached across the table and put his hand on hers. "Thank you for considering it. Me." He cleared his throat. "I mean it, Jaime. I'll prove to you that I've changed. That I'm ready for us now. I'm a lot more patient."

The urgency in his voice made Jaime feel put on the spot despite his words. Like she needed to make a choice right then. In the back of her mind, her mother shouted at her to marry him. To undo all the damage she'd done before and accept Jonathan.

A movement in the periphery, and the waiter was back at their table. "Can I get y'all anything else?"

Jonathan rechecked his watch. Grinned. "It's after two. Let's have a couple glasses of wine. Rosé because it's hot as hell out there?"

"House?" the waiter asked.

"Please," Jonathan said. He winked at Jaime. "See? Told you I remembered what you like. Now, remind me, does your family still go to Myrtle Beach every summer?"

Chapter Five

The next day, Jaime woke to a good morning text from Jonathan and a splitting headache. She wanted to burrow under the covers, grab her book from the nightstand, and read with a flashlight the whole day. Instead, she dragged herself out of bed and into the bathroom where she dry-swallowed two over-the-counter pain killers and took a shower. Hair pinned back with her favorite barrettes and extra mascara applied to accentuate the green of her eyes, she headed out of the apartment with her second coffee in hand. Anxiety be damned.

With this headache, and the unease that had settled into the pit of her stomach—maybe leftover from that scary customer encounter—it was likely going to be a three-coffee sort of day.

By the time she'd made it to the shop, she'd decided she was going to respond to Jonathan but continue to avoid his question a little longer. He'd said he could be patient with her. And he knew that she did take a long time to make decisions. A few days wasn't excessive. It wasn't too long to keep him hanging. And she really did need the extra time to mull things over. Because she truly didn't know how she felt about jumping back into a relationship.

He checked all the boxes. Handsome, smart, kind, occasionally funny, and interesting enough. To cap it off, he'd achieved all his professional goals and was living his life the way he wanted to—something to be admired by anyone. Her parents would be thrilled. Her mother positively gleeful. And yet, that nagging claustrophobia that had forced Jaime's hand before continued to sway her.

Maybe she had some sort of syndrome where nothing was allowed to be easy.

At Plant Life, after switching the sign to open, a trickle of customers came and went, but nobody bought anything. Ryan had remained at the front of the shop with her, true to his word ever since *the incident* as Jaime now thought of it, but after a phone call from a customer who had the wrong date for their order and needed their plants before they went out of town the next day, had to run out for the delivery.

His concern before leaving, his insistence to call right away if she felt at all uncomfortable, had left her feeling embarrassed on many fronts. It was as if she now needed minding even more than the shop. Worse, his attention, the constancy of him nearby, made her aware of every single hair out of place. It didn't make any sense, but she was glad of the extra mascara. And if she was honest, she'd spent the extra time trying to tame her curls, knowing that Ryan would be around to see it. Why she wanted him to notice her, to focus on the parts of herself that she liked: her green eyes, the fullness of her lips, her hair if it was in a cooperative mood—she didn't know. She couldn't explain the compulsion.

Once Ryan left, Jaime chastised herself for being silly and got busy. Watering. Checking the soil for bugs or weeds. But for such things to exist would mean Ryan had somehow missed something in his soil mixing process. Jaime had come to appreciate that from every speck of dirt or compost to every new plant shoot, he was attentive to a fault. It also meant there wasn't much for her to do but twiddle her thumbs and wait for customers.

Jaime trailed the rim of a triangle *ficus* pot with her finger and walked up and down the store, studying each plant with the intent to memorize more of their names. The Swiss cheese plant was popular, and she could now identify it easily. She paused at the carnivorous plants, examining the cartoonish fish mouths of the purple pitcher and the toothy clamshell body of the Venus flytrap.

The bells on the shop front tinkled and a woman walked in with a little girl that Jaime would guess was six or seven-years-old. First grade, maybe second.

"Hello," Jaime said, glad of the company that was female, young, and therefore, definitively safe. "Can I help you all?"

"Just looking." The woman bent down to the girl. "You don't have to stay next to me, but use your eyes only, understand? No touching."

"Okay," the little girl said.

The woman immediately stepped away, heading for the palm varieties, but the little girl stayed in place, her eyes sweeping slowly across the shop. Jaime could almost sense the force of her curiosity. A knock to Jaime's heart, triggering an irrefutable wakeup call.

Jaime crouched beside her, putting their faces at equal height. "What's your name?"

"Isabelle."

"Hi Isabelle, I'm Jaime."

Isabelle lifted her right hand though her arm stayed locked by her side, offering a tight, barely-there wave.

"Can I show you something really cool?" Jaime asked.

The girl's expression remained guarded, still quiet, but she nodded.

Cautious, thought Jaime. And brave. Isabelle knew her boundaries and wasn't afraid to protect them. Jaime beckoned for Isabelle to follow her, leaving plenty of room between them, as she walked to one of the displays by the window.

"These are called terrariums," Jaime said. On the table, glasses of all shapes and sizes held small alienish worlds of miniature plants—tiny leaves shaped like whale fins circling round into rosebud structures and feathery ferns. Each accented by carefully chosen rocks and pebbles atop a thin layer of soil.

"How do they grow in here?" The shyness forgotten, Isabelle's eyes held that cartoonish gleam, luminous in her hunger to see more.

"They recycle their own nutrients. A well-made terrarium—" (all of Ryan's were) "—should need little to no care ever. My boss told me that some terrariums hold plants that were placed inside over fifty years ago and are still growing after all that time. With no extra water or food."

"Can I make one?"

Jaime had to bite her cheeks to keep from blurting that *yes, of course, what a great idea.* "I—"

"Please?" Isabelle's face scrunched in earnestness, her entire body positively twitching with the need to put her hands on something, to get the full sensory experience of this place, to see the plants up close. To learn.

"Well." Jaime considered. Ryan had made it very

71

clear that she wasn't allowed to work in the back room. The back room which had a wide butcher block counter going down the center, the shelving beneath host to all sorts of soil mixtures, pots of many varieties, and the different nutrients. Enough nutrients to keep any plant happy and thriving. There, Ryan's tools were hung, each in their specific place along a pegboard wall. Jaime was allowed in for only the space of time it took her to grab whatever she needed and then get out. If she got the supplies for a terrarium and left, she wouldn't be overtly breaking Ryan's instructions.

"Okay," she said. "I'll be right back."

She checked in with Isabelle's mother who clapped her hands. "Isabelle would love to do that, you're sure you don't mind helping her?"

"Not at all."

Inside the back room, Jaime's confidence melted away and she felt as though all the plants in the room were shifting slightly to confer amongst each other, storing up their secrets to share with Ryan once he returned. *She came in here without you. She grabbed the round, globe-style glass with the big, child-friendly opening. She's taking plants that weren't already marked for sale up to the shop front.*

Jaime ignored the voices inside her head that were making the room pulse with a sense of wrongdoing and lined up several containers on a cart in front of the terrarium station. In each, she threw some pebbles, moss, charcoal, soil, and then grabbed a *fittonia* and a fern from the selection Ryan had set out already.

Before she left the back room, she took a deep breath and reminded herself that she was catering to a customer. That was good for business. And this was—no matter how much Ryan's eyes gleamed as he explained pruning techniques—a business. Still, dread made Jaime want to peek her head out before fully leaving the back room. So that if Ryan were around, she could quickly put everything back. Hopefully, before he noticed that she'd touched anything.

She squared her shoulders and walked back out into the hallway. She wasn't doing anything wrong. Not really.

In the shop, Elise now loitered by the front door, looking at the shelves with ornamental pots.

"Hello," Jaime called out, waving.

"Hi." Elise smiled at Jaime, starting forward only to stop when Jaime made a sharp turn back toward Isabelle, whose mother had joined her in the terrarium section.

"Now," Jaime said to Isabelle. "We have all our supplies and tools. Are you ready?"

As Jaime explained the step-by-step instructions, Isabelle slowly scooped the substrates from their containers into the terrarium, creating a water-catch at the bottom, a barrier for the roots to save from potential rot if they were to meet the excess runoff with moss, and finally, a thin layer of soil. They were ready for the plants and then any decorative elements.

The whole time, Elise hovered, slowly drifting from one end of the shop to the other. Several times, Jaime half-straightened from the dedicated project space, made eye contact, and nodded to imply, *I'm here if you need anything.*

Elise had reciprocated the nod at first, maintaining that same tight smile she'd first offered. Yet with each check-in, her expression became more reserved and definitely more strained. What Elise wanted, Jaime couldn't guess. Elise was clearly comfortable in the shop. Anyone who walked in with no knowledge of the place would think that she was the one who worked there because of her authoritative air of ownership. The possessive hand she placed along the back counter, her watchful gaze. A slight, but audible, sniff anytime Isabelle spilled substrate onto the flooring. As the girlfriend of the actual owner, Jaime supposed that Elise was entitled to that sort of behavior.

More likely than not, Elise was waiting on Ryan and was growing irritated with him for not responding to her texts or getting back to the shop—to her—quickly enough. Jaime couldn't help her with that. If that was the issue.

It wasn't any of Jaime's business, whatever it was. She refocused on Isabelle and after the tropical-style plants were snug inside the bowl, she encouraged the girl to choose from the selection of decorative rocks and multicolored pebbles to finish the terrarium off. She answered her questions to the best of her ability and encouraged her to think of the globe as a mini world that she was getting the chance to create. And next, watch grow.

A loud, annoyed huff came just before the slam of the shop door and the violent ringing of the bell on the handle. Jaime jerked upward. No one new had come into the shop.

Elise had been the one to make the disturbance.

Ryan must have messed up somehow—maybe he'd forgotten a date. The relationship would be brand new, since he'd only just finalized the divorce that had kept them apart. But after the last time Elise had been in the shop, there was no denying that something beyond the

normal vendor-client relationship existed between the
two. Clearly something that had begun before the
divorce was official and Jaime was in the picture. The
fact that the idea of Ryan with Elise made her hands
clench into fists? Well, that was a mystery she'd have to
solve later.

Once the finishing touches were laid inside, Jaime
wiped Isabelle's terrarium down with a glass cloth and
placed it inside a box for transport. "You're the proud
owner, and maker, of your first terrarium," she said with
an enthusiastic, happy voice.

Isabelle's excitement, and her mother's happiness,
were infectious, and whatever pause Elise and Ryan's
troubles had given Jaime, she quickly forgot them. She
felt overwhelmed with warm, fuzzy feelings of having
merged this new job with her favorite thing in the world.
She was a teacher once more and she felt transformed—
taller, stronger, better.

"What do we owe you?" asked Isabelle's mom.

"This was all my idea. Because I sprung it on you,
it'll be on the house," Jaime said. It could come out of
her pay. It'd be worth it.

"Absolutely not. Other ones about this size are going
for about eighty. Does that sound like enough to you?"

"Only if you're sure. I'd hate to make you pay for
something that you'd never intended to buy."

"Honey, I'd pay a lot more than eighty dollars for
what you just did for my Iz. The summer has both of us
crawling up the walls and ready to take to the blue
mountains like wild creatures. Charge it."

Jaime rang the woman up and tried to keep herself
from smiling too widely at the little girl cradling her self-
made plant world, already freed from the box.

After she signed the receipt, Isabelle's mother pulled out a small notepad. "Would you mind telling me your name again?"

"I'm Jaime."

"And do you own this place?"

"No, I just work here. The owner is Ryan MacLeod."

After they left, Jaime cleaned up. Restaurants further down the boulevard were opening for lunch, which meant that restaurant-goers not ready to end their day out would soon be popping in and out of the shop. She surveyed the front and back rooms to make sure that everything looked the same as always. Nothing was out of place. Once the plants were noticed missing from the back, Jaime would be ready with an excuse. Ryan would never have to know about this morning's impromptu class.

****

The lunch hour typically meant more customers, but Jaime couldn't have anticipated the mad rush of people in and out of the doors all afternoon. By four, she was ready to drop. Her feet felt like they did on Friday afternoons after a whole week of standing. Maybe the difference was in the concrete floors of the shop versus the laminate and carpet of the classroom.

Either way, she deserved a drink tonight, or the large bucket of balls at the driving range instead of the usual, economy pail. More than anything solitary though, Jaime wanted to call up Bree and turn the evening into a celebration. Because today was a day worth toasting. Not only had she been allowed to show Isabelle a small niche in the cool world of plants, but she'd made more sales than all of last week's workdays combined. All despite

Ryan's delays, keeping him away from the shop and leaving her to run it alone. Jaime was coming into her own, and the success made any leftover fear from that one encounter with the awful customer and the nagging doubt over leaving at summer's end, vanish.

She smiled at the last customer in line, calling her forward and ringing up the order. One snake plant and an ornamental pepper. Jaime finalized the transaction, thanked the woman, and then helped hold the door for her on her way out. After the gentle click of the latch and the tinkle of the now overly familiar bell, Jaime slumped against the glass panes not caring how it would look outside on the street, absolutely wiped.

Deep breath. Jaime still had a half hour to go. And falling asleep at the front door wasn't an option. She made her way to her phone over at the far end of the shop behind the counter. Maybe Ryan would have messaged to let her know what had waylaid him. At the very least, she'd check in with Bree about getting together tonight.

Jaime opened her messages tab where Jonathan's name sat at the very top of the list, his name bolded, because he'd sent the last, yet unopened text. She considered his offer yesterday and all of the day's goodness, all of the bubbliness dissipated. To avoid losing the feeling completely, she texted about actualizing her plan for drinks later.

Bree's response was immediate.

Bree—*Of course. I was starting to think I wouldn't get to see you this summer bcz of that fancy new job.*—

Jaime grinned and texted back.

Jaime—*You're not getting off that easy.*—

She was still grinning when the back door slammed. Footsteps loud from the hallway. When the door to the shop opened, Jaime automatically braced herself.

"What are you playing at?" Ryan's voice wasn't loud enough to be considered yelling—but that's how it hit Jaime.

Her mouth dropped open, working to find a response to his unexplainable anger. She couldn't guess what had caused Ryan to be so red-faced, his jaw flexed and still except for the tick of a muscle just below his ear. She closed her mouth and tried to swallow but it had gone dry in the space of seconds. "I was only sending a quick text. Is that—"

"Elise is my best customer. In all honesty, my only customer. She keeps this place in business."

"I—" She'd thought that Elise was waiting for him. Queasiness washed over her, making her want to hold her stomach.

"You spent the morning playing pretend classroom, ignoring the single most important person to this business." Ryan's intensity, so alluring before, drawing her attention anytime he was nearby, now made her feel cornered.

The high from earlier made the fall that much quicker. The emotions that much more intense. Jaime's eyes and nose began to burn, threatening tears that her pride would never allow her to shed.

"This place may seem like a fun little break from teaching while you figure out what's next for you, but it's my *life*. I can't afford to have anyone treat it like a playground for whatever whim takes hold."

The walls shrunk around Jaime. Her head tight and pressurized. Squeezing, provoking her fight or flight response. Flight was preferential. "I—"

"No. I'm not finished—" Ryan took a step back and

reopened his mouth.

Before he could keep talking, the pendulum of panic swung the other way. Action it was. She did the unthinkable. She interrupted. "Neither was I." Pushed too far, despite that she still felt on the verge of crying, she was not going to let him speak to her like this. "I *saw* Elise, but I didn't coddle her because I thought she was waiting for you. It's clear that you two—"

"Us two?" demanded Ryan, throaty and hoarse.

He must be unused to raising his voice if he was already going hoarse with the effort. The small sign of weakness dried Jaime's tears. The cord inside her that was constantly wound tight by the stress over money and pent-up anxiety over her family, still thrumming from the encounter with that customer the other day, finally snapped.

She was about to show this waste of a plant-shop, reactionary, good-for-nothing just who she was. "Don't tell me that you two are nothing. I *saw* you. And for whatever stereotype of the cutesy, naïve schoolteacher you want to throw my way, you can think twice. I can say the word sex as easily as the next. *Sex*. Sexual tension. It was here in this shop the last time that she and you were together, and that's a clear sign that your relationship—whatever it is—isn't purely professional. So, mister—" Jaime's schoolteacher, sit-back-down voice was in full effect. "I figured that as a grown woman, Elise was very capable of either texting you, or better yet, simply walking the ten feet over to me to ask for whatever help she needed. She acted like a child. And now, so are you."

Jaime's breath was ragged, her chest heaving.

Ryan looked away. "You should go."

She straightened, stepping closer to him and trying to match his height. Though still shy more than a few inches, the effect made her feel like she could do what needed doing. He really was a man-child. And Jaime knew how to handle children. She'd already decided what was going to happen next. "I'll be done for today—which, by the way, was a great day for sales—but I'll be back tomorrow morning. Your mother said that she needed my help so that she didn't have to sit here all summer. All because you can't bring yourself to grow up and trust anybody."

"My mother—"

"Is going to Greece next month because I'll be here to field customers." Jaime grabbed her bag and her keys. "See you tomorrow."

She slammed the back door on the way out as hard as he had earlier, and only then, began to cry. To sob. To let out all the tension that she'd allowed to consume her as she got into the car. Then shouted at her windshield like someone possessed.

She'd spent the last six years having to defend everything about herself to nearly everyone. That she'd thought this summer, this green oasis, might be any different was laughable. And if Ryan thought that he could use his own insecurities to bully her then he had another thing coming. She'd been through this before. And she wasn't doing it again.

****

"I can't believe that you told the owner of the place that he's not allowed to fire you." Bree leaned into the table, her boobs getting precariously close to the edge of her pasta, several strands of linguine hanging off the plate. "Right after you told him he was acting like a child." She was finding way too much joy in Jaime's terrible afternoon.

Surrounding restaurant-goers swiveled in their seats to look at the two women after the eruption of Bree's honking laughter.

"You're going to end up with stains all over your shirt," Jaime said, pointing her fork at Bree's chest.

Her friend leaned back in her chair and cupped her hands together in front of her face. Her smile stretched beyond her interlaced fingers.

Jaime groaned. "Ha." She emphasized the last part of the pretend laugh. "Ha. I'm glad that at least somebody can find some enjoyment out of all this."

"I mean," Bree said, pushing her thick curls back behind her ears. "You have to admit that it's pretty hilarious. You've had this job for like one week and the dude tries to fire you. But you whipped out your best angry schoolteacher and used his mother—*his mother*—to cow him into keeping you."

Jaime hid her own smile with the back of her hand. "Technically, I walked out before he could respond. Maybe I am still fired."

"Are you going back tomorrow?"

Jaime considered it. Was she still red-hot over the whole thing? Absolutely. But did she want to go back to the applications and the desperation for a job? That felt even worse. She shifted in her seat, placing her elbows on the table. "That's what I need your help deciding. If I don't return, I'll just have to find another job. And based on how the process was going several weeks ago, I'm about a month late for finding something with an immediate start date. Except for maybe fast food."

Both women wrinkled their noses, squinting at one

another with an accusatory look that encapsulated the thought of working for minimum wage, smelling like burnt oil, and possibly having student families walk in, only to shake their heads at the state of affairs for teachers in this country.

"So," Jaime continued. "I go back. I go back to a job where I work for an absolute jerk. But, before that creep happened, Ryan was never really around anyway. Maybe it'll go back to that. And, it's temporary. I can completely ignore him for the five minutes per day that I see him. And, I can do it knowing that there's literally only two months left before I can say goodbye forever."

"And good riddance." Bree nodded, her dangly earrings bobbing.

"Enough about me, though." Jaime took a bite of her risotto ignoring the weird flip of her stomach when she'd talked about forever goodbyes. Because despite everything, the idea of leaving Plant Life, never seeing the bright shop again, sent a pang through her. She swallowed. "Tell me about you. How's the job? Life? And Patrick?"

"Patrick. Well, he's probably two hours deep into some gaming tournament right now. He practically squealed when I told him I was meeting up with you tonight. Sometimes I wonder if he really does love me, or if I'm just there to complete the basic needs triangle. Food, sleep, and sex. Video games being his one true love, of course."

"I think the hierarchy of needs goes way further than those three things." Jaime wagged her finger at her friend. "And Patrick is crazy about you."

"Yeah. As long as the glow of the computer screen is somewhere in the background." Bree shook her head.

"And work's work. Supply chain issues mean the shelves are emptier than normal which freaks customers out—no one wants to have to fight for their groceries, you know—but otherwise, it's still just people management. I feel more like a parent than a manager most days."

"Any good bagger gossip?"

"It's early days yet for the summer. Give it another month and then there'll be the first breakup. When it happens, we'll get drinks and hash out who's to blame. I've got my eye on one pair. I'm pretty sure that he's possibly seeing one of the other girls on the team too, though. That's about to be a mess." Bree snorted.

"Before we go down the road of making fun of teenagers—again, I want to ask. Maybe it's the stuff about Jonathan. The way he talked about teaching. But it's got me thinking. Do you ever feel like leaving? Like doing something else?" Jaime sat back in her seat.

"No." Bree twirled her fork into her noodles, then speared a shrimp. "I'm not like you, Jaime. You're always trying to get me to talk about my great passion for leadership and make my job into a—" She took a deep breath, widening her eyes. "*Vocation.* Maybe even a life calling. It's a job. I like it enough and find ways to make it fun. And sometimes I want to scream at the walls of my office and pull out my hair. Because it's a job. I don't have to feel like it's meeting the needs of my soul. It pays the bills and that's mostly good enough for me."

"I didn't mean to imply—"

"I know you didn't," Bree interrupted. "I got all high-horsey because sometimes I think that you believe everyone is as intense about stuff as you. I'm the type of person who wants comfort. You're the type of person who needs passion to feel fulfilled. Which is also why

I'm questioning this new Jonathan angle."

Jaime pretended to melt in her seat. "Let's not get into that. Not after all the stuff at work today."

"It's the *perfect* time to discuss it," said Bree.

"There's nothing to get into, yet. There's not much there. We went on one maybe-date, and now, he wants me to consider getting back together. And I—well, I'm considering it."

"Go on," said Bree in a mocking, deep voice.

"Honestly, he couldn't be more perfect," said Jaime. "He's attractive. Nice. Loved by my family and close to his own. Happy in his job and all that. There won't be any surprises with him. And he says he's never stopped thinking about me, which does make my stomach go a little fluttery."

"A little?" Bree arched an eyebrow. "Despite the shithead tendencies of his?"

"I'm ignoring the last part, there."

"Did you want to jump his bones immediately?"

"Excuse me?"

"You know what I mean." Bree grinned and rested her chin in the bowl created by her fingers, her elbows perched on the table.

"We were in the middle of a restaurant. In broad daylight." Jaime waited for Bree to respond. When her friend continued to stare at her unblinking, she threw up her hands. "At lunchtime."

Bree maintained the eye contact. "No passion. Probably because he's so effing controlling."

"Again, ignoring the last part. And you think there's no passion because I didn't want to straddle him in front of a bunch of seniors on break from the retirement home?"

"Yup. And because there's no passion, it means it won't work. Remember what we just talked about?"

Jaime took a long drink of beer. "After the last few days, I like the idea of comfortable. Jonathan is comfortable. I know him, and everything around me will get better if we start dating again. Think about all the issues with my family." Jaime fluttered her fingers, trailing them into the air. "Gone. How comfortable does that sound?"

"About as comfortable as an arranged marriage with a known douchebag. Who already has you questioning your job and all the things you've decided for yourself."

Jaime shook her head. "No. I'm not questioning. I'm just taking a page out of your book and choosing comfort over passion."

Bree rolled her eyes. "Should we go bathrobe shopping later tonight?"

Chapter Six

Rain meant that the shop would be lonely. With little to interrupt the monotony of the plants' silent respirations, the drip of condensation sliding down the sides of terrariums, the routine clicking of the ceiling fans that spun round and round overhead. Jaime had come into work every single day in the week since Ryan's blowup. And as if the city had conferred about their fight, the haze of it still lingering like something poisonous, people avoided Plant Life. There had been hardly any customers the last few days.

Ryan, who hadn't pushed the firing issue, was still insisting on staying up front whenever she was in the shop. Bringing all his work from the back on a wheeled trolley that he stopped at the front, as far away from the counter where Jaime sat as he could get. Beside the wall of decorative pots, across from the front door, he took cuttings, repotted, fertilized, and pruned silently. All while Jaime sat behind the cash register in the back of the large, open room just waiting for a customer. For instructions. For anything.

It was awful.

The stale conflict leeched her energy and by noon each day, she needed a nap. Several times, Ryan had cleared his throat, made eye contact, and even started toward her. But then nothing. The look in his eyes each time made Jaime want to be the brave one. To acknowledge that it was time to address the fight and move on. To ask him point blank for his apology. If she were reading him wrong though—if he wasn't actually feeling sorry—then she'd be setting herself up for another fight. And she couldn't stomach that. She let their awkwardness ride.

Later in the day, another set of deliveries took Ryan out of the shop again. Leaving her alone to another brand of silence. Simply being alone. At first, it was better. And then, just as difficult. Everything about this place reminded her of Ryan—and thinking about him made the lead weight in her stomach only heavier.

Jaime nearly panted with relief when the bell on the front door handle announced a customer. Not a customer, though. Jaime smiled, placing her book down on the counter as she called out, "Helen! Hello." In her happiness at seeing the woman, she forgot that there was a chance Helen might be angry at her, too.

"Hey, sugar. I brought you a coffee. I figured you could use something to keep you warm on such a miserable, wet day."

If the moisture fogging the glass at the inside corners of each window was any indication, coldness beyond Ryan's wasn't a real issue, but Jaime accepted the latte appreciatively. The warmth of it was a comfort she hadn't realized she'd needed. "Thank you," she said, surprised that her eyes were suddenly as misty as the rest of the room.

"I hear you went to war with my boy," Helen lifted her cup as if in salute and raised both her eyebrows. "And won."

Jaime tried to regain the feelings from when Helen had first walked into the shop, but the sense of isolation from this past week was made clearer, contrasted by Helen's kindness. Jaime's smile faltered, tugging her lips into something that probably appeared weak and watery from the outside. "I'd hardly call it winning."

"Oh honey, bunny. I'm sorry." Helen reached out and grabbed Jaime's shoulder, squeezing and then running her hand up and down the length of Jaime's arm.

"I promise I'm okay." Jaime leaned into the touch a moment, dabbed at her eyes and after, her nose. "I won't start crying." She hoped. She took a deep breath. "Did he tell you what happened?"

"Yes. And per his telling, he treated you terribly."

"I lost him his best customer." Though, that still didn't excuse his temper tantrum.

"Pshh." Helen waved a hand in the air. "That girl is a bloodhound with his scent shoved up her nose. She used the whole situation to ensure that she's got a private, twenty-four seven line to Ryan."

"Before, it sounded like that would be a good thing."

"Well, it turns out, I may not have been listening to Ryan. It wasn't just that he was still technically married to Ashley. He's not interested in Elise."

"Oh." Jaime studied her coffee, trying to avoid the memory of shouting sexual tension at her boss. Over a woman whom he wasn't dating, and apparently, wasn't interested in. It took a lot to make Jaime lash out, but when she did, she always lost it. Saying the dumbest things.

Helen took off her glasses and inspected them for smudges. "Elise is his best customer, and that puts him in an uncomfortable place." She squinted, and then put her glasses back on.

Jaime swallowed. "And I made that worse for him."

"You didn't do anything but your job. She's the sort of woman who's catered to wherever she goes, and that day, was given a reality check. Ryan ought to know better than to string someone along, whether it helps the business or not. It's not right."

"You think he's been encouraging her?" Jaime tried to make sense of that with the man that she'd worked alongside these past weeks. It was hard to imagine him stringing anyone along—ever—with his silence and rough-edged frankness.

"I think he's been walking a fine line. I don't know. There's something there I don't fully understand." Helen took a sip of her coffee and beckoned toward the stool behind the counter. "Mind if I sit?"

"No, not at all." Jaime pulled it out and cleared her book and water bottle from the space directly in front of the seat.

"He cares about this little place more than anything else. And I think he's desperately afraid that he's going to lose it." Helen looked over the top of her glasses, forcing eye contact. "His protectiveness is misguided, but that doesn't make him a bad man. Please don't think that of him."

Jaime nodded, but it was hard for her to accept Helen's words. Jaime loved her job too, and though people were constantly nitpicking at her choices, she didn't fly off the handle at them. *Try putting yourself in their shoes*, she always told her students. As she took a drink, Helen suddenly busy with her phone, Jaime tried to imagine herself owning a school. Each teacher in the building hers to manage and every choice they made the potential difference between keeping the doors open to students versus not. She imagined herself handling a situation where one of the staff had angered their largest benefactor. Without having to entertain the 'what-if' any further, adrenaline had started to build, making Jaime's palms sweat and heart quicken.

She still liked to think she would have handled it better.

"Did you do the crossword this morning?" Helen asked, breaking the silence.

"Do you need a hint?"

"No, no." Helen narrowed her eyes at her phone and jabbed at the screen with her pointer finger. "I'll figure it out. If I could just figure out what the hell they mean by *modern laugh*, I'm sure I'd get the rest."

The back door opened, and a draft announced Ryan's presence, cooling the room with the same stiff awkwardness of the past week. His neck was bent so that his chin touched his chest. Now, apparently, he couldn't bear to even look at her. Jaime considered finding a rag to wipe the moisture from the windows, just for something to do. But that was conceding in some small measure, and she was tired of their avoidance game. This was the workplace environment *he'd* created. He'd have to deal with it.

"Hi Mom." Ryan glanced Jaime's way. "Jaime." His voice cracked on her name and both women looked up, Jaime's sudden alarm echoed by Helen's jump from the stool.

"You're bleeding," Helen said.

"It's nothing."

Jaime realized that Ryan hadn't been hunched over to avoid her, but instead, because he held one of his hands cradled against his chest. A paper towel with wilted, blood-soaked edges just visible. "The knife slipped. Dumb mistake."

"Do you need stitches?" Jaime asked, starting toward him.

"No, there's super glue in the first aid kit."

"Such a stupid, man thing to say," Helen said. "I can't stay and watch this. Force him to put some antibacterial on it at least, will you please, Jaime?"

Jaime nodded, almost to Ryan when she remembered that they were fighting. Would he even want her help?

Deciding that their issues needed to take a backseat, she got the first aid kit and beckoned for him to sit on the stool that Helen had just vacated. For all her talk, Helen still loitered, watching as Jaime pulled out a disposable packet of antibacterial cream, and a roll of gauze.

"There." Ryan pointed. "That small tube is the superglue."

Helen tsked.

"Thank you," Ryan said, as he took the glue and other supplies from Jaime. He pulled the paper towel back, winced, then dabbed until there was what could roughly be considered, *less* blood. "I got a call from The Roam Rover this morning."

"Ryan!" Helen exclaimed, clapping her hands, then wrinkling her nose as Ryan unscrewed the glue cap with his teeth.

Jaime had no idea what the rover was, but it was obviously a good thing. She stayed quiet, waiting to hear if Ryan would need anything else for his hand. He finished gluing himself, and pinching the cut closed, signaled with his elbow for help opening one of the nonstick pads from the kit. Jaime opened it and held it out for him to grab. Their eye contact went on a beat too long, a silent acknowledgment of the sudden drop of all hostility. Without shifting his gaze from her, Ryan placed the pad on the now sealed cut.

"Do you need help with the gauze?" Jaime asked.

Ryan finally looked back to his hand. "I can do it," he said.

Helen lifted her clasped hands above her head triumphantly. "You may be an idiot, son, but this is amazing. The Rover is a culture magazine that recommends restaurants and local shops." She gestured to Ryan. "Are they going to feature Plant Life?"

"They're going to put us on the front page. They called for permission, and to set up a time to take photographs." His gaze resettled on Jaime.

That feeling that he wanted to say something, to talk, came over her again. The same intuition that had made her sit straight several times throughout the week, somehow aware that Ryan was fumbling for words—then, unable to find them.

"That's wonderful," Jaime said, flushing with the second, less situation-provoked instance of prolonged eye contact. She'd forgotten the way that her chest tightened whenever he looked directly at her.

Ryan dug his foot into the floor as if there was a scuff there that he wanted to buff out, his hand apparently forgotten. "They—" He cleared his throat. "They want you here for the pictures, Jaime. The woman writing the article said something about the way that you helped her daughter. That it was an experience that defined why shopping local is different from big box stores."

"I knew it." Helen whooped. "I knew that she would transform this little place from the moment I saw her.

Around here, The Rover can make a business an institution." She toggled a finger at Jaime. "You clever girl, you."

"Wow." Jaime slowly sat down on the second stool opposite Ryan and leaned against the counter that ran the length of the back wall. "Do they have to include me in the story?"

"She talked about potentially bringing her daughter back in for the shoot. Ms. Flores said that the impromptu workshop you were willing to create was what makes this a frontpage worthy story."

Seconds ticked by without anything more said. Jaime grabbed her wrist, squeezing until her thumb sat on top of her middle finger. She let go.

"Hey Mom," Ryan said. "Could you give Jaime and I a minute?"

Helen's brows shot up, and she made a show of exiting. "I think I'll just use the ladies' room and peek in on what's happening in the back," she said.

She closed the door to the hallway behind her.

It was quiet once again, and Ryan rubbed his face with his good hand, the other still in his lap. "I'm not good with words." He put his free hand in his pocket and caved his shoulders.

"But Jaime, I'm sorry. Not just because it turns out the person you helped was a journalist, and now, she's going to do good things for the shop. I've been wanting to say it—I just didn't know the right way to do it. I was embarrassed. I overreacted because I'm a fucking asshole. And stressed. You didn't jeopardize this place; I did. Everything you said to me that day was true, and even though I haven't said this yet either, I'm glad you didn't listen to me. I'm glad you're here."

Jaime gripped the edge of her seat hard. She couldn't begin to count the number of times she had apologized in her life. Thousands of times. Saying *sorry* came as easily as *thank you*. Yet, she could count on one hand the number of times she'd been apologized to. Really, apologized to. Without any request for her to somehow step down from what she knew to be right. From what she'd wanted.

Not only had Ryan taken responsibility, he'd praised her for her defiance. Jaime's stomach somersaulted.

"And I want you to stay." Ryan raised his head, meeting Jaime's eyes. "Please, will you stay?"

Chill bumps raised along her arms and the back of her neck. The intensity of his continued gaze and the promise of settling all that tension from the past week was almost too much for her. "Of course," she managed to respond.

She wasn't quite sure why his request felt like it was about much, much more than a simple summer job.

"I'll stay."

****

The next day was sunny. The clouds gone and the air sweet smelling, as if the overnight rain had scrubbed Roam of all the car fumes and haze. Jaime set her phone in the cupholder of her car and clicked into the video messaging app, opening the group chat that she shared with Bree and Talia. Bree was in town, but Talia lived in South Carolina, so most of their conversations were virtual via the communication app. Jaime started the car as the load icon circled round on the screen. The longer it took for the messages to begin, the likelier it was that Jaime would have to covertly listen to them, hunched behind the counter while waiting for a customer to show up at Plant Life.

Fridays were typically the busiest day, yet there were always pockets of slowness. Fifteen-to-twenty-minutes at a time, perfect for catching up on texts, sending off a quick video message or reading an article. Scanning social media. Jaime didn't want to have to wait for one of those stolen moments. She hit refresh and pulled out of her apartment's assigned parking spot, weaving through the lot before taking a right on the main street.

Bree's voice echoed from inside the plastic ring meant for water bottles. Lined with receipts and gum wrappers, it was a phone holder when Jaime was driving. "I can't believe that you not only finagled your way into keeping the job after you got—let me say it louder for the people in the back—*fired*, but you also got an apology? Like down on knees, *thank you for getting my dumpy little store into a magazine. You're the best and I'm the worst.*"

Jaime chanced a glance at the phone for Bree's facial impression of Ryan, whom Bree had never actually met, yet still somehow managed to nail his grumpy, long faced expression.

Then Bree changed topics, discussing a showdown she had with a man who had to be escorted into the stock room to confirm for himself that the store was truly out of his favorite canned soup, then calling out to Talia, who she had plans to travel down to over the weekend.

"But back to you, Jaime-baby, I heard you slip in that last little detail about *your* weekend plans. Don't think I missed it, even though it came out like one of the side effects in a medication commercial." Bree pitched her voice lower and began to rattle off what Jaime had said at lightning speed. "Oh and, last thing, I agreed to go on a date with Jonathan (who sucks, by the way) this Friday. Dinner and drinks. Tell me I misheard you."

Jaime grimaced at the phone and then realized that the light ahead had turned green. She pressed on the gas as the car behind honked, waving a hand in apology for being distracted.

She came to another red light and looked back to the chat where the circular loading icon had returned. The grayed-out thumbnail was of Talia, whose short hair always made Jaime consider the possibility of chopping hers off too. If she did, her mother was likely to have a heart attack. If she did, and it looked terrible, she wondered if Jonathan would still think of her in the same way. When she cut her hair to shoulder length after college graduation, he'd been so upset. Clear that he preferred her long hair, and with it so curly, that she'd done herself a disservice. It was only an inch or two longer now. Did he care? How far did his dedication extend?

But it had been years since his blowup over her post-graduation haircut. And where Jaime had thought that he was a memory, he'd apparently kept a candle burning for her in the recesses of his heart. Jaime couldn't say the same, yet everything else about him was so right, so easy. That back-and-forth was why she suggested a trial, one date before they settled into anything more committed.

Her lane was given the go ahead, and Jaime let off the brake, flicking her blinker, and tapping the steering wheel as she waited on Talia's message and the line of cars ahead.

Talia's service must have been bad when she

recorded because her voice fuzzed in and out. "Jonathan? As in *the* Jonathan? PS, congratulations on not getting fired and all that. Crazy. But *Jonathan*?"

Jaime kept her eyes on the road. She didn't need to look at the phone to know that Talia was getting closer and closer to the screen, her nose likely rubbing it as she shook her head in disbelief. If Jaime weren't driving, she'd probably be able to see Talia's pores.

"If you two get married, will you count your little hiatus as part of your time together? Because I have to admit, that's one of my biggest pet peeves. If you have a breakup where you're separated for more than a year— by the way, this isn't really about you, Jaime, more about other people that I know—but say you breakup for a year and get back together, then you haven't really been together for ten years, have you?"

Bree's video took back over the screen. "I know who's not going to be giving the maid-of-honor speech at their wedding. Just imagine Talia up there, *so these two haven't actually been together that long because they were busy boning other people for the seven years they were split.*'"

"I wouldn't say that in a speech. Just to you. In private."

The two women were still going back and forth when Jaime pulled into her now usual parking space behind Plant Life. She leaned across the console, accidentally pausing the videos when she brushed the phone with her boob, trying to grab her bag from the passenger footwell.

She restarted the chat and fumbled with her keys, trying to find the shop's brass one, different only because she'd had her apartment keys recut with one of the printed designs. Her favorite cartoon snowman's carrot nose was now scratched up from fitting in and out of the lock, but it made it easy to differentiate between her house key and her parents', who had been assigned pink flamingos.

Talia and Bree argued on, silences occurring between each of their videos as the service continued to struggle and then adjust to the shop's Wi-Fi. Jaime pushed through the door, into the back hall of the store.

Talia was certain that sex on the first date was a good idea. "They need to just get it over with. If the chemistry's not there, then they can avoid wasting time."

Bree couldn't be convinced so easily. She made a disgusted sound at the start of her video. "I don't trust any of this. Jonathan doesn't deserve our girl. Especially not in bed."

"But look at it this way: if it's really boring, then Jaime will know exactly what she's getting herself in for. Three-minute missionary for the rest of her life—"

A rustling sound punctuated Talia's words, making the bottom of Jaime's stomach drop. No. No, no, no. Of all the mornings for Ryan to get here before her. When she'd let her guard down and kept her phone volume loud. She hit the screen hard with her thumb, desperate to stop the video. Pausing to try and keep Talia from saying anything more.

"That sounds like an interesting conversation," Ryan said from the back room.

When she'd first walked in, Jaime hadn't even noticed that the door was open; she was so used to it being closed that she now rarely gave it any notice. And why should she pay attention to it? Other than the time that she'd gathered supplies for Isabelle's terrarium, she'd never been in there. It had the vibe of the Beast's lair. But Ryan's fairy-tale rose would probably be in constant bloom thanks to his plant-daddy magic, even if he was nowhere near to shedding his beastliness.

Beastliness that looked a lot like a very well-fitted gray tee shirt this morning, and pecs that Jaime was trying to avoid staring at as he leaned against the doorframe on his forearm. It was all the sex that her friends were talking about. Curse those women and the way they celebrated her hormones, championing them into a flurry.

Jaime clicked the side bar of her phone twice more to keep from accidentally unpausing the conversation, restarting the sex banter, and straightened, matching Ryan's intense gaze. Too intense for a Friday morning after only one coffee. And much too intense after the week of conflict that they'd shared. Jaime needed more caffeine and then, to get back to business as usual. Avoiding this man who had made her life a lonely, silent sort of torture for the last few days.

"Did I ever show you around the back room?" Ryan asked, dropping his arm and angling himself so that the large butcher block workstation was visible beyond. Jaime shook her head and then said, "No," because he was still looking away from her.

"Well, if you're going to help yourself in here, you might as well learn where stuff is, and how to put it back properly." His mouth twitched. "The charcoal has its own space you know. It doesn't go in with the river rock."

Jaime crossed her arms. "I know for a fact that I put everything back exactly where I found it."

"Is that so?" Ryan folded his arms, matching her

pose.

"Yes," Jaime said, making sure he knew that if he tried to push the matter, she'd bring back that teacher voice that had talked him down last week. One benefit of their fight was that Jaime felt strangely powerful around Ryan. She had been allowed to flex and assert herself and it was still him who had wound up apologizing and feeling ashamed. The new feeling of power—of bravery—that came with that knowledge was, well, it was invigorating.

"Is this how you treat customers, too?" he asked, releasing the stern pose, breaking first.

Jaime brought her crossed arms even closer to her chest, staying firm—winning. "If I need to."

"No wonder our sales have shot up. They're all afraid you'll smack them with a ruler if they don't walk out of here with a *hedera helix* for the top of their kitchen cabinets."

"No, I just don't lord the Latin names over them like they're dumb-dumbs. I say, *this English ivy would look great in your kitchen*. And because I'm *nice* to them, they buy it."

Ryan arched an eyebrow. "Still doing your homework then?"

"Your sales may have gone up, but it's still nowhere close to busy around here. There's not much else to do but study plant tags." Talk of how few customers there were toed that uncomfortable, miserable topic of possibly losing him his best one, though. Jaime dropped her arms and hiked her bag up her shoulder, slipping her phone into it. Wanting, needing something to do with her hands.

"Why don't I take your bag and you head in? Start

to get acquainted with the back area. I'll be in right after I put this away for you."

Jaime didn't move. "You don't know where I like to keep it."

He met her eyes. "I know exactly where you like to keep it."

They stood there, stalemated.

Until, once again, Ryan broke first.

He sighed. "Look, I know everything about this place. If dust resettles in a different corner, I make it my business to know. You always put your bag to the left of the mini fridge in the cabinet with all the spray bottles."

She did.

"Why would I pay you just to steal from you? And you're obviously more comfortable breaking into the backroom without me there. So, go on. I'll take care of this, and then we can pretend I'm catching you snooping around back there again."

"I wasn't snooping—"

"No, just helping yourself." He grinned and leaned closer.

Jaime didn't smile back, though she was tempted. Instead, she handed over her tote, taking her phone back out again to stow it in the pocket of her jeans. If Ryan found something else to get angry about, she'd record him yelling about how she'd somehow breathed on the wrong plant, then force Helen to listen to it when she tried to give Jaime the *he's so nice* speech again.

After a few tentative steps toward that once off-limits door, Jaime paused in the doorway, turning to watch Ryan walk down the hall. She cleared her throat. "It's not right to be nice to a person only when they get you a front-page article, you know." Her pulse raced as soon as she said it, but it felt necessary. He wasn't off the hook for being a jerk.

"I'm not being nice because of The Rover, Jaime. I'm being nice because you took the time to learn that *hedera helix* is the proper name for English ivy."

He'd said it so softly that she repeated his response to herself, rocking from her heels to her toes in surprise. She tried to swallow the pride his words provoked and hold onto what was important. What needed saying. "You should be nice because it's the right thing to do—with anybody."

Ryan pushed through the door at the end of the hallway and walked through it, disappearing from view. "And that," he called out.

Chapter Seven

The bottles that lined the wall behind the bar sparkled in the light of the old-fashioned bulbs frequently used in modern fixtures. Brick and exposed wooden beams signaled that this place was one of those old downtown shops or warehouses, renovated to suit the growing number of breweries or sustainability-focused restaurants. One of many businesses that catered to the outdoor enthusiasts that made up the bulk of the tourism in the area.

Jonathan had reserved a table by one of the tinted windows, all the light from the bar a twinkling reflection, lighting up the long wall of glass on their other side. The effect made Jaime feel like a fish in a bowl, the clinking of ice in whiskey tumblers and the rattle of the martini shaker like taps on the glass. Jonathan looked perfectly at ease. His dry-fit polo was tucked into chino shorts, boat shoes occasionally finding Jaime's open-toed sandals under the table, grazing her foot in a way that made her settle further back into her seat, pulling her legs in closer.

"It was all hands-on deck," Jonathan said, continuing a story from work that would have delighted Jaime's medical mother, but made Jaime slightly nauseous. "I mean, the chainsaw was literally wedged into his thigh—it's amazing he had the capacity to stop the thing when he did."

"Thank goodness he wasn't on a ladder or anything." Jaime channeled her guided imagery lessons for kids with behavioral issues to avoid picturing what Jonathan was talking about. A golf club lined up perfectly, blue sky stretching out over an endless green lawn. The sound of the club connecting with the ball. She breathed out slowly through the slightest part in her lips.

Jonathan guffawed, slapping his leg as if to confirm there was no chainsaw stuck in his thigh. "Enough about me, though, how's your work going? Still at it with the plant shop, huh?"

Jaime sipped her tea, catching and chewing a piece of ice, considering just how much she should tell Jonathan about the past week's drama. She'd been strangely hesitant to tell anyone but Bree or Talia about Ryan trying to fire her, the words dying on her mouth when her mom called or her dad texted. And now here, with Jonathan asking. Why she felt protective of Ryan, or the job, she had no idea. But she did. "It's going fine."

She took another drink. "Actually—this is pretty cool. A local magazine wants to feature the store. With a front page spread and everything."

"Wow." Jonathan flagged down the waiter, not looking at Jaime. "Excuse me," he said to the woman dressed in all black that approached their table. "Can we get the charcuterie starter, please?"

"Of course, and are you ready to order?" She pulled a pen and pad of paper out of her small apron, camouflaged with the rest of her black-on-black ensemble.

Jonathan rubbed his chin, considering the menu. "Yeah, I think we are." He cleared his throat. "I'll have the filet mignon, done medium-rare, please. Jai, you always liked fish. Do you want the grilled salmon?"

Jaime's hand slipped on her menu. "I—" She'd been considering getting the crabcake sandwich. Salmon did sound good, though. And it'd be a treat, seeing as it was typically out of her price range. "Uh, okay." She gave her menu to the waiter and nodded, embarrassed that she'd been so unprepared with her order.

"Thank you." Jonathan's smile was confident as he handed his menu over. "And," His eyes cut to Jaime. "—Are you ready for a drink? Maybe wine? To go better with the fish." He put a finger up, silently commanding the waiter before gesturing toward the bar. "What would you recommend for pairing with the salmon?"

"We have an oak-aged chardonnay from a local Blue Ridge winery that's fabulous."

"Does that sound good?" Jonathan and the waiter both looked at Jaime expectantly.

She hesitated, uncrossing then recrossing her legs. "Sure."

"Great," Jonathan said. "And I'll have another of these, please." He tapped the side of his nearly empty Manhattan.

The waiter confirmed his whiskey choice and then walked away.

"Now, back to where we were." Jonathan drained the last of his drink. "Your work. Or the summer gig, that is."

"I was just saying that it was going well. I'm enjoying it."

"Does it bother you? Needing to find these odd jobs to make ends meet in the summer?"

The same defensiveness that had kept her quiet before returned as swiftly as the real answer—*yes*—

formed in her head. Jaime let that protective instinct guide her. "No. In fact, it's actually kind of neat, getting to do and experience lots of different things. This summer, I've learned so much about houseplants, plants in general, really, that I never would have if not for needing this job."

"Hmm." Jonathan traced the outline of his glass with his finger, making a slight ringing sound that complemented all the other noises of the busy restaurant. "But you don't want to do that forever do you?"

"What do you mean?"

Their drinks arrived and Jaime suddenly wished that she'd ordered another of the iced teas that Jonathan had first gotten her, instead of the wine. She'd let it sit until their food arrived, since it was meant to go with the fish anyhow.

"I just mean that we're over thirty-years-old now, Jaime. You don't want to be slinging burgers or working retail every summer for the rest of your life, do you?"

"No." Jaime was back at her parents' table, answering prying questions about finances and whether the insurance her school provided could cover even general doctor's visits. It could.

"It's a great job for a mom, though." Jonathan's eye contact made Jaime blush.

"Yeah," she said. "I suppose so." The smell of the wine drifted over. "For dads, too," she added.

"Sure, sure." Jonathan leaned back in his seat. "Would you ever consider not working for a while after you had kids. Staying home with them until they're school age?"

"This is starting to feel like an interview," Jaime said, trying to manage a laugh. As if to imply that she understood his questions as jests, and she was joking in return. Her remark hadn't been a joke, though. She considered excusing herself for a quick break to the bathroom so she could gather her thoughts and steel herself for any more questions that assessed and probed the future. The future that felt less and less like hers to control every second that passed. She picked up the wine glass and set it back down.

"Not an interview. Just trying to get a feel for where you're at. And what you want next."

"What do you want next?"

"To settle down. A family. You know I've always wanted kids, and I guess that I'm at a point in my life where I don't feel the need to keep exploring. I know who I am, and I know what I want."

"You've always been like that," Jaime said. It was the truth. One of the things she'd always admired about Jonathan. And at times, been intimidated by.

"You have, too."

Her eyebrows shot up, her forehead wrinkling. "Really?" This did not sound like the Jonathan who had ridiculed her indecisiveness, who had lost his patience when *for the millionth time already* she didn't know what she wanted for dinner or which movie to watch. Maybe he had changed after all.

"Yeah." Jonathan nodded and paused as the cheese plate appetizer was set on the table between them. "You had talked about teaching even before you realized that you weren't up for medical school. And you're honest to a fault, Jai. Everyone always knows where they stand with you. You don't mess around."

The old, never-appreciated nickname wasn't the only thing that nagged at Jaime. She squirmed, trying to figure out what felt off about his words. "Have you been messed around with?"

Jonathan puffed up his cheeks. "Cutting right to the heart of the matter as usual. I feel like you're just proving me right here. So, I'd better be honest." He thumbed at his jawline. "Yeah, I have."

"What happened?"

"Well, after we broke up, I was still carrying around a lot of hurt from the way that you ended things. Out of the blue like that. And I was in medical school. Stressed to the max." He glanced at Jaime and the way he looked at her forced her to sit back, curling her spine and pinching at the inside of her wrist. It was as though she was in trouble for hurting him all over again. Her stomach felt queasy.

He looked back down at his drink. "And then I met someone."

Jaime stayed quiet, waiting. She hadn't had any serious relationships since Jonathan. None of the men she'd dated had ever sparked that desire to commit. To go back to that life where her entire purpose was to smooth things over. Never looking forward because she was too busy sweeping up the messes and keeping her head down to avoid trouble.

"We dated for about three years, and I thought that—once again—I'd found the one. But it turned out, after I'd put my heart on the line—again—she'd found someone else. I found out she'd been cheating on me for months the same day she left me for said guy."

Jonathan took a long drink and rubbed his mouth with the edge of his index finger. The smell of whiskey drifted across the table, overpowering all the other scents of the restaurant. "And after that, I couldn't help but remember you. We may have had our issues, but you were honest with me at every turn—you respected me in a way that I couldn't appreciate until after Ashlynn."

The name made Jaime think of Ryan's similarly named ex. Thinking of her conjured an image of Ryan—his woody smell that was slightly reminiscent of the whiskey, when he leaned closer to show her the proper way to clean secateurs after each use.

"I didn't realize how much more mature you were compared to me back then. But I think I've finally grown enough to match you, Jai. And that's why I want this second chance. For me. For us."

Jaime reached for her wine glass, trying to chase away both the memories of how comfortable the morning had felt, working side-by-side with Ryan in the backroom, and also, the sense of interview-like tension that this conversation kept bringing up. "I said it earlier," she said, measuring her words and trying to ground herself back in the present. "I want to take things slow. Start back at friendship and see how things go from there."

As soon as her mother found out they'd been on what was probably not just one, but two pseudo-dates, the option for slow—and remaining just friends—would be out the window. Her mom would be picking out names for their children. Children Jonathan would want Jaime to stop working for and stay home with. And it made sense. Her salary would primarily be spent covering childcare if they had more than one. Yet, even if it was temporary, the idea of giving up her job felt like she was right back in school, considering her life as something pre-arranged and obvious, no twists or turns. No adventure. No passion.

"I want to do things however you're comfortable," Jonathan said. He reached across the table and grabbed Jaime's hand, squeezing and lingering. When he withdrew, Jaime did as well, twisting her fingers in her lap. When that wasn't enough to offset the surge of anxiety, kneading the napkin there.

"Thank you," she said, hating that both their tones indicated he was doing her a favor, versus the other way around. Wasn't he supposed to be grateful that she was considering his offer at all?

It took another five minutes for her fisted grasp to unknot, for their banter to lighten, and for Jaime to relax again. But she did. And the rest of the dinner passed by in easy, less intense conversation and, as the evening wore on, Jaime even found herself laughing. Letting go of the tightness in her shoulders that was left over from the earlier topics of discussion. Another glass of wine was brought to the table and her blood warmed, a faint buzz making everything softer around the edges, including Jonathan. As she ate her dinner, she felt bad for the knee-jerk reaction of irritation when he'd ordered for her; it was delicious. And she couldn't help but imagine him at her parents' table for Thursday night dinners. It would make her mother so happy to see him again—to see them together again.

Jonathan paid the bill while Jaime was in the bathroom, and though she protested him covering all their food and drinks, the fuzzy feeling that put everything in such a positive slant intensified. It was nice to be taken care of, versus always on the hunt for ways to make ends meet.

Their rideshare back home stopped at her place first. The sedan waited by the curb, motor purring softly in the night as the cicadas and other bugs chirped noisily. Moths danced in the streetlamp glow. Jonathan walked her into the building and then to her apartment door.

She pulled her keys out of the wristlet that she'd brought to dinner. "Jonathan, I—"

"I'm not asking to be let inside. We said slow."

A wave of relief washed through Jaime's chest, carrying her long exhale with it. "Thank you," she said. Aware of how many times she'd thanked Jonathan tonight. It was better than *sorry*, which used to be her mantra around him. *Thank you* was a definite improvement.

As if he'd heard her inner dialogue about how this time, maybe it would work, maybe *they* would work, he reached out and cupped the side of her face. Before she knew what was happening, before she could think to draw back and remind him they were taking things slow, he brought his lips to hers. Modest and tender. Yet, still a far cry from the friendship-zone she'd asked for.

"Goodnight," he said, the whiskey on his breath no longer woody and earthy, but syrupy and stale.

"Goodnight," Jaime echoed, the word as flat as she felt during the kiss. Not only was it something she hadn't wanted, it was a kiss that spoke of a future she knew well. A three-minute missionary kind of kiss. The kind of kiss that would follow sex performed mechanically—without feeling—until he finished and immediately after, rolled over in bed. Snoring seconds later.

Jaime opened the apartment door, and before she could slip through, was pulled back and kissed again. Her arms slackened at her sides, and as Jonathan's tongue pushed past her closed lips, she was reminded of the creepy customer's hand on her wrist. The queasiness from the beginning of dinner returned.

Jonathan inched back, assessing her. "That was a little preview of what might happen after we're past the friendship stage." He leaned in again, smelling her neck, his breath hot on her skin. "A sneak peek."

A faint headache had sparked along the top of Jaime's eyebrows, the usual pressure that replaced a wine buzz. She pushed through it and managed to smile. "Goodnight," she said, stepping the rest of the way through the threshold and into her apartment. She closed the door as he said it back, and then leaned heavily against it, listening to his retreating steps on the landing.

Guilt made her want to call back out to him and clear the air. Just to dissuade the tension building inside her. Wasn't this how early dating worked? Small moves past the friendship zone that indicated something more was coming. A kiss to end the night. And who was she to think that she needed butterflies before that kiss was allowed? Soulmates and such were for books. Passion was eked out of effort. Working to make the relationship better by showing up time and time again. Jonathan had shown up. He was trying. And he had changed. At least a little.

Jaime traced her lips with her finger. She knew as well as the next person that relationships where clothes were torn from bodies, the connection instinctual versus hard-won, weren't real. What was real was the image that she'd conjured over dinner of being with Jonathan at her parents' house—of having that family that he'd said he wanted, and that, if she was being honest, she did too. Jaime wanted to get married and to have kids. To grow old with somebody. And everything about Jonathan fit that dream perfectly.

She crossed the living room floor in time to see the taillights of the sedan they'd hired disappearing onto the main road. The tingly feeling that she longed for was a fantasy. The revulsion she'd felt about the kiss simply a matter of not having been prepared for it. Next time, it would be better. Because there, in that car disappearing down the main road, was a man who wanted her. Who would be good to her. Who would help provide for children in a way that she couldn't do alone on her teacher's salary. Who she would try to get excited about.

This time, she could make this work.

****

The shop had been closed an extra day that week because of the Fourth of July and it seemed as though customers hadn't caught on that they'd reopened. The fans clicked. The plants breathed silently. And Jaime sat with her phone in her hands, overthinking what to text Jonathan. She had celebrated the Fourth with Bree. Watching the fireworks from the green, Bree sitting on a picnic blanket and drinking while Jaime smacked ball after ball. Bree ignoring the light show and instead, insistent that Jaime needed to drop Jonathan before it got any more complicated.

You didn't give him permission to kiss you. You said friendship.

The memory of their conversation twisted the base of Jaime's stomach into a knot as she hit send on the text. The blue box appeared on her screen, marked sent, at the same time as the shop door opened, the bell tinkling. She put her phone away and looked up, the "Hello," dying on her lips as soon as she saw who it was.

Elise stood in the doorway, her red lipstick stark against her pale skin. Her stance rigid and despite being shorter than Jaime, intimidating as hell.

Jaime swallowed and stood. "Can I help you?" She'd do better this time. She'd make sure that Elise got the customer service that she deserved as the shop's main source of income.

"Isn't Ryan here today?"

"He's working on-site with a customer. I don't think he'll be in until tomorrow."

"That's not what he told me," Elise said. She hitched her designer bag further up her shoulder, the logo flashing in the room's bright light, so bright that it was impossible for Jaime to make out the brand.

Probably something wildly expensive, and yet, with the emblem so small, tasteful.

Elise wandered the shop, tracing the edge of the plant-bearing tables with her pointer finger, her nail polish perfect and an identical match to her lips. Whenever Jaime did her nails, they wound up chipped or fully ruined within a couple days. She sat back down on top of her hands, hiding her bare nails, and waited for whatever Elise wanted.

"You're lucky that Ryan's such a nice guy," Elise said idly. "If this were my place, I'd have made sure that you never sat in that seat again after the stunt that you pulled the other day."

Jaime took a deep breath and assumed her parent teacher conference persona. Even if hard words were shared, she wouldn't rise to the bait of turning a fraught moment into a fight. "I'm glad he's my boss too."

"Is that why you're here? Because of him?" Elise pulled a sprig of rosemary and ran it along the underside of her nose.

Jaime's mouth opened and closed several times.

Was she here for Ryan? No—she was here for a paycheck.

Elise tore a sage leaf from the plant, dropping the rosemary to the floor as she rubbed the sage between her thumb and forefinger, the pads of each finger becoming green. The herby scent drifting. "I looked into your employment status, you know. I figured that Ryan wouldn't. He's trusting." She tossed the sage leaf aside. "Too trusting, it turns out. Because I found that you're still a teacher with the public school district."

Jaime's heart slowed, thudding painfully in her chest. Her mouth was too dry to speak.

"So, this is temporary, then?" Elise snapped a twig of lavender from the plant, sprinkling the pellet-like petals onto the floor.

"This is—" Jaime started and stopped. This *was* temporary. And she owed Ryan the truth. But last week had been so horrible that she didn't want to relive that anytime soon—and she needed this job. Her chest began to ache. Friday had been wonderful with Ryan, when he'd showed her how to replant an orchid, explaining just how picky they were—the gentleness with which he handled their sensitive roots. His methodical approach to cleaning every tool lest it introduce some harmful pathogen to the delicate, tropical flowers.

Elise flicked a small container of oregano off the table. "Oops," she said. She nudged it out of her path with her heeled sandal, one that looked a lot like the designer copycat that Jaime had added to her list of potential splurges, hopeful that they might go on sale during the holiday. Elise walked down the path between plants until she was directly in front of Jaime. "How about this," she said. "You make yourself completely unavailable to Ryan. Especially since this is just a quick summer job anyhow, yes?"

Jaime nodded, her mouth now painfully dry, her confusion overriding her discomfort. Unavailable was an extremely general term that could mean any number of things. But now didn't seem like the time to question Elise's word choice. Nor ask for clarification.

"You leave it at that, and I'll keep your secret."

Jaime had to clear her throat, rallying her nerves, but she managed a quiet, "I'm just an employee here."

"You're obviously blind." Elise inspected her nails as if her herb table destruction had made a mess that she would need to clean instead of Jaime. The red polish was still perfectly intact. "I won't bore you with the details. You stay out of my way, meaning, away from Ryan, and I won't tell him that you're just using him and this place." She thrust out her right hand.

When Jaime didn't immediately reciprocate, Elise inched closer, the tips of her fingers almost touching Jaime's chest.

"Do we have a deal?"

Meeting Elise's hand with the weakest, most pathetic shake she had ever given in her life, Jaime shook, promising to something that felt both unknown and like a scene from a reality television show. Where love was a game to be maneuvered and manipulated. Elise was manufacturing the plot, though. Because if she thought Jaime was responsible for hurting her chances with Ryan, she was delusional.

Elise gave Jaime one last appraising look, making Jaime flush harder, her thoughts continuing to flurry, attempting to rationalize the encounter. How was she supposed to stay away from Ryan when they worked together?

Elise turned and marched out of the store.

The silence that followed was accusatory, like Jaime had been the one to go crazy. She couldn't decide if she wanted another customer for the distraction, or if she should turn the open sign to closed so that she could cry in peace. The need to talk to someone, anyone, for reassurance was a squeezing pressure quickly developing into outright nausea.

Jaime grabbed her phone from where she'd stuck it out of view when Elise had first come in and bypassed all the notifications from Jonathan, going straight for Bree's number. She called her friend—an immediate sign of an emergency for them, since neither ever called. Typically, relying on video messaging apps and text.

Bree answered after the first ring. "Is everything okay?" she demanded.

"I need you to meet me for lunch. Please?"

"Can you come to my office? I really can't take off right now."

"See you in twenty minutes."

Jaime wrote, *Out to Lunch. Back in 1 Hour,* on a blank piece of paper and taped it to the door, turning the Open sign to Closed. She grabbed her car keys and practically flew out the back hall and to her car behind the shop.

* * * *

"What a conniving bitch," Bree said. She slumped in her tall-backed, black office chair, swiveling it back and forth as she processed the story that Jaime had faithfully repeated, trying to include every detail. Jaime wiped her nose with the tissue that Bree had given her from the box by the computer.

Bree did a slow three-sixty rotation. "I don't understand it—she essentially came in *just* to yell at you to back off her man."

"But I'm not on her man. We weren't even speaking for almost a week. We're only now at the point where he'll look at me again."

"Yeah—but after your lover's quarrel, I'd say you two quickly made up for lost time." Bree proceeded to look everywhere but at Jaime.

Jaime blew her nose then ducked to find the trashcan, throwing away the tissue. "Lover's quarrel? What's that supposed to mean?"

"I mean, I'm not trying to give crazy-lady any extra ammunition, but you do kind of get this faraway look whenever you talk about Ryan."

"What?" Jaime's jaw dropped. She certainly did *not* get a dreamy look. "The only time I've talked about him is when he tried to fire me."

"Umm, no. You talk about him all the time." Bree fluttered her eyelashes and adopted a falsetto, sing-songy voice. "Oh Bree, *Ryan* has taught me so much about this whatever plant that has all these whatever magical properties. Oh, and even though he totally flew off the handle about something dumb and was an asshole about it, I still think he's a good person deep down and I'm going to be super defensive of him like literally days later—"

"Stop," Jaime said, starting to laugh. "I do not talk about him like that."

"You do."

Jaime rubbed the creases of her eyes, trying to dry any leftover tears. Her fingers wet, she used them to slick her eyebrows. "Say I do—and I'm not saying I do talk about him like that, because I don't—but say I did. I think it's just because I—" She faltered. "It's been a long time since I've... *been*, with a guy, and all this stuff with Jonathan—"

"Has you all hot and bothered?" Bree's cheeks dimpled.

Jaime smiled back. "Maybe?"

"Next time, if you're feeling it, let Jonathan into your apartment. You can get it out of your system and then you won't want to bone literally every guy who walks past."

"It's not every guy," protested Jaime.

"Okay, your boss then." Bree turned in her chair when her phone began to ring. She read the number out loud and then shook her head, sending the call to voicemail.

"I think it's just because I'm with him every day. It's a proximity thing."

"I looked him up, you know. And I can tell you right now that it's not just a proximity thing. Plant-daddy is hot, friend. Like super hot."

"You what? When?"

Bree laughed. "Like as soon as you took that job. There was a picture of him from some feature when he first opened the store. He didn't have any socials for me to stalk—which now seems very on brand."

"On brand for what?"

"Slightly elitist, possibly hippie dude who grows all his own food and probably dreams of living completely off grid while giving all his money to save the whales."

Jaime untwisted the cap from the smoothie that Bree had tossed to her when she'd first walked into the office. "Don't forget blowing up dams in the cover of darkness

119

every weekend."

"Oh, for sure."

Bree returned the call from a minute ago, talking while Jaime drank the blueberry-apple smoothie. When Bree hung up the phone, she pointed the pen that she'd been taking notes with at Jaime. "I know that you just promised wacko that you'd stay away from Captain Planet, but I for one, am much more in favor of him than Jonathan."

"Jonathan actually wants to date me. Ryan..."

"Ryan requires a little risk." Bree smiled, leaning back and chewing on the end of the pen.

"It'll only last as long as he believes I'm not going back to teaching."

"Sounds like enough time for some fun."

Jaime drained the last of the smoothie and threw the bottle into the trash. "Sounds like a great way to lose the job and make a fool of myself." She grabbed her bag from beneath Bree's desk. "I've gotta get back, I'm already late."

"Tell Ryan hi for me, please." Bree winked.

Jaime shook her head and walked out of the office. They were all crazy, every single one of them, but at least Bree's insanity had made her feel better. Dry-eyed and ready to deal with customers, Jaime headed back to Plant Life.

Chapter Eight

Ryan was already in the shop when Jaime arrived the next morning. She paused in the hallway when he called out a good morning from the backroom, clenching her bag strap as she waited for the next words. *I need to talk to you. Elise told me that you haven't actually quit teaching.*

They didn't come. Instead, all she heard was the continued clack of typing.

He said that he did ordering on Mondays—but he'd been gone all of yesterday, so maybe that's what he was up to this morning. Jaime didn't know. What she did know, was that she wasn't getting fired (again) just yet. To avoid inviting it, she made her way quickly into the front room.

After watering, after dusting, and after turning the lights and main computer system on, Jaime switched the sign to Open a few minutes early. A group of elderly women came in shortly after, each buying several plants and requiring help getting their purchases out to their cars and put safely into trunks. Later still, a young woman came and bought a peace lily and a new ceramic planter to repot it in.

The morning went by at a moderate pace as people continued to come and go in waves. A woman with three children stopped to shop—but her stress levels were ceiling high as the kids began to pull at leaves, and though Jaime was happy to redirect them, pointing out the Ponytail palm and comparing it to the hairdos of a Dr. Seuss character, the mother quickly dragged them right back out.

Jaime had gone back to her book when Helen walked through the door.

"No coffee this time, I'm afraid. I'm trying to avoid having to raise the dose on my blood pressure medication, so now, it's the one cup in the morning and that's it."

"You don't have to be sorry," Jaime said, hopping down from the stool. "It's almost lunchtime anyhow, and you never needed to buy me coffee."

"I like buying you coffee. I know how sleepy this place can get sometimes. Is Ryan around?"

"In the back."

"I'll just go check on him. Be back in a jiff."

Jaime held the back door open for Helen as she stepped through, and after, went back to her book. Five minutes later, Helen and Ryan both walked into the front shop.

"Skipping meals isn't healthy, you know," Helen was saying, her tone huffy and authoritarian. The heels of her shoes stamped the concrete in a brisk, steady drumbeat.

Ryan shrugged.

"I bet that Jaime brings a lunch every day. Don't you?"

Jaime bowed her head, trying to give Ryan apologetic eyes. "It's a habit at this point."

Helen rounded to face him again. "So, you're just not going to eat?"

"I'll eat later."

"You'll eat now. Go on, go out for something. There's that new Greek place round the corner. Go try it out and tell me if it's worth visiting."

"If you want to eat there, why don't you just go?"

"Because I can feed myself young man, and I've already had my lunch." Helen walked over to Jaime and patted her arm. "Have you eaten, yet?"

Jaime shook her head.

"You two go. I'll watch this place. My treat. Let me see, I might even have cash." She dropped Jaime's arm and proceeded to root in her purse, pulling out her wallet.

"Stop that." Ryan gestured for his mother to put her money away. "I'll go. I promise. Jaime, do you want lunch?"

"I—"

Helen nudged her. "Go on, dear. I know how dull this place can get. Go get some fresh air. Take a break."

"Are you sure?" Jaime asked Ryan, feeling embarrassed and like she had somehow imposed herself on him.

"Please?" he said.

She grabbed her purse and then both were shooed out the door by Helen who closed it with a firm click. The bells just barely audible through the glass amidst the noise of passing cars. A couple of pedestrians waited at a crosswalk a block away, but otherwise, it was only Jaime and Ryan on the sidewalk. Despite having been alone with him many times the last several weeks, this was different. It was entirely new to be with Ryan away from the shop. And Jaime was suddenly hyperaware. Of herself. Of everything. Her clothes felt wrinkly and wrong, and she wished that she'd popped into the bathroom to reapply her deodorant before going out into the humid, summer heat. Or at least to check that her hair was behaving, her curls clipped back to avoid them becoming a frizzy halo.

"Come on," Ryan said, and he began to walk past the metal streetlights and parked cars. Pausing only to shake his head at the newly hewn crape myrtles, branches knobby without the flowery tops. "Crepe murder," he said.

Jaime tutted beside him. "Should we outline the bodies?" Her joke earned her a smile from him, though he didn't respond, and she resented Bree for planting the idea that she had a secret crush on Ryan. Because it was only that strange influence that could account for Jaime's sudden need to see that secret, sly smirk again. Immediately, even.

They arrived at the restaurant a little more than five minutes later, both with lines of perspiration beading their foreheads. Ryan held the door. "I say we eat inside, yeah?"

"Thank God." Jaime didn't return the accompanying smile that indicated his question was a joke, too aware that if she spent any more time outside, she was likely to sweat through her shirt and stink worse than the teenage boys who slinked into the shop three paces behind their mothers, rolling their eyes whenever they were asked their opinions or to help hold something.

She and Ryan ordered at the counter, and he insisted on paying though Jaime did her best to shove her card at the cash register attendant in front of his.

"Sorry ma'am," the middle-aged man who took their order said. He threw up his hands. "The gentleman insisted that he was covering yours."

Jaime put her credit card away, giving Ryan a dark

look.

"You and I both know that Mom would rip my throat out if she heard that I made you pay for your own. This was supposed to be her treat, remember?"

"But instead, it's yours." Jaime grabbed a pile of napkins and waited for Ryan to choose a table.

"She's probably hiding cash in the *dracaena* as we speak, practicing her money tree joke. This will still somehow end up being on her. Either that, or she's about to help some customer win the Helen lottery when she forgets which tree she put it in and we never find it."

Jaime laughed. "We should post about it on your social media."

Ryan grimaced. "The shop doesn't need any accounts."

"You'd get a lot more business if you had an online presence."

"You sound like Elise."

At that, Jaime went silent, not pleased with the comparison after her last run-in with the woman, and worried about what bringing Elise into the conversation would do for the atmosphere between her and Ryan. She didn't know for sure that Elise hadn't told Ryan that she was still employed by the school district. At this point, would he even care that she was leaving? Helen's initial words resurfaced in Jaime's memory. Probably.

"Which table do you want?"

"I was waiting on you." Jaime realized they'd been standing by the food counter for an awkward amount of time, creating a traffic jam for the people whose orders would be ready first.

"You choose," Ryan said.

Jaime sighed. Readying herself to be ridiculed for

not already having chosen. For taking too long to decide. She pointed to the table closest to them. "Is this one okay?"

None of the usual commentary came. He simply nodded and followed her lead.

Chairs pulled out, then scooted back in with loud scraping noises against the floor, they sat facing one another. Neither spoke right away. Jaime's eyes traced the line of Ryan from his hands resting on the table, then up his arm, past the pulse ticking steadily in his neck, and along his jaw until she was looking directly at him and aware that he'd been observing her ogle him. As if she were some middle-aged creep gawking at a young woman in a sun dress. She blushed, folding her lips inward as she took a deep breath in and looked away.

Ryan cleared his throat. "So, how do you feel about the job? Is it the relief from teaching that you needed?"

Jaime narrowed her eyes, a flicker of pressure making her blink harder. She continued to stare at the front of the restaurant as if something very interesting was holding her attention there. "It's been good," she said. Her gaze slipped to meet his again. She rested her mouth and chin in her palm.

"Even when you were supposed to be fired and I was acting like—how did you put it?—like a big man child that can't bring himself to grow up?"

She burrowed her face in both hands. Rubbed her cheeks and looked up. "If you want an apology—"

"I don't." Ryan waved his hand and grabbed his water bottle from the table, undoing the top. "We needed to clear the air again. And it'd probably be best if I dwell in my assholery a while longer."

"It's that serious?"

"Chronic at this point."

Jaime's bottom lip tugged down, making a pitying face. "You should probably get that one put on your medical record right away."

"Yeah?"

"Definitely. Then we'll need them to prescribe you something strong for the condition. Something very strong."

"I don't know that Mom's hiding enough money right now to help fund a bunch of random new prescriptions. Plus, she tells me she likes me just the way I am."

"Mothers are supposed to say that." Jaime laughed.

"Maybe so, but who am I to call the woman a liar?"

Jaime interlaced her fingers and leaned forward. "I think it's wonderful how close you two are."

"I mean, you're saying it like we're weirdly close. She's just my Mom—there's no *Psycho* story lurking in the background—I'm not going to keep her skeleton in the attic or anything."

"I wasn't saying that."

"You went from laughing to serious in some two seconds flat and then said," Ryan set his jaw and intensified his eye contact, "You and your Mom are so close."

Jaime fell back in her chair, hand against her heart, play-pretending that she was hurt. "Well, you are."

"What about you then?" He took a drink of his water, his Adam's apple bobbing. The metal rang out against the plastic tablecloth when he set the bottle back down. "Are you close with your mom?"

Jaime straightened. "Yeah, I'd say I am. I mean, I'm close with both my parents. But I don't know, it seems easy for you and Helen, where I feel like I'm arguing with my mom as much as I'm ever having an actual conversation."

Ryan nodded appreciatively. "Family is tough."

"But does it have to be?" Jaime asked, wanting the answer, needing the answer. Yes, in the future, she wanted a family of her own, but not in the way that she saw some bickering and slogging through their days. As if living together was a chore that had to be dealt with rather than enjoyed. If she took Jonathan up on all that he was offering, would that be how it was for them?

"I don't think I'm the right person to ask." Ryan's voice was serious, and he gripped his crossed arms, squeezing his biceps as if the room had gone cold.

Their names were called from the counter, and he jumped up, seeming eager for an out from their conversation. When he returned, he balanced two blue, woven plastic baskets piled with fries and steaming pitas sporting lots of lettuce, tomatoes, and feta on top.

Ryan lifted one of them. "You got the gyro?"

She accepted it and pointed to his. "What'd you order?"

"The falafel."

"Are you a vegetarian?" she asked, thinking of Bree's assessment.

"No. I'm just not one of those people that feels like a meal means meat and potatoes."

Jaime grabbed a fry and ate it in one bite. "What kind of person are you?"

"Are you always this philosophical at lunch? If so, it's no wonder you bring yours all the time. It'd be exhausting to go out and get into the weeds of family and souls and whatever else you're going to ask next when all your fellow teachers probably want is another cup of coffee and a cigarette."

She threw one of her fries at him. "Not all teachers are jaded and burnt out."

"The brand-new ones aren't. And maybe the ones that teach the little, little kids. They're probably not as bad."

"What are you talking about? Kindergarten through second grade is the most exhausting work there is. Fourth grade is where it's at. They're like full-fledged kids. They can make real jokes, have good discussions, and all of it without any of the hormonal rage that is headed their way in a couple years."

Ryan finished chewing and swallowed. "Then why did you need out?"

The food settled in Jaime's stomach like a lead weight. She coughed. "It was time for a change, I guess."

"Well, I'm sorry for the fourth graders, but I'm glad that you found the shop."

"I'm not sure I had much to do with it," Jaime said, regaining her footing as she got further away from the lie of whether she was still a teacher. "Your mom found me. She really didn't give me much of an option, either."

"Now that, I believe." He wiped his mouth with a napkin.

Their conversation lightened, lunch passing quickly, and before Jaime knew it, they were back out on the downtown sidewalk, walking past gray-stone buildings, interspersed with red and painted brick shop fronts. Many of the places were empty, downtown not quite the revitalized destination hotspot of Richmond's or any of the other big, more coastal cities. But for every old business like the shoe shop that looked like it hadn't been updated since the day it was opened in the early fifties, there was another new, trendy boutique or café. With hanging flower baskets, chalkboard specials, and menu signs that brought life to the area.

Almost to the shop, Jaime stubbed her toe on some broken concrete and tripped. Ryan grabbed her arm, helping her steady herself. It wasn't until minutes later that sensation anywhere but where his hand had been returned. The pain in her toe was a delayed surprise, the heat from where they'd touched still her focus.

****

Since their lunch the day before, and since that moment when Ryan had grabbed onto her arm, rescuing Jaime from faceplanting in front of the coffee shop that served her favorite lavender latte, she hadn't been able to stop thinking about him. Something had changed. Whether it had changed only for her was the real mystery.

Now though, she felt aware of Ryan all the time. Like a part of her mind was reserved for tracking where he was in the shop and what he was doing. When he brushed past her to help a customer who had questions about their dying *philodendron*, the hairs on her arm raised. Every part of her was suddenly reaching for him.

There was no good reason for the shift. He hadn't done anything that signaled to Jaime that he was interested in her beyond the employer, employee relationship. And she'd been given the very clear *stay-away* warning by Elise.

Maybe that was it. Being told that something Jaime had never given a second thought to was actually a possibility, then to have it be denied, put these thoughts into her head. Before Elise's blowup, Jaime hadn't watched Ryan. At least, not like this. She hadn't leaned across the counter when he bent over to grab an extra pot from their storage beneath the succulent table, unable to resist the glimpse of his bare skin as his tee shirt rode up.

Or maybe it circled back to what Bree had suggested, that Jaime was simply crushing on him out of physical necessity, sex starved after years of having given up on dating entirely.

If that was the case, then Jaime needed to immediately text Jonathan back and take him up on his offer for dinner tonight. She should anyhow. Jonathan had reached out hours ago. Except—she'd spent the morning checking out her boss. Focused on him as he made his way around the shop, Jonathan's message notification forgotten and ignored in the background. Jaime felt like she was starting down the road of cheating, cheating just as the potential relationship was beginning. Though she hadn't done anything more than look. Though her and Jonathan were far from official, and she'd said she only wanted to be friends.

Jaime stood and rung up the customer that had simply needed fertilizer for their nutrient-deprived, yellow-leaved *philodendron*. That and some small sticky inserts to catch mites and gnats that seemed to commonly plague plant owners. Ryan stayed in the area dedicated to vine-style plants, inspecting gem-shaped leaves and clipping drooping foliage. Ryan's attention to the plants was more like a father's than a businessman's—Jaime couldn't imagine a coffee shop owner obsessing over a display of mugs or cellophaned treats the way that he did.

The customer with the sickly *philodendron* said, "Thank you," refusing a paper bag before walking out of the shop. Ryan straightened, replacing his clippers in the leather waist apron that he always wore at work. "I've got a delivery run this afternoon; will you be okay here alone?"

"Of course," Jaime replied. That day where she hadn't been okay seemed so far away. Nothing like that had happened since. And yet, Ryan still acted as though leaving her alone was a risk.

"Can I get you anything while I'm out?"

She wanted a giant milkshake and a burger, craving one since she'd seen a photo from a local restaurant advertising their summer special that morning, but she could hardly demand that of Ryan. "I'm good." She shook her head.

He lingered, massaging his hands and grazing his lower lip with his teeth. Jaime waited on what felt like an impending question.

The silence stretched and Jaime became aware of her own hands, not sure what to do with them as they hung lamely by her sides. Could he tell how awkward she was? Was she the only one feeling like this? She crossed her arms, grabbing hold of each elbow. "Is there anything you need me to do here?"

"No. Not at all." He cupped the back of his neck and looked around the shop. "Have you got plans tonight?" he asked.

Jonathan's name lit up Jaime's phone on the counter. He had texted a screenshot of the same burger photo that had Jaime ready to throw money at Ryan and demand a second lunch. She turned her cell over. "I might have dinner plans." She still hadn't decided whether she should see Jonathan or not. "Why? Did you need help here with something?"

"No. No. Just being nosy, I guess."

Their back-and-forth continued another minute until they finally said their goodbyes and Ryan walked out of the shop. Jaime's phone began to vibrate against the counter, whirring a buzzing accompaniment to the soft background music in the shop. Secret Sisters playing over the speakers. She silenced her phone, then as her mother's name continued to drift across the screen, picked up.

"What's this I hear about you and Jonathan?" her mom immediately asked.

Jaime's tongue thickened. Her throat tight. "What are you hearing?" It was possible Jonathan had run into her mother in the emergency room and told her that they'd met for lunch, and then for dinner. But that was the opposite of taking things slow—involving families felt about as fast as putting the relationship into a bubble topped jet plane and then waving to approve take-off.

"Patti called me. Apparently, she saw your name pop up in Jonathan's phone and got it out of him that you've been out a couple times."

So, his mother had found out and then updated hers. Great. "Mom—" *Don't get your hopes up. Don't force me to make this more than I'm ready for right now.* Jaime swallowed hard. "We're just seeing how things go. It's not—"

"I invited him to dinner on Thursday," her mother blurted. "I know that'll probably upset you. And I've likely stuck my foot in it, but sweetie, I've missed Jonathan. Your father has, too. We just want to see him, and who knows, maybe having a family dinner will help you to see things more clearly as you both decide what comes next."

The back door opened, and the smell of Ryan

distracted Jaime from her mother before she even saw him. As he walked past, the hairs on the back of her neck raised, dotting her skin. He grabbed his sunglasses off the counter, waved them. "Forgot these."

Jaime's mother was still talking about Jonathan. And with chill bumps still sending shivery tingles down her back, Jaime struggled to concentrate. Ryan started to walk away, but stopped, narrowing his eyes. Pointed at the phone. He mouthed, "Everything okay?"

Jaime nodded. Awareness slipping back to what it had been before he'd brushed past, her mother's voice getting louder and more insistent, she felt increasingly tired, and Ryan must have sensed it. She muted and lowered the phone.

"Everything's fine," she said.

Ryan stayed still. "If you need to leave, I can stay here. The delivery can wait."

She unclicked mute and put the phone back to her ear, waving him on. "It's okay, I promise."

He didn't move. He watched her. Jaime waved him on again.

With a slow nod, he said, "If you change your mind, call. I'll come right back."

Jaime shook her head, offering a smile as assurance. Phone to cheek, she studied the door an additional heartbeat after it closed behind him.

Her mother continued discussing the options for Thursday's menu, whether they should dress up a little more than usual. "He's no stranger, but it still seems like maybe a less casual approach might be best. Especially since you two aren't a definite item yet."

The decision about what she and Jonathan were felt like it had already been taken away from her. The word item, in no way corresponded with her request for friendship from Jonathan. "I'm not wearing a ballgown, Mom."

Her mother's laugh was twittery. "Well, obviously not."

Jaime listened to her excitedly plan, going past this week's dinner to suggest what future ones might include instead. Her mother trying to remember what Jonathan's favorite dessert was. If he had a preference for craft beer or domestic.

The music playlist restarted, its cycled songs highlighting the foreboding sense of repetition from the phone conversation. She'd been here before. Done this before. Jaime got up and walked through the rows of plants, rotating them to face the light differently simply for something to do. Finally, she couldn't take it anymore. "Mom—mom? There's a customer," she lied. "I'm going to have to let you—yeah. Yeah. Okay, bye."

She clicked out of the call and stared at the plants, unmoving and yet, invisible to the naked eye, growing. That was how life felt—everything happening outside of Jaime's vision and control. Scenes in the periphery were what guided the direction of her future.

Her job was the one thing she'd been able to direct autonomously. But not without significant clapback. Clapback that Jaime didn't fully understand yet felt weighted down by. A life with Jonathan ensured the end of that battle—her pay no longer a point of contention with her family, whom she wanted to be close to, whom she wanted to share her future family with. Jaime brushed some dirt from the rim of a pot back into the well and clicked into her text messages, her mother still very much on her mind.

Jaime—*I'd love to have dinner tonight*—

Jonathan—*Wear something blue. You know I love you in blue :) —*

****

"I'm telling you," Jonathan said, gesturing empathetically with his hands, "Mom should have been a detective. I couldn't get away until she got it out of me. I swear I didn't mean to involve our parents."

"It's okay." Jaime gave him a half-smile. Frustration scraped at her insides. Making her feel itchy and restless. "It was bound to happen eventually."

"I know. But you wanted to take things slow. And I promised."

Jaime picked up her glass of wine, which Jonathan had said came from one of the best vineyards in Virginia when he'd ordered a bottle. She considered the dinner just two nights away. How to set her and Jonathan up for better success when it was them plus her family? What she wanted for this night was another conversation as easy as it had been with Ryan at lunch. "Do you feel like you're close with your parents?" she asked, reusing the question.

Jonathan nodded. "Absolutely. You know how they are."

"You don't ever feel like it's hard? Like sometimes you have to choose between them and what you want?"

"No." He shrugged. "Do you?"

It was hard to want to share when it felt like the disclosures would be completely one-sided. She shook her head. "I guess not."

"I'm going to get the burger," he said, picking his menu back up. "Did you want the chicken sandwich? It's got pesto—you love pesto, right?"

Jaime opened and closed her mouth, her mother's excitement nagging at her to quit being so picky. To let the small things go and simply enjoy the fact that someone wanted to take care of her. Whether it be in life or this one meal choice. "Pesto's great, but—"

"Okay, I'll go up and order then. Seems like they're short staffed or something tonight." Jonathan frowned, craning his neck as he looked around.

Jaime's phone buzzed against the table where she'd had it out to show Jonathan a recent picture of her parents. Both of them smiling and windswept on an impromptu weekend getaway to Myrtle Beach last month. The text was from her mother.

—*Have a great time tonight, sweetie.*—

Heart emojis made the message a paragraph instead of a single line. Jamie stowed her phone back into her purse without responding.

"Jonathan," she called out, stopping him a few feet from the bar counter. "I want a milkshake, please. The chocolate stout one." She pushed the wine to his side of the table. If this was going to work, she'd need a voice, even if it was smaller than she'd like. But that was part of the growing pains of fitting into community and partnerships. It wasn't about just her. She settled for the chicken sandwich, looking forward to the milkshake.

Chapter Nine

"What are you having for lunch?" asked Ryan, walking over to inspect the peanut-butter and jelly sandwich that Jaime had just taken out of her lunch bag.

She held it up to show it off.

"That's depressing," he said, wrinkling his nose. "We've talked about this before, haven't we? I still think it's food for children. Come on, let's go out."

"Where?"

"The Notched Tree, my treat."

"You paid last time."

"But I suggested it, therefore, I feel responsible. Come on, their burgers will stop your heart—in a good way—and the beer's great."

Jaime's stomach rumbled; the chicken sandwich last night had done nothing to curb her craving for a burger. "Sold."

They gathered their belongings and switched the Open sign to Closed, Ryan smiling at the handmade 'Out to Lunch' memo that Jaime taped to the window. The walk to the brewpub was only ten minutes, and she and Ryan spent it talking about all the changes to the area and comparing their memories of Roam from childhood.

Inside the restaurant, only one of the downstairs tables was empty, a tall, bar-style two-seater directly in front of one of the windows facing the street. Ryan pulled her chair out for her and then pointed to the beers listed on the wall. "Tell me which one you want, and I'll go order."

"Drinking on the job?" Jaime teased, squinting to try and make out which of the choices were IPAs.

"The plants won't mind. And the customers probably prefer me after a drink. Or two."

Jaime gave up on the wall and looked at one of the paper menus stuck to a clipboard. Pointing, she said, "This one."

"You got it." Ryan walked to the counter, waiting behind three other people wearing matching conference-style badge necklaces who laughed loudly, filling the room with echoey noise.

As time stretched, Jaime pulled her phone out and briefly scanned the messages from her mother. Dinner with Jonathan was that night and Zofia had been texting continuously since nine in the morning, worried about everything from the salad dressing she'd made to what she should call Jonathan.

Zofia—*Can I call him your boyfriend? Or should I just say friend?*—

Jaime—*Who are you introducing him to?*—

Zofia—*Just in case. I don't want to say the wrong thing*—

Ryan returned with the drinks, and Jaime put her phone back in her bag, her mom's question unanswered. The real answer would have been that everything about the dinner felt wrong—it was too rushed, too much too soon. The snowball had left the mountain's edge and was picking up speed, Jaime caught beneath it. She accepted the sweating glass from Ryan gratefully and took a long drink.

"So, what's on the table of discussions today then?

After getting through family history and what makes us *us* last time, maybe it's time for politics or religion?"

Somewhere in the back of Jaime's mind, Bree was shouting *Sex!* loudly. The only taboo subject that Ryan had missed. Jaime took another drink to try and quiet her friend's voice, or at least, to avoid accidentally giving it airtime.

Ryan stretched in his seat, his legs straightening in front of him, his quads flexing so that the hint of muscle created a shadow along his pant thighs. "You do dinner with your family on Thursdays if I remember right. Yes?"

Jaime looked from his legs to her bag, as if his question had prompted her to search out her phone again. Better he thought that she was rude than checking him out. "Good memory. Six-thirty tonight."

"You also said that family was complicated—are the weekly dinners a good thing?" He returned his legs to beneath the tall chair.

"I didn't mean to imply that I don't like them." Jaime shifted in her seat, trying to get comfortable on the hard wood. "Just that sometimes I feel less myself when I'm with them. And I don't know how to get over that."

She twisted her beer on the paper coaster, creating a wet ring that stretched beyond the edge of the glass. "But that's what family is, right? If everyone was intent on making it all about themselves—what they wanted—there'd be no group, no family. Not a functional one at least."

"I don't know about that." Ryan sat facing her, hands in lap, not using any of the distracting devices that Jaime was busying herself with. His stillness made her self-aware of how twitchy she must seem.

Leaving her drink alone, Jaime sat back. "What do you mean?"

"I guess what you're saying just kind of reminded me of what it was like with Ashley. I loved her—still do in some memory-centered sort of way—but sometimes it felt like I was constantly trying to fit into some sort of mold to make things work. And obviously, she could tell."

"I'm sorry."

He shrugged. "It's for the best. She's happier, now."

"Are you?"

Ryan sighed. "Yeah. It's strange to say, but I am. It was a lot of work, trying to maintain a certain persona— maybe that's not the right word, but you know what I mean—trying to fit what that other person wanted all the time."

"My mom wants me to get back together with my ex-boyfriend," Jaime blurted, needing to be equally vulnerable even though Ryan had done nothing to force her to share. These were things she needed to save for Bree, but the words kept coming. "She's invited him to dinner tonight."

Ryan arched an eyebrow. "How do you feel about that?"

"Well." Jaime traced the knuckles of her left hand. "I feel kind of stuck. I want to make my parents happy, but I feel like every time something makes me happy, it somehow takes away from theirs. And I'm tired of feeling like a disappointment."

He cleared his throat. "I don't know them, and I've known you about a month. But even so, I can all but guarantee they're the furthest thing from disappointed when it comes to you."

"They worked hard, sacrificing a lot to make sure that every door, every opportunity, was open for me and my sister, Gretchen. They wanted better for us. Especially my mom. Her parents immigrated here, and she's taken on their reasons for leaving Poland as a sort of mantra. The chance for wealth, respect—you name it. But I chose a job with a salary maybe half my mom's alone. It's hard for my parents to be proud when they feel like I'm taking all their progress toward that life my grandparents dreamed of and moving backward."

"Yeah, but you're not teaching anymore."

Jaime's throat constricted, an immediate pressure that made her feel almost sick. She wanted to come clean right then and there and be done with it. Either he'd fire her, or he wouldn't. But it was no longer the job that was holding her back. Not exclusively. Every day that passed, the idea of disappointing Ryan—of hurting him—grew harder to stomach. She no longer felt that grip of power that made confronting him easy. Now, it was as if there was something to lose, holding her back from saying whatever she wanted. Same as she did with all the other people she cared for. All the other people she loved.

Jaime went back to making circles of condensation on the paper coaster, not speaking, and Ryan seemed to take that as her signal that she was finished talking. They stared at the menu in silence and then ordered.

Sipping their beers, facing each other, they both waited on the other to restart the conversation.

Ryan tapped the table twice and gave Jaime a look that was almost searching, his forehead scrunched. "Look, I'm sorry if you felt like I was overriding your feelings or trying to tell you they were wrong. It wasn't my intention."

Jaime resisted the urge to reach across the table and grab his hand. She grabbed one of the napkins instead. "Not at all. If anything, I cut you off while you were talking. I'm sorry I distracted you from your stuff with Ashley with my own problems."

"I don't really want to talk about her." Ryan scratched at his beard. "You heard that we just got divorced. But we've been separated a long time. It's been a couple years since I needed a big heart-to-heart about all that."

"Who'd you talk to?"

He shrugged. "A counselor. Friends. And then after a while, I found it was easiest to just not talk about it. Shifting my focus gave me the space to realize all the things about myself that I'd been denying or ignoring— good and bad."

Jaime nodded. "I should probably talk to someone. It might help me be kinder to my parents at the very least." And figure out what she truly wanted from Jonathan. If anything.

"Then, we need to look into getting you benefits. You've been with the shop nearly a month, and coming to the end of your probation," Ryan said. He raised his glass in salute.

The sick feeling from earlier came back. Jaime had five more weeks until she was back in the classroom prepping for the school year ahead. And he was here discussing getting her insurance—making her more permanent.

Their food arrived, distracting her from the growing sense that it was past time to tell Ryan that Plant Life was a summer gig. She could lessen the blow by promising herself to the shop for a few hours every day after school let out and working every weekend—she could even help him stay open on Sundays too if he liked. It wouldn't disrupt his weekend either, he wouldn't need to come in. Maybe then he could also make Monday his closed day as was common with most local businesses in the area.

She didn't tell him. Every time she looked up, something new gave her pause. The now familiar bob of his Adam's apple as he laughed, the way his shirt collar hugged his neck, the rough callouses on the pads of his hands. The healing cut that ran a rough line across his palm. Jaime shook herself and took a bite of her hamburger.

Loneliness was making her insane.

Halfway through their walk back to Plant Life, Ryan paused, touching Jaime's shoulder lightly. "I hate to be that person again, but you shouldn't walk around thinking you're a disappointment. You're one of the bravest, best people I know."

Jaime laughed but stayed as still as possible, fearing he might take his hand back if she moved. "Give it another month, then we'll see what you say."

"In another month, I'm going to say the same thing."

The blush that had started in her cheeks ran down her neck. Deliciously hot. "Okay, years then," she countered.

"Years from now, you check back in. But I bet my answer'll be the same."

They walked side-by-side the entire route from restaurant to work, close enough to one another that their arms brushed every few steps. Jaime couldn't be sure—she was probably imagining it—but she felt that the touches were anything but random. She couldn't be sure who exactly was to blame for them, though. Had he moved closer? Or was it her, drifting naturally to his side of the sidewalk. To him.

****

The pot roast that her mother had stressed over all day was falling off the bone, vegetables so soft that they could have served them to a retired food critic who had forgotten their dentures. It was her mother's claim to fame, the dish she made whenever she wanted to impress, but always with the proviso, *Oh, it was nothing.* Her outfit might seem a relaxed choice to anyone that didn't know her, but Jaime recognized the pearl earrings that were her favorites, the ones that came out for special occasions and for dressing up. And the shirt her mother wore was new, definitely not the one that she would have worn all day while cooking. It smelled like the detergent that Jaime associated with home when she'd given her mom an extra-long hug after she and Jonathan had walked through the door.

Once she was sitting at the table though, Jonathan's musky evening cologne was all that Jaime could smell, replacing that of home. His scent was the kind that came in dark bottles—designer, meant to be worn with a camel hair coat, and by the sort of man who traveled to DC often. Jonathan didn't travel for work, or at least, not that Jaime knew of, but she could almost guarantee that he had a topcoat that would label him as a local in the capital city if he did.

And watching the ease with which he had slid into the seat in the dining room, pulling Zofia's chair for her first and then Jaime's, she could almost imagine herself on his arm, walking through the DC snow in long coats and cashmere scarves, stopping for hot cocoa before hitting an ice rink and then waiting in the long lines to watch the tree lighting. It was the sort of life that her sister Gretchen lived. With Jonathan, Jaime could too.

She picked up the glass of wine in front of her, a Bordeaux-style blend that had made Zofia tut over the price when she'd taken it from Jonathan. Jaime took another sip. The small amount she'd had already sparked a slight headache, like the point of a newly sharpened pencil just starting to dig in. Bunching her eyebrows to try and force it away, she returned to the conversation, aware of Jonathan's leg drifting closer to hers.

"You don't think you'll ever work for the business, then?" Ed asked Jonathan, pushing the carrots from his pot roast to the side of his plate.

Jonathan dutifully speared the vegetables onto his fork, and with it half raised, responded, "I honestly can't say never. But I love what I do, sir. And for now, Mom and Dad have got it handled. I think I'd just get in the way."

"What do you like to do with your free time?" Jaime's mother had been peppering Jonathan with questions all evening, then yelling at Ed for doing the same.

"You can find me on the green most days that I'm not working." Jonathan nudged Jaime's leg under the table. "Though I'm hoping that won't be the case forever."

Jaime's jealousy was immediate. He probably belonged to a club where he could show up at any time, never needing to wait his turn for the small section of a driving range to hit balls, but instead, using the long, scenic courses at his leisure. He'd never wanted to golf with her when they were together, when she was still using her dad's hand-me-down clubs. He'd never bought her balls either, even though that's all she asked for each Christmas.

Zofia smiled into her wine, curved mouth mirroring the line of the glass. "Where do you golf at?"

Ed slid his watch round his wrist, eyeing Jonathan's, and pushed his plate aside. "I'm a member of the Hills myself."

Jonathan replaced his fork by the side of his plate. "I actually became a member of Berryside this year."

It was only the nicest course in the entire area. Maybe the entire state. Jaime couldn't believe that they'd gone out for dinners when they could have been golfing *there*, instead.

Her dad whistled. "I'd give anything to hit a ball out there. I've heard the views alone are worth the drive."

"You should come with me some time." Jonathan's voice held such a beseeching note of generosity, like it would be *his* day made to have Ed join him. Jaime both wanted to hug Jonathan for his invitation and acceptance of her father and slap him for his lack of overture to her.

"I'd love that. Really." Ed beamed.

Jaime would love that. She waited for her dad to say something about how much she loved to golf, garnering the extra invite for her without forcing her to throw herself on the ground and beg.

"Your mother was also telling me that you bought a house recently?" Zofia's expression was fixed. Like she had a secret, seated all the way to the back of her chair, free hand cupping her elbow as she rested her wine glass in the other hand against her cheek.

Jonathan cleared his throat. "Y'all are going to make me blush now, but I'll confess. I did just close on a place by the beach."

"Where?" Jaime was genuinely curious. He hadn't said anything about a beach house during any of the times they'd gone out.

"Myrtle Beach."

They'd just been talking about Myrtle Beach the other night. When she'd shown him the picture of her parents. Jaime opened and closed her mouth several times, her hand resting on the neck of her wine glass.

"We've got a timeshare in Myrtle Beach," her mother exclaimed. "We were just there last month." The surprise in her voice was genuine, not at all the voice she put on after opening every Christmas gift each year. *Oh, a new e-reader, thank you so much.*

"Maybe we'll see each other seaside, sometime." Jonathan's voice was honey, and Jaime had to admit, he probably was a fantastic anesthesiologist. Something about the slight Virginian lilt mixed with the enunciation that came with years and years of education and living in the best neighborhoods encouraged trust and confidence in him. Even as he spoke about buying golf memberships that costed more than five years' of her pre-tax deducted pay, purchasing beach houses—such an easy thing to do that he completely forgot to mention it—Jaime couldn't help but feel as though he was somehow letting her in on it. He made it seem normal—they all had that kind of money. If she married him, she would.

"We're headed there again next month, actually." Ed tipped his glass toward Zofia, a request to fill, but Jonathan jumped first, reaching for the bottle and walking it over to do the honors himself.

"Gretchen will be there," Zofia said. "It's meant to be a family vacation, but Jaime hasn't been since college.

Maybe you can convince her." Her voice was bubbly, riding high on having Jonathan back at dinner, but with the slightly threatening undertone of the fight they had every year over the ritual summer vacation. And tonight, both Jaime's mother and father had gone past their usual two-drink standard, her mom's cheeks flushed and her dad's neck beginning to mottle with pink splotches.

"Brody should be there too," Ed said. "Gretchen's husband."

Neither he nor Zofia made eye contact with Jaime, and the pink faded to pale on her mom's cheeks. The same color shift that happened whenever Gretchen's husband was brought up after last Christmas. Jaime stilled in her seat, waiting for an accusation. Waiting for the fight that had been lingering overhead like a storm cloud threatening to break.

Without blinking, without looking to either of her parents to see if they'd finally meet her gaze, she did her best to explain the first part of her parent's resentment to Jonathan. "I won't be there because I have work."

They would pay for Jaime to go, they offered every year, but giving in would make her the baby that they all thought she was—continuing a long tradition of highlighting Gretchen's independence and Jaime's supposed dependence. She'd rather miss it despite the fight. That way she could look her parents in the eye at the next Thursday dinner.

And if the threatening storm cloud hanging over their family since last Christmas hadn't broken before Myrtle Beach, Jaime going—especially with Brody there as well—would only strengthen the storm. No more sprinkle of rain but a deluge that would soak them all, inducing a chill that might last forever. Gretchen's silence had lasted this long, Jaime didn't want to risk it becoming permanent.

Jonathan, to his credit, didn't weigh in on the old conversation, nor did he seem to pick up on the undercurrent of tension surrounding the mention of Brody. His thigh met Jaime's under the table, pushing slightly, and she felt a small tug of connection amidst the feeling of being alienated from her family, from her sister.

As he maintained the contact, it became more and more familiar, taking Jaime back to her teen years. High school's risked touches at dinner which led to car kisses that left her hair a mess and her cheeks flushed for the rest of the night. Later, when Jonathan had braved the trellis into Jaime's upstairs bedroom, they'd lain next to one another, whispering promises for the future—clothes directly next to them in case the dreaded knock ever came.

Those promises had become stifling in college, reaching a strangle hold by grad school. But now? Now, Jaime could almost taste that perfect future—vacations in Myrtle Beach in a house that was their own. Dinners on Thursday with a highchair pulled up to the table. Her parents' eyes sparkling like they did when Gretchen walked into a room, but for once, with Jaime's arrival, too. She nudged Jonathan's leg, keeping her body as still as she used to when the touches were considered off-limits.

Ed had absorbed Jonathan into a discussion on deep sea fishing. Had he ever gone? Of course, Jonathan had. They traded stories about boating—argued about the best time to visit the beach. All while Jonathan's hand drifted to her thigh, stroking her lightly. Until Zofia scooted her chair back and he threw his chair back to rise with her.

"Let me help with this," he said.

"Jaime's going to help me." Zofia waved Jonathan back to his seat with the swan armed gesture of a beauty pageant winner.

In the kitchen, she rinsed the dishes and Jaime stuck them into the dishwasher. Their rhythm was unconscious because of the weekly dinner ritual, working around each other with the well-timed regularity of practice. That ache for her mother's full confidence and trust grew the more Jaime could feel just how close it was. It was there in the way her mother smiled, scraping potato mash off a plate, the slight hum as she handed utensils over, the extra touches that she sprinkled over Jaime. Jaime wanted this all the time.

"It was really nice having Jonathan over," Zofia said, squeezing soap onto a sponge to begin on the hand washables.

"It was."

Her mother slowed, the vigorous scrubbing downgrading to a gentle massage as frothy white soap suds built in the sink basin. "Should we invite him next week, again?"

Jaime heard her father's laugh from the dining room, could feel her mother's held breath like an ache in her own chest. "That'd be nice, Mom."

Zofia's exhale was long and loud. That of a kid's during a birthday party, blowing at the candles on a birthday cake. Full of hope and a certain wish. She dropped a serving platter into the water covered by bubbles like frosting and dried her hands on her apron before pulling Jaime in close.

"I'm so happy for you," she whispered.

Jaime's heart thudded in her chest as she rested her cheek against her mom's. She could say the exact same thing back to her. She was so happy for her.

Chapter Ten

Jaime's head bobbed and she lost her place in the book as it began to slide out of her hand, her finger slipping out from between the pages. She set it on the shop counter and stood to stretch.

"Sleeping on the job, huh?"

Not anymore. As if jolted by adrenaline, she was wide awake, all her senses cued in on Ryan's voice. She swung round. "Never."

He smirked, crossing his arms. "Wild weekend?"

Hardly. She'd gone to the driving range yesterday evening, but it was packed with people taking advantage of the heat and last day of the weekend. She'd been forced to wait long periods between swings. The highlight had been hiking with Bree. Bree was decidedly not a hiker, though it had been her that suggested the exercise as a means of getting together while also hitting her insurance-discount's step goal mandate.

Jamie squared her shoulders and picked a piece of lint off her pant leg. "Did you need something?"

Ryan's gaze traveled to where her hand still rested near her lap. His jaw clicked. "I was going to see if you wanted to repot snake plants with me. But maybe I should send you on a coffee run?"

"Snake plants."

"Come on. The bigger ones aren't selling, so we're going to break them up into smaller pots. The five-to-ten-dollar batches always go fast."

She followed him into the back room, propping both doors open in the hallway so that they'd hear the bell if any customers came in.

"There's an apron for you there," Ryan said. He pointed to her left, just inside the doorway where a new canvas apron hung on a peg.

"This hasn't always been here."

"Neither have you," he said, back turned.

"Thank you." She reached up and touched it. The canvas was the rough, unmovable fabric that she associated with drop cloths for painting—not the soft, pliable fabric of her tote bags and book carriers. She slipped it over her neck. "Help me tie it up?" She tried to smooth it over her torso, but the apron fell like an old army tent over her hips.

She felt Ryan before she heard or saw him. A tightening of the apron around her waist. The shush of the strings sliding against one another. That she had been nearly asleep five minutes ago was laughable now. Every part of her was awake and tingling with anticipation. Of what, she wasn't sure.

"Is that too tight?" Ryan's inflections soft. Like he was trying to have a private conversation in a quiet room—each word crystal clear, yet said with a muted breathiness that spoke of intimacy.

Jaime's own voice failed her. She was too distracted by the pressure of his handhold on the apron strings. She wanted him to keep pulling. To pull until he was holding her, her back pressed into the broad expanse of his chest. She wanted to feel him. To press herself against him and mold her body to his.

This was different from the fuzzy comfort of

Jonathan's leg against hers just a few nights ago. This was a need that was making her body a traitor to everything she'd thought she wanted with Jonathan when she'd walked into the shop first thing this morning. *Don't let go* she wanted to tell Ryan.

When he did let go, the lightness made Jaime's joints slacken. She could barely turn round for want of his hands back on her, somehow, someway.

"These are *Sansevieria trifasciata Laurentii*. I already prepped soil. So, all you're doing is filling these." He gestured to the row of ceramic white pots lined up along the butcher block work counter. "Let's do four to six leaves per pot."

His lack of eye contact as he spoke made the somersaulting inside Jaime's lower belly leaden. Maybe he'd sensed her sudden desperation and was doing her the favor of avoiding further embarrassment by refusing to look at her. If he were to, he'd see that her cheeks were flushed, her breath so shallow that her chest was barely rising. Jaime swallowed, trying to rewet her mouth, trying get ahold of herself.

"Use your fingers—gloves are there—" A new, purple, floral pair sat on the bench to the side of all the materials he'd prepped. "Use them to loosen the soil around the leaves, then gently, keeping as many of the roots intact as you can, pull them apart. Dip them in rooting powder, and they're ready for their new home."

As Jaime put on the gardening gloves, she felt him watching her, but this time, she didn't dare look up to check. Not with the flush that was already giving her away and the steady thrum of her heartbeat pounding in her ears. If someone walked through the front door, she doubted she'd hear it. She wriggled her fingers.

"Anything else?"

Ryan grabbed the back of his neck, bicep flexing in his black tee shirt. "Only that we really shouldn't be doing this now. Spring is the better time for repotting."

"Should we wait then?"

"No. They're impossible to kill. It'll be fine."

He leaned across the table and pulled one of the large, full plants over to Jaime. As they worked, taking turns dipping roots into the shallow tray of rooting powder, she tried several times to think of something to say. The silence felt heavy—the collective anxiety in a classroom before a test. But she had no idea what was going to happen next, and she was afraid to say anything in case it altered whatever she was waiting for.

She pulled her bottom lip in. "Should I be watering them as soon as I'm done?"

Before he could answer, Jaime knocked something with the side of her elbow. A slight pressure and then nothing. The resulting crash made both of them flinch. One of the ceramic pots lay in jagged, shattered pieces on the concrete floor. Jaime looked from the broken pot to the space on the counter from where she'd accidently hit it. "I'm—I'm—" The embarrassment was much worse because it was multiplied by the shame she felt over her distraction. Distraction that just broke something. How she couldn't stop thinking about the way that his hands had felt at the base of her back, tying the silly apron.

"Don't move." Ryan knelt down to gather pieces and put a hand out to stop her from doing the same, the tips of his fingers resting just above her knee.

His words hadn't been necessary. She couldn't have moved if she wanted to. The spot where his fingers rested on her skin burned, heat tunneling up and between her legs.

A second passed. Ryan hadn't gathered any of the broken pieces. He seemed as stuck in place as she. The backroom was golden amber, trapping them in this moment forever.

Jaime wanted so much more than this moment.

She lowered herself just a fraction of an inch, but it was enough to jostle Ryan. His hand slipped and she grabbed it, pinning it back to her leg, her mouth still dry both from the embarrassment and the urgent knowing that whatever came next would be entirely up to her.

"Don't," she said, voice strangled and hoarse. "I don't want you to stop."

He tightened his grip, inching his hand up her thigh, and then she was falling to the ground in front of him.

Ryan tugged her into his lap to keep her from kneeling directly onto the broken pot. Pulling her against him and bracing her as they both stood—sliding up against the worktable.

Jaime leaned back, arching. Aware that her pupils must be as dilated as his. Ryan's hands eased down her back. Longing thrummed inside Jaime, making everywhere he touched resonate to the beat of her desire. They watched each other until their proximity made the stare dizzying. She maintained the eye contact anyhow, coming up on tiptoes. Her chest against his, nipples tight. The friction of her small movements enough to make her want to cross her legs and finalize this slow build of release.

He focused on her lips and the shift reinitiated the dizziness that made her want to sway. Jaime slipped against him, losing the leverage she'd won by tiptoeing.

Hands clenching his tee shirt, she thrust herself into him and used his shoulders as leverage. As soon as their hips met, Ryan groaned. He lifted her in one fluid motion and set her on the counter, settling between her legs. Noses nearly touching.

"Do you want this?" he asked, voice like gravel, eyes still on her lips.

She'd never wanted anything more. She nodded, her throat tight. Slowly, she positioned herself so that her forearms rested on his chest, hands grasping the back of his neck. The space between them was negligible, their bottom lips now nearly touching.

"Please," she said. It had to be him that kissed her. She wanted to be wanted. She wanted to be wanted by him.

His mouth was on hers. There was no time to close her eyes. Whatever self-control he'd been exerting unleashed. Molding all of her to him. Jaime clung to him with her legs, circling his hips and thrusting herself into him. He tugged on her bottom lip, and she responded by licking into his mouth. Finding his tongue with her own. She heard herself moan, and Ryan shuddered, deepening the kiss until Jaime's jaw ached. Ached because she hadn't had enough. She needed so much more.

"Jaime?" came a voice from the shop front.

She and Ryan broke apart, forearms pressing bruised lips, patting down crumpled clothes, and breathing hard.

"Jaime?" her mother called again.

Jaime hopped down. Made to leave but Ryan drew her back. "The pot," he said, pointing shakily to the broken shards on the ground. She nodded—she could have stepped across a field of razors and not felt a single cut. Her body was buzzing, blanketed in Ryan's smell, the feeling of his hands still pressing into her lower back. His lips on hers. It would be so easy to slam the door shut, lock it, and let him map her body with his mouth.

She threaded her fingers into his and then let go. "It's my mom," she said.

He slumped, resting his hip against the countertop. Using a hand to brace himself. Then, drawing up to his full height, he picked her up and carried her the two paces past the broken ceramic before setting her back down. Sliding down his body elicited a shiver. And, skin on fire, Jaime walked into the hallway, sure that she looked exactly how she felt. Undone.

"There you are." Zofia's hand was raised as if to knock right outside the hallway.

Seeing her mother there was the cold shower that Jaime needed. Her body temperature cooled several degrees and anticipation became trepidation. "Sorry, we were repotting in the backroom."

Zofia arched an eyebrow and looked Jaime up and down.

"There's no AC back there," Jaime said, grasping at excuses that sounded just as flimsy to Jaime as they likely did to her mom.

"You certainly look flushed." The words hung there, accusatory. And with an aftertaste that Jaime knew well—disappointment.

The sunny brilliance that had swollen every fiber of Jaime's being under Ryan's touch hardened into something brittle and fragile. "What are you doing here?" she asked, eager to redirect her mother's attention.

"I just came to see where you worked. I thought that

I'd pick up something to bring some color into the living room."

Jaime drove her thumb into her opposite palm, engaging the pressure point there to try to steady her breathing and slow her heart. She walked her mom over to the snake plants. "These are what we were repotting," she said, reinforcing her story. "Ryan says they're impossible to kill."

"Well, that's certainly a plus. Is Ryan your boss? The grumpy one?"

"That's me," Ryan said, closing the back door. He looked how he always did except somehow more intense—the air around him shimmered like the first day of new glasses, when the details of the world were suddenly sharp enough as to seem unreal.

Zofia turned from Jaime to Ryan and back again, eyes not exactly narrowed, but as close to slitted as she'd ever get in public.

"Nice to meet you," Ryan said, crossing the space to shake her hand.

"Likewise."

Zofia's expression remained unchanged the duration of her time in the shop. Lips pencil thin and tight, she didn't buy anything, unusually quiet as Jaime explained the merits of different houseplants, ultimately refusing to be lured by even the fully in bloom pink *anthurium*.

When Zofia finally left, after closing the door behind her, Jaime leaned against it, the bells pressing into her back. Her stomach hurt, thinking about the tension in the air around her mom. Her mom, who desperately wanted Jonathan as a son-in-law, who long ago had gone into her room and shut the door to sob privately when Jaime announced that she was going to use her biology undergrad degree to teach instead of pursuing medical school like Gretchen. Her mom, who now had one more reason to be disappointed in Jaime. The ache in Jaime's chest that had felt so good, so *right* with Ryan twenty minutes earlier, was now more like heartbreak.

All the trust that had been regained, her parents' renewed confidence, was gone once again. It had disappeared as quickly as it had last Christmas when Gretchen had screamed, and screamed, and screamed.

The opening then shutting of the back door made Jaime turn around. Her eyes met Ryan's, the oily slick feeling in her stomach rising to make each beat of her heart seem to slip, smacking her ribs.

"Is everything okay?" Ryan set aside the wheeled cart of newly potted snake plants, ready to be put on display.

Jaime shrugged, stepping forward so she wasn't blocking the door anymore. She grabbed her elbows and chewed the insides of her cheeks, unsure what came next. Was what happened earlier a fluke that they now needed to be appropriately embarrassed about? Was what happened, something that shouldn't have?

After seeing her mother's face when Ryan had walked into the shop—Jaime's cheeks likely brick red and the stiff apron unyielding in its exhibition of every single wrinkle they'd made, making out in the backroom—she felt that deep down, she knew the answer. Her mother's expression couldn't have been further from the smile that she'd worn last Thursday at dinner.

Ryan cleared his throat. "Look, now that we've both

had a minute to think, do you—"

The confirmation from him that the kiss had been wrong pitched inside of her. One of those weights attached to a pulley that yanked her mouth open and forced her to say, "It was probably a mistake," before Ryan had the chance to say it first.

No matter what, Jaime had a month left before she had to leave, probably ruining whatever could have been between her and Ryan anyhow. Earlier, Helen had made it clear that her temporary approach to this job would make him retreat to the stony distrust that she had associated with him in the first days of working here. Leaving would lump her in with the group of people that had hurt Ryan. And although a part of her still wanted to throw herself at him, she couldn't imagine working at Plant Life for the rest of her life. It was easier to imagine herself at dinner every Thursday with Jonathan in tow. At least she would still be doing what she loved during the daytime.

Nothing came without a cost, and one of those possible scenarios for her future had a cost that she felt she could swallow. The other was too unknown, too risky.

"I'm sorry," Ryan said. Taking a hold of the cart again and looking down. "If I—"

"No." Jaime let go of her elbow and waved her hand. "It was me. I'm responsible for what happened. But…I… I shouldn't have."

His knuckles whitened around the cart handle, forearms tightening into those channels of muscle that had been holding her only minutes ago.

She looked away.

"Why don't you head home? I'll give you all your

hours for today, but I think—I think we both need some time to reset."

His words were the spark of a match, igniting Jamie's sinuses, triggering a burning that threatened to make her nose run and her eyes blur with tears. But he was right. They couldn't be here together, spending the rest of the day trying to pretend what had happened hadn't. Or, recreating it.

Ryan headed over to the space under the counter where Jaime kept her bag. "Can I walk you to your car?"

"No." The cardboard box was all that would be missing to really complete the scene of being fired, were he to walk her.

He handed Jaime her bag, holding on an extra beat once she reached for it.

"You'll be back tomorrow, though?" he asked, releasing his handhold.

Jaime hiked her tote up her shoulder, focusing on not giving into the urge to cry that was pressing the corners of her eyes. She nodded.

"I'm sorry," he said again. Arms at his sides, tucking his chin and bringing their eyes to the same level.

The space between them was two, maybe three steps wide.

Jaime closed it, walking into his scent and stopping herself until she could feel the softness of his tee shirt but not yet the hardness of his chest. Her breath made the cotton fabric ripple. Time stretched like an elastic band pulled tight, motionless, and yet full of possibility. All it would take was letting go.

"I can't," she said.

Ryan stepped aside. He cleared his throat. "Have a good night, Jaime."

She swallowed hard and nodded.

"I'll see you tomorrow?" he asked.

"Bright and early." Jaime tried to smile but could feel the heaviness of her cheeks, the weariness of always seeming caught between what she wanted and what she was supposed to want.

Nothing felt right anymore—not what seemed like the best option for pleasing her parents. Not what her sister still felt was Jaime's fault. And not walking away from Ryan now, encouraging the belief that what had happened was a mistake. Indulging that interpretation doubled Jaime's guilt over lying to him.

Not only was she going to leave Plant Life in a month, but that kiss was the opposite of regrettable. It was the best kiss she'd ever had.

Chapter Eleven

The shop was cluttered and tight because of the extra people and new apparatuses that looked like a cross between a giant satellite dish and a projector screen.

"For the photos," said one of the men setting out equipment.

Ryan had avoided the shop the last few days.

In fact, this was the first that Jaime had seen him since Tuesday, and she was grateful that their first meeting after the kiss was happening surrounded by people and plenty of distraction. Still, it was as though he was the brightest thing in the room—drawing her eye even from the periphery and somehow standing out amidst all the hustle. What had seemed so clear before was now muddied—why they shouldn't be together no longer relevant. It was hard to remember what other people wanted of Jaime when what she wanted pounded through her, louder with each heartbeat and sidelong glance.

Isabelle's mother had interviewed Ryan, but she wasn't here now. It had been decided that the shop should remain the focal point of the piece, not the impromptu class, nor Jaime's relationship with Isabelle. Accordingly, Jaime wasn't sure why she was needed for the photos. The article was now about Ryan and the plants, not her. And there was no chance of a customer here in all the mayhem. They'd closed the shop for the duration of the shoot anyhow, anticipating how tight things would be inside, and to avoid interruptions that could make the shoot drag on longer than necessary.

"Can we get one of the two of you together?" asked the photographer with the man bun and facial hair. Facial hair that could loosely be called a beard, though was more like scruff framing a goatee, nothing like Ryan's beard. The comparison triggered a cascade of thoughts about the feel of his face against hers. Jaime's chest squeezed.

"Sure," Ryan said. "Where do you want us?"

The men shuffled them over to a cluster of Fiddle Leaf figs.

"Can you do something with the plants? Take care of them in some way?" The guy was looking down at his camera, clicking the buttons beside a small screen.

The best part about Ryan's immediate, disgusted reaction was that for once, it wasn't Jaime who had prompted it. She hadn't overwatered, missed a brown leaf while pruning, or put the wrong plant in a certain section dedicated to one particular genus. This was someone else messing up, and honestly, the slack look of disbelief that Ryan always gave when someone didn't treat a plant like it was royalty made Jaime want to laugh out loud. His overprotectiveness had become endearing instead of infuriating. She could now appreciate the care that was easily misunderstood as standoffishness and condescension.

Ryan's mouth was still thin with the slightest hint of an upturned lip. "These particular *ficus*'s are sensitive. They won't appreciate being moved just for the sake of photos. When they're bought, they'll get jostled in a car—put in a new location, probably without enough light—and we need to do our best to prepare them for all that trauma by not messing with a good thing."

The photographer, Man-Bun, as Jaime had started to think of him, snapped a photo. "Rad, man. What's something that you can touch?"

"We could water the ferns?" Jaime suggested. "We have those new watering cans that are so cute."

Ryan's face stretched into a broader mask of revulsion and Jaime had to put her fist to mouth to stifle a snort. "They're very cute," she said again, drawing out the consonants of very for extra emphasis. "And I didn't water this morning."

"Great," said the other photographer. "Let's have you do it together."

"You want both of us watering at the same time?" Ryan's forehead was like a child's drawing of the sea, thick line waves showing exactly what he thought of this entire experience.

"Could one of you use a spray bottle?"

Jaime didn't even need to look at Ryan—she could feel his eyeroll.

"Sounds good to me," said Jaime. "I call the watering can."

She grabbed both and filled them from the tap in the back of the room, on the other side of the counter. As she handed it over to Ryan, her triumphant smile faltered at the look on his face. It was no longer the frustrated, disbelief that he'd been wearing most of the morning. He was looking at her—really looking at her, as if there was no one else in the room, or at least, no one else that mattered. It was the same look that made her throw herself at him on Tuesday. The ache low inside her that had been a faint flutter coming and going when she remembered those minutes in the backroom was now a gnawing pressure that was building, pushing into the deepest parts of her. All in front of a photographer who might put her picture, hungrily staring at Ryan, into an article that thousands of people might see.

"Great, guys. Now, I want you here." Man-Bun directed Jaime directly in front of a Maidenhair fern, then positioned Ryan so that he stood directly beside her. Their elbows bumped and for the first time in her life, Jaime's elbow was sexy. Warm and tingly, she wanted to lean into Ryan until the rest of her felt equally electrified.

"Maybe a little closer?" The sound of the camera shuddering through shots filled the space.

Jaime's breath held as Ryan edged closer—so close that she could feel the heat of his body. Only one more step and she would be hip to hip with him. Another and she would be pressed against his body. Temptation gnawed, urging her to forget the camera and simply lean into the impulse to straddle Ryan right here, right now.

"Hold the watering can a little higher please?"

After a few lighting tweaks, and a few deep breaths on her part, Jaime and Ryan fell into a rhythm of looking at the camera when directed, then back to watering for action shots. The awareness of him so close was still a pressure chamber squeezing her little by little.

If Bree could see her now, with chills from the closeness of a man, she would die. Her cackling would be heard across the whole state. She'd already told Jaime that the off and on desire to jump Ryan's bones was a sign that it had been way too long since Jaime had last had sex. And maybe she was right. But, Jaime hadn't ever felt like this around anyone else before. Her desire was something beyond a quick fix. It was a slow burn. Something she wanted to luxuriate in, allowing for dreams of a future that was easy to consider.

Until she thought about the lies that would have to be addressed, sure to infuse reality's sting into those fantasies.

"A few more and we can get out of your hair. This time though, I want you looking at the camera," Man-Bun said to Jaime. He pointed to Ryan. "And you looking at her. A smile would be great."

Jaime blushed as she tried to maintain the smile without blinking. If they used these photos, they would need to be liberal with the photoshop because the redness making her neck feel swollen with heat was heading for her chest. Once there, it would grow only blotchier.

Definitely not a good sell for the shop. *Please buy our plants, said the lady who looked like she was allergic to said plants, battling either anaphylaxis or the worst fever of her life.*

"That should do it." Man-Bun was back to looking down at the camera, the other man already starting to pack the gear that they'd scattered around the shop.

Neither Ryan nor Jaime made any move to help them, or to move at all. They remained side-by-side, quiet, supposedly watching the men work, though Jaime didn't let a fraction of her attention slip from Ryan's hand—so near to hers. She could care less about how the equipment got packed. Where Man-Bun had left his car keys. She was studying Ryan the way ants navigate underground tunnels, incremental. Feeling, trusting. As though her skin had developed extra sensors that were all tuned to him, detecting even his smallest movements, a shift from one foot to the other, the rest of his fingers on the table, exhalations making his chest rise in a rhythm that Jamie could use to pace her own breathing.

It was overwhelming then, when Ryan stepped away from the table where they'd been positioned for the photos—taking that hand that had been so close—and heading over to Man-Bun and the other photographer to shake hands and say goodbye. Jaime followed behind him, copying the social politeness in the automated, stock gestures of a grade-level graduation ceremony. Had to be done, and certainly a nicer experience than being forced to plunge a classroom toilet, but ultimately meaningless. It was the actual last days of school that got to Jaime during the graduation season, often making her tear up as she hugged her students goodbye, wishing them luck in fifth grade, preparing herself for the empty classroom devoid of energy and sound that would be the teachers' last days before summer break.

Ryan walked the men to their cars outside where they'd parked on the street and Jaime hovered by the till. Likely, he'd leave as soon as their car pulled away. At most, he'd stick around another five minutes, doing whatever needed done in the backroom. He'd say goodbye and then be gone for the rest of the workday, and she'd leave here for her mom and dad's and the usual Thursday dinner.

Except it wouldn't be the usual dinner—Jonathan would be there. Jaime groaned before she could stop herself. How anybody could juggle multiple relationships was beyond her. Just having kissed Ryan, and the persistent need to kiss him again, and again, and again, made the thought of Jonathan and her non-relationship though not-*no*-relationship pull at the back of her throat like a hangover.

"Are you alright?" The bell tinkled as Ryan shut the door, locking it again. One look at her expression and he was across the shop in what seemed like three steps. His progress stopped at the end of the counter, leaving space between them that Jaime longed to close.

"I'd forgotten that I have dinner with the parents tonight." She smiled, doing her best to try and convince Ryan that he wasn't the reason she was groaning. It wasn't him that had done anything wrong.

The longer they stood there though, the more Jonathan faded into the quiet space of memories packed away and labeled as the past. As the minutes ticked by, as Ryan and her eye contact went long past the normal length of social custom, the only thing on Jaime's mind was the man in front of her. And the desperation with which she wanted Ryan to stay here, with her.

He continued to stand, quiet and still. All the weirdness that they'd been able to avoid by having the other people in the shop was back, so blatant with each passing second that one of them would soon have to address it before either of them choked on its noxious presence.

They'd kissed, and she'd said it was a mistake, despite that it had been her that had initiated it, and her that wanted it again now. And she could feel, she *knew*, that if they stayed alone in the shop for more than another minute, she'd try again.

"Would it be better if I left?" Ryan asked, apparently reading her mind.

Thinking of dinner with her parents and Jonathan later that night, the right answer was yes, he should leave. But Jaime was no longer thinking about them. She was thinking about herself.

Her brain had shut off in favor of her heart, gravitating toward Ryan like a magnet to metal. Maybe if he'd dropped the eye contact, she'd have stood a chance. Maybe if his shoulders didn't look so good in his heather-blue, clingy shirt, she'd have been able to focus on how right things were with Jonathan. How happy the idea of them as a couple made her family. But Ryan was still staring at her as if she was beautiful, as if she was a woman worth the wait, and his shoulders *did* look that good, the pulse in his neck like morse code encouraging her to approach. It wasn't her parents, it was her, just her, without anybody's influence, who wanted to learn what it meant by taking the time to unravel him, and all the hidden messages of his body.

As if he'd once again read the direction of her thoughts, he said, "Jaime, you told me last time that—" He cleared his throat. "Jesus, as your boss, it should have been me to say it. But I'm not thinking clearly, not feeling… feeling like this."

Jaime's breath caught. "Feeling like what?" Her heart pounded in her ears, and she took a micro step toward him. Her body was the encroaching tide, washing over him would be a force of nature, the most natural thing in the world.

"You know like what."

"I don't." She stopped. She wanted him to say it. To say that in the last couple of weeks, he'd thought of her as much as she'd thought of him. To say that those thoughts weren't strictly about work—in fact, they weren't about work at all.

"I'm no good at putting things into words. I just—" He tucked his chin and grabbed onto the back of his neck. "I didn't feel like it was a mistake the other day."

She took one last step and then put a hand onto his chest. She wanted to lean in, but it was wrong with what she'd said Tuesday hanging between them still. "I said that, but I didn't mean it. I want—"

He kissed her. As soon as she figured out what was happening, she opened her mouth to his and then his tongue was pushing against hers, his hands on her lower back before moving up her shoulders. Back down and then up her front. Urgent. She craved him everywhere. Jolts of pleasure sent shockwaves that made every part of her tingle with possibility. She shuddered, digging her fingers into his back, pulling herself up onto him until she was cocooned within his arms.

The comfort made her melt. She sagged into him and Ryan responded, tightening his grip and helping her as she arched up to straddle him. Running kisses from her mouth to her neck and lingering there. Jaime wedged herself against him, shimmying herself up and enjoying every second of the journey. He dug his fingers in, and she wrapped her legs around his waist, begging him to find his place between her legs. Ryan lifted her, cupping her butt and groaning.

Jaime tightened her hold and ground herself against him—the desperation to be closer, to have more of him, making her whole body buzz.

She nudged him until his lips were on hers again. Sucking on his bottom lip to deepen the kiss. He leaned back, exposing his throat, groaning again until she quieted him by finding his mouth. Jaime already felt on fire, but she burned when he hiked her further up around his hips and then began backing toward the door and into the hall. Away from windows. Away from interruptions.

Groping for the knob without breaking apart, she

started to slip downward, and he laughed, the throatiness of it reverberating through her like a purr. Jaime smiled, a slick expression against his swelling lips, clenching his shoulders harder to help him keep herself glued to his body. The door finally gave way. As soon as they were through, they banged into the wall of the back hall, refusing to break the kiss. Pushing their tongues in a tug-a-war that had to be played to its fullest. It was slow moving progress. One step further, then a kiss that stopped them. One more half step. The pattern continued on down the hallway. Ryan clutched her like a dying man as they finally backed through the door to the work room. The lip of the counter bit into her back as he sandwiched her between himself and the table. "God Jaime." He swiped a finger across swollen lips.

"What?" she asked, feeling powerful as he jerked in response to her shimmying against him, feeling all the variation of his body. Where there was give. Where there was none. She had turned Ryan's shirt into a crumpled expanse of her desire, his lips a bruised, dark pink and his breathing a pant.

"You fucking slay me," he said. "I don't know how I'm so lucky right now. Doesn't feel real."

Crushed together, they staggered, searching for the cracks in clothing, for any skin that could be kissed, licked, touched.

"Jaime." Ryan gasped her name. "Jaime."

She'd unzipped his pants, and her hand was around him inside of his boxer briefs. It still wasn't enough. She pushed herself into him further. Ready to guide his hand to her if he didn't start touching her beyond her clothes soon.

That they'd let another two days pass without doing

this, without giving in, was painful now. Today marked one day shy of a full month left at this job. Every one of those remaining days counted.

"Yes?" she finally breathed, the word one large exhale as she continued to cover his shoulder in kisses and bites.

"I don't have a condom."

And for the first time since the camera men left, Jaime felt the world come into focus around Ryan despite the heat making the pulse between her legs an insistent drumbeat. She wasn't on birth control anymore—not having a boyfriend, and not having sex, made the side effects seem pointless. She cursed herself for trying to avoid the hormonal belly pooch, the headaches and moodiness, because right now, right here, that was nothing compared to how badly she wanted to have Ryan. All of him. Here, on this countertop, in this moment. She withdrew her hand from his underwear and tried to ignore his look of pain. The push of his hardness against her thigh when the space between them closed again.

"I don't have any at my place," she said. Any that she may have would probably be long expired, the search for them as embarrassing as the wait time that would make her aware of the last time that she'd shaved. Even in the height of shorts season, her legs had a shadow of prickles that it was hard to care about, working behind a counter, with no one to rub against at night. And she didn't wear a bathing suit to the golf course, she'd let her pubic hair grow in like the landscaping around her favorite sport. She hadn't been prepared for this, and part of the beauty of having it progress randomly was that she hadn't had the chance to dwell in the self-consciousness that usually guided her approach to nakedness.

"You're more than welcome at mine, but—" Ryan pulled back, then sagged into her, speaking into her collarbone as he traced her arm, finger lazily moving up to her shoulder and then to the very tip of her pinky finger, sending shivers that traveled the path of his touch and then down her spine, again, making her forget the once imperative need to groom before sex. His breath made chill bumps stipple her arms.

As she nestled her face into his shoulder, he sighed. "But don't you have dinner with your family on Thursdays?"

Chapter Twelve

Jaime grasped the door handle then stilled, closing her eyes and visualizing the moment just before the club hit the ball. The smell of the grass, more fragrant in the summer because of the heated soil, the shifting breeze as daytime faded into evening, the stillness and yet anticipation. The thrill of something about to happen that was fully, completely under *her* control.

Dinner was more likely to be a fore, where the ball went careening toward another group of golfers, than an ace. She opened her eyes before the daydream went on too long and pushed through the front door.

"Hello," she yelled, dropping her keys on the entry way table, and placing her purse beneath after slipping her phone into her back pocket. "Sorry I'm late."

The house was quiet and didn't smell like food. Jaime walked through the foyer, passing the empty dining room and into the kitchen where there was a prepped salad sitting out and several loaves of bread on a thick, wooden cutting board. Movement through the glass sliding door at the breakfast nook finally alerted her to where everybody was. Smoke billowed past, obscuring any view of who exactly was on the patio.

Her mom and dad must both be out there, otherwise she would have heard one of them inside by now. Jonathan had texted his apologies that he was being kept late at work and wouldn't make it to dinner. The relief

Jaime had felt, when halfway to the house, stopped at a redlight, she read his text, was like having her hair chopped off during a heatwave. She hadn't known how heavy the burden was until it was gone.

But not gone for good. She'd have to talk to Jonathan sooner rather than later. Things had already gotten too out of hand, and if nothing else, this past week with Ryan had made clear that although Jonathan may be a good guy, no matter how much he had changed, he was never going to be the good guy in her story. And the longer she kept him around, the more likely it was that he'd become the villain in her narrative. Same as what had happened before. Jonathan didn't deserve that. Neither did Jaime.

The door opened and Jaime's mother stepped through, looked up from her watch—and screamed.

"Surprise," Jaime said in a sing-song voice, smiling.

Zofia's eyes were still wide, and she bobbed her head forward, catching her breath, hand to chest. "Where's Jonathan?"

"He got held up at work, so he won't be able to come."

A cough sounded from outside as the door reopened. "Sounds like you were right then, Mom." Gretchen stepped through, waving away the smoke, and gave a sneering sort of half smile to Jaime before shutting the sliding door behind her.

The air left Jaime's chest in one exhale, leaving her limp and off balance. She'd thought she'd caught a break with Jonathan's cancellation. She'd thought it might make tonight easier. Instead, she'd stumbled, blindfolded, into a minefield. "I didn't realize you were coming into town."

"Mom asked both me and Brody to come down, but like Jonathan, he wasn't able to get out of work."

"Mom wanted you both here? For what?" Jaime narrowed her eyes at her mom, trying to recall if there was anything special about tonight, and dug her toes into the groove between the planks in the floor. Forcing herself to keep her shoulders straight around her sister. More than anything, Jamie wanted to cave them in and slink away home, curling up into the fetal position as soon as she was through the doors. To sleep as soon as she was in her bedroom, the light turned off, her sound machine whirring in the background.

Zofia sighed. "Can't I ask for our family to get together just because? You're not coming out to the beach ever again it seems, and I feel like we haven't been together since the holidays. With Jonathan coming, I thought it'd be nice."

"But now he's not here," Gretchen said. As if Jaime was to blame for that too.

"Well, then it'll be just us four again." Zofia clapped her hands and walked past Jaime, giving her shoulder a quick pinch. "Come help me set the table. Dad grilled chicken."

Like someone had hit rewind on the VHS of their life, the two sisters fell back into the pattern of their evening chores. Jaime grabbed napkins and utensils and Gretchen helped her mother by putting the right tongs into the salad, cutting the bread and placing it in the basket before bringing it out. They passed each other, making plenty of space for one another as they crossed under the archway from the kitchen into the dining room and back again.

A knock on glass signaled that the food was finished

Rachel Cooper

cooking. Ed stood, nose to door then held the blackened chicken, piled onto a plate, up to show how full his hands were. Too full to open the door. Zofia responded to his nonverbal request for help first, crossing the room to help him. Jaime sidled from the table to the archway, angling herself so that she could watch her mother and father's interactions.

They were the type of couple that bickered, only rarely displaying overt affection. It had always been easier to be with her dad. Ed was quiet, preferring activities that he could do alone, whether it was reading, watching television or walking. Zofia liked to be around people, preferring the noise of the hospital to Ed's quiet university office, enjoying shopping and large parties that she could only occasionally drag him to as well.

Jaime had a hard time imagining them falling over one another, desperate to touch each other like she and Ryan had been earlier.

"Thinking about trying to break up their marriage, too?" Gretchen said in a monotone.

Despite the low pitch, her words gut punched Jaime. She didn't know what to say to her sister. What would help? Dread pulled like a hangnail inside her, and once again, Jaime wished she could somehow make the bargain to pay all the money she had—do anything she could—to go back to last Christmas. To have never gone upstairs that night at Gretchen's party.

Zofia led Ed through the door, forcing him to pause and wipe his feet on the carpet. As they passed by, she waved at Jaime and Gretchen. "Sit down, sit down," Zofia said, still motioning them toward the table. "Start serving yourselves, I just need to grab the pasta salad from the fridge."

They assumed the chairs that had been rigidly theirs throughout Jaime's childhood, though dining room seat assignments had never been expressly verbalized. Food was passed clockwise starting with Zofia, while Ed twisted a corkscrew into a wine bottle, hunching over it with the effort.

"So, Mom says that you're spending the summer in some sort of plant shop," Gretchen said, cutting her chicken with a look of concentration that likely mirrored the way she sawed through bone during surgery.

Jaime nodded, swallowing, hesitant to do anything beyond the bare minimum of interaction. The fight that Gretchen wanted was a fifth guest, sitting at the table and staring Jaime right in the face. The force of its presence enough to bury her. The ensuing claustrophobia slowed all her movements and distracted her from anything beyond the impending battle.

Glasses of wine were set by each plate. And Ed took his seat. Jaime looked for any other reason to get up, to take a small breather in the kitchen. Everyone already had cutlery. The napkins were set out. There was nothing else needed except the stamina to stay put.

Her sister's knife scraped the plate, a screeching sound that Jaime felt in her core. Unphased by the noise, Gretchen asked, "Will you always have to work odd jobs? Or will you find someone to take care of you so you can continue to play victim?"

"Girls..." Ed raised his wine glass, looking over its rim, forehead wrinkled, and eyebrows raised in warning.

"You were trying to catch a doctor last year. And now that you know Jonathan's an anesthesiologist, he's back on the menu. What was wrong with him before?"

Here it was. Internal sirens warned that Jaime

needed to take cover now. She slid her chair back from the table an inch. "I wasn't trying to *catch* anyone last year. And nothing was wrong with Jonathan before. Nothing's wrong with him now." Except that he claimed Jaime and he were in a relationship when she explicitly asked for friendship. Except that he kissed her after she'd asked for slow. All of that was wrong. And allowing the illusion of their reunion to continue was as well. "And I haven't caught him. I've simply caught up on his life."

Zofia set her fork down. "What's that supposed to mean? What's happened?"

"With Jaime, something is always happening."

"Gretchen, I—" Ed didn't get to finish because Zofia stood, cutting him off.

She put her napkin over her full, hardly touched plate. "It's that man, isn't it?"

Ed swiveled in his seat. "What man?"

"Her boss." Zofia spat the words then leaned over the table and grabbed her glass, downing her wine in one gulp. She held it out to Ed for a refill.

Gretchen huffed. "Figures."

And Jaime, seated at the table, growing progressively redder, progressively more estranged from herself, like she was disassociating so that she could watch the impending implosion from a safe distance, suddenly felt as though she'd slammed back into her body with the force of a golfclub smacking a ball. Now, though, she was holding that club. This was *her* life they were splashing around the table in bits and pieces of misinformed headlines.

Enough was enough.

Jaime took a deep breath in through her nose and released it. "I broke up with Jonathan the last time

182

because I knew he wasn't right for me." She stood so that she was level with her mother and looking down on Gretchen, which shouldn't have mattered but did. It was good to finally gain some leverage on her older sister.

"I should have trusted that intuition again, instead of ignoring it to try and make all of you happy. I'm tired of doing that. I like being a teacher. I really, really, do. And I'm sorry that it's not as prestigious as being a surgeon—" Jaime forced eye contact with Gretchen. "Or a professor—" She set her jaw, jutting her chin toward her father. Then, throwing her napkin across the table until it landed in front of her mother, she said, "It may never pay what you'd like me to make, but I don't care."

Jaime took a deep breath, teeing up. "This is my life, and teaching makes me—*me*—happy." She gulped air, forcing herself onward. "And it matters, the difference that I make if not daily, then weekly. Monthly, yearly. So, please, for the love of everything holy, please explain the problem you have with my choices. Because I don't understand what the issue really is."

Both Jaime's parents stared.

Her mother slowly sat back in her chair.

"No one gives a shit about the fact that you got scared of medical school and then chose an easier route." Gretchen's voice was a scalpel, slicing through the balloon that had blown up until Jaime felt large enough to speak her mind.

Gretchen bullied on, both her hands set firmly on the table, white with the tension that was rippling like heat waves off her rigid posture. "What we care about is your lack of respect. Your inability to think of anybody but yourself."

Always needing the last say, Gretchen had the

resilience to maintain an argument where Jaime caved every time. Jaime could feel herself folding inward now. Getting ready to hide, to curl up and sleep until Gretchen's words no longer stung. Switching to that too familiar dull ache instead.

Zofia cleared her throat. "Girls—"

"She tried to have sex with my husband," Gretchen shouted.

Ed coughed. Zofia snorted.

Jaime's mouth opened and closed. "What—" She couldn't find the words.

Finally, she gathered herself enough to sputter. "Did Brody tell you that?"

Gretchen stared straight ahead at the wall.

"I caught him having sex in your upstairs bathroom with one of your colleagues." In her mind, Jaime was back at that party, the one she'd been invited to only because their mother had insisted Gretchen include her. She hadn't wanted to go, knowing that she'd be a stranger amongst all her sister and Brody's resident friends. Then she'd made the mistake of needing to pee at the wrong time. When the downstairs bathroom was busy. Forcing her upstairs. Upstairs where Brody had another woman in the unlocked hallway bathroom. Up on the counter. Knees digging into either side of his hips. Seeing him with that other woman—driving into her as if he wasn't married to Gretchen who was just downstairs—had made Jaime's anger boil over, the way it had tonight, forcing her hand and prompting her to find Brody later. To demand that he tell Gretchen, or she would.

When Gretchen had been so furious the next day, ranting that Jaime was the worst sister in the world, screaming to their parents about her selfishness, her inability to care about anyone but herself, Jaime had just figured that she was the messenger being shot down in her sister's hurt. It had been so similar to the way Gretchen routinely spoke about Jaime anyhow. She'd never even questioned whether Brody had done as she'd asked and told the truth. How naïve.

The dining room pulsed despite the silence. Ed appeared transfixed by his hands in his lap, twiddling his thumbs as Zofia ducked her chin to try and catch Gretchen's eyes.

Gretchen looked up. "I don't believe you," she said, her lip quivering. "Brody wouldn't."

"If you can believe that I would ever want to sleep with Brody, then I'm never going to be able to convince you. Anyone who knows me also knows I've always thought he was scum. He *was* cheating on you, but not with me."

Zofia broke the stalemated posturing of everyone at the table. Standing and following the circle of chairs until she was at Gretchen's side. She pulled Gretchen into her, cradling her head against her chest. "Honey."

A sob ratcheted out of Gretchen. Only one. A heaved cry that sounded as if it had been brewing for much longer than tonight's dinner.

Ed, pink cheeked with bright red ears, turned to Jaime. "So, what's this about you and Jonathan not working out?"

"Ed," Zofia snapped. "We're focusing on Gretchen right now."

"I thought she'd like us to shift that focus, was all," he said, squirming in his seat and back to playing a solo game of thumb war.

Jaime's knees shook and she braced herself against the back of her chair. It was probably time for this overdue conversation as well. "For a minute, Jonathan seemed like a good idea. He made you all so happy." She grabbed her napkin from near her mother's plate and sat down. "But he's not who I want."

Her father nodded, and Gretchen pushed Zofia away, wiping her eyes.

Jaime thought better of sitting and once again rose, walking out of the room to go grab a box of tissues from the half bath opposite the kitchen. Back in the dining room, she handed them to her sister. "I'm sorry that I played a part in extending your pain," she said. "My intention was to avoid prolonging it."

Gretchen buried her face in a tissue, turning herself in her chair so that she faced away from the table and toward the window where the light had gone soft with evening. Pale pink filtered through the shuttered blinds, softening the edges of everything inside.

Zofia tutted and tried to pull Gretchen back into her, but Gretchen shook her head and angled herself further from view.

Jaime strode to her seat, thinking of Ryan, and what Helen had revealed about him being let down and abandoned by all the people he loved. She sat down hard. Letting the *whump* sound the exhaustion that she felt. She didn't want to add to the number of people that had hurt Ryan. But it didn't seem possible to avoid any damage. Nor was it feasible to continue to be with him while pretending that she wasn't going back to teaching. Prioritizing what she wanted, indulging her own agency, meant that first, Jaime needed to tell Jonathan that he deserved better. She'd keep to herself that so did she.

Then, she'd tell Ryan the truth.

****

The walls of the bar were red, the shelves that hosted rows of glittering bottles nearly black their wood was so dark. Jaime looked around, grounding herself in all the details despite the dim, yellow mood-lighting, because she was having trouble believing that she and Gretchen were out together. Just the two of them alone in a bar in Roam. A month ago, this would have only occurred in a dream. And even then, it would have been more like a nightmare.

"Tell me what happened, again?" Gretchen said, her voice fuzzy from the cocktails.

Jaime sipped her beer, the only one that she would have all night since she'd be driving Gretchen back to their parents' as soon as Gretchen made it clear that she was done. "I'm not sure that's a good idea."

"If Jonathan had cheated on you, you'd have wanted to know every detail, wouldn't you?"

If that had happened, Jaime would have been given the out she'd been secretly craving since the night sophomore year when Jonathan had mapped their lives, detailing the type of house that they'd live in, the parties they'd host, the vacations they'd take, the children they'd have. Baby names and all. She'd felt so stifled by the solidness of his vision, one where she could've been exchanged for any willing woman, ready to wear a matching sweater in the holiday family photos that fit so well with the rest of his vision.

There was nothing particular to who Jaime was that directed his dreams for their future.

"Well—wouldn't you want to know?" Gretchen slumped back in her chair, twisting the stem of her martini glass until the olive bobbed.

Jaime took another small sip of beer. If it had been Jonathan, then maybe—if only because it would arm Jaime with the means for a breakup. But when she framed that question with Ryan's name instead, her feelings changed. They weren't a couple. Never even been on an official date. In many ways, they barely knew each other. But the thought of him with someone else made her stomach clench so violently that any more details would be painful. "I don't think I would."

Gretchen made a *pshh* sound and sat forward.

"Really," Jaime said, trying to avoid dwelling on thoughts of Ryan with somebody—anybody—else. "It would only make me more miserable than I already was."

"I knew Brody was cheating," Gretchen said, her eyes glazing over and her tongue darting out to wet her lower lip. "Of course, I knew that he was. But you've been such a mess lately that I didn't know if—if… And even if you hadn't, it was easier to be mad at you. Easier to just go with the flow of what had always kind of been there."

"What does that even mean?" Jaime folded her napkin lengthwise then along its width. "Why does everyone think I'm such a mess?"

"Because you were all set to go to medical school, majoring in Biology, checking all the boxes. Last we knew, you'd both gotten into medical school and were planning a wedding. Then you rejected your spot at school and got your teaching license. No explanation. There was no heads up when you went to grad school for education, either. Or when you randomly broke up with Jonathan days before the party to celebrate your engagement. It all just happened out of the blue with zero warning."

Jaime groaned. "I tried to explain. Loads of times." Medical school was her mother's dream for her girls. One that Gretchen had been on board with from their first doctor play-kit. The plastic stethoscope slung round her neck whether she was wearing a princess costume or a superhero's cape. Jaime had gone along with those designs because it had been easier. Until it wasn't. And when she'd finally found the force inside herself to make the change, she'd needed to do it right away. Without asking for the permission she knew wouldn't come.

Gretchen pinched her nose. "Why break up with Jonathan, though? You know that he's the only reason I'm here today. Mom was like desperate for me to come out for dinner with him. I sort of thought he was going to propose again tonight."

Jaime burrowed her face in her arms. "Please, no."

"Uh-huh. And honestly, I'm not sure why you're not going for it. It doesn't get any more Ken-like. So don't be a rebel, Barbie. You'd never have to work another random summer job again, married to him."

"I really like my summer job this year." Jaime unconsciously angled herself in the direction of the shop just on the other side of where they were downtown. She wondered if Ryan was there now. Setting out the new Zig Zag plants with the rest of the succulents. Scouring the inventory with his index finger set against his lips in that habit of his.

"At least one of us is happy." Gretchen swirled her drink and downed it. "I'm probably heading home to a divorce. Mom and Dad know about Brody, now. That's hard to recover from. And not something I want to dwell on right now. So, give me something else to think about. Please? Starting with whatever the issue is with Ken-himself?"

"Jonathan makes me feel like some lesser version of myself. Like I'm just a picture instead of a person." Jaime became sidetracked by the bartender with a martini shaker, moving it so fast it appeared to blur, his black apron signaling that whatever was about to be poured was likely to be a masterpiece. She sighed. "Bree says that he doesn't let me shine. That he wants arm candy while I want to be the star."

At Gretchen's questioning look, Jaime added, "My best friend. You've definitely met her."

Jaime licked her lips, trying to overcome the flair of frustration at how little her family listened. "Bree sometimes accuses me of wanting all eyes on me. That's why she says that I like teaching. But that's not entirely true. I just love the feeling of being able to help—I like seeing those connections made. When we were little, everything felt halfway... like it was hard to tell if Mom and Dad were ever happy—with each other or with us. All our conversations had to be figured out after the fact because nothing was ever direct or obvious. Teaching is literally the opposite of that, it's all about making sure that people understand."

"Okay, okay." Gretchen stood. "The second we start talking family drama, I need another drink. And no more, save-the-children-be-a-teacher talk. Keep that for your billboards or annual reviews or whatever's done in education." She walked, wobbling on her heels when a man scooted his chair into her path. At the bar, she ordered another drink.

When she returned, she said, "Tell me about needing

attention. Jonathan seemed to give you plenty all the times I've seen you together."

Jaime thought about the way that Ryan had looked at her during the photoshoot at Plant Life. "I feel like Jonathan sees what he wants to see. And sometimes that doesn't add up to the person I really am."

Gretchen nodded. "And this random dude that Mom brought up, he does?"

Jaime smiled despite herself. "I think so."

"Well then. Maybe I'll meet him when you bring him to my divorce party."

"Funnily enough, a divorce party was the first reason he and I went somewhere besides work."

Gretchen narrowed her eyes. "Whose divorce?"

"His, of course."

Gretchen spat out her drink and then wiped her mouth, ignoring the long-haired blonde's disgusted reaction from the table beside them. She smiled and said, "Okay, now I really want to meet him. Oh my God, Jaime. You really are such a mess."

Jaime raised her empty glass. "Cheers."

Chapter Thirteen

Back at the shop, in between customers, Jaime's cell phone buzzed—not with a response from Gretchen who she had texted two hours before to check on, sure that Gretchen was suffering not just from heartbreak this morning but likely a torrential hangover as well—but with a message from Bree. Bree wanted to know on a scale of zero-to-ten just how badly dinner the night before had gone. And if it had been a ten out of ten, worst dinner ever, she needed Jaime to know that she had a grocery bag full of golf balls that she had collected to drop-off later that night. Alongside a six-pack, of course.

Jaime—*You're too good to me*—

Then she rated the night a six. Because although it had been painful, it had also been cathartic. Freeing. Her parents had both responded to her outburst with a level of respect that had even afforded the question about whether she was excited for the next school year later that night. And Jaime had gone out for drinks with Gretchen after, a milestone in and of itself. Though, Jaime wanted to hear back from her sister before deciding whether that was simply a one-time fluke.

A rush of wind blew into the shop as the door opened, the summer day breezy, making all the trees that dotted the outside sidewalk, bordered by small, black cages to protect from deer, or, most likely cars, sway. After the door was firmly shut, everybody through, and the shop resettled in the steady white noise familiar to a slow day at Plant Life, Jaime put down her phone.

"Are y'all looking for anything in particular?" she asked, rising from her stool.

"Just looking, thanks," said the couple who'd entered. They held hands as they began to wander the aisles, pointing to different plants and talking about where they might fit in their home. A Red *aglaonema* for the television stand, *bromeliads* for the kitchen windowsill. Jaime listened, busying herself behind the counter to cover the fact that she was watching them. She couldn't help herself. Drawn to their eagerness, it was clear that the couple was talking about decorating a space they were new to sharing, and the openness that both approached the others' opinions made a warm, fuzziness blanket her insides.

That feeling intensified with the sudden pressure of a hand against her lower back and the low, breathy voice in her ear. "These two are happy enough that I'd recommend an olive tree. They have enough time ahead of them that they may get to enjoy watching it fruit."

"Do we have any?" Jaime asked, leaning the back of her head against his shoulder.

"Nope," Ryan said. He laughed. "I want them in someone else's shop, so you'll be all mine again."

"You're supposed to want to make sales, you know? That's part of owning a business."

"I'm transplanting in the back. Come find me after they leave." He briefly rested his chin on her head, then the warmth of him was gone. The soft shush of the back door closing accented the murmurs of the couple in the shop.

"Will these grow well in low light?" The woman let

go of the man's hand and gestured to a Swiss cheese plant, turning expectantly to Jaime.

"I wouldn't try, not with that one." Jaime moved out from behind the counter. "But certain palms are a great option for a dimmer spot if you're looking for a larger plant."

She rang them up for two Areca palms and a small *pothos*, offering to help them get everything into their car multiple times. They assured her that they could handle it, and she rushed to get the door for them as they juggled their new plants, giving up on hand holding as they exited the shop.

There was no one else on the sidewalks outside, no new cars pulling up, so Jaime went straight to the back, propping the hallway door open in case anybody did come in while she wasn't up front.

Ryan's back was to her when she walked through the open doorway of the workroom, his earbuds likely in because he didn't hear her, nor did he stop what he was doing. He had apparently finished repotting and was mixing soil, prepping for whatever project he had in mind next. Jaime smiled and leaned against the open door, watching him for a moment. She loved the concentration, the exactitude with which he approached everything. He stretched a piece of painter's tape across the bucket lid, labeling the soil mixture.

Once her attention was noticed, he turned around, smirking as if he knew that she'd been checking him out. He removed his earbuds and leaned against the counter. "Did you get rid of the lovebirds?"

"I did," Jaime said, crossing her arms and trying to keep her smile from becoming too big.

"Let's get lunch, then."

****

"Just so you know, I'm setting a timer," Jaime said after ordering at the bar.

Their drinks arrived at the same time that Ryan put his hand to his chest, mock appalled. After the waiter left, he said, "You don't think I'm a responsible business owner?"

"It did take you forever to hire some help."

"I was waiting for you." Ryan's smile was butter, melting into Jaime.

She wanted to surrender to this offer of lunch dates every day. Or at least, a few times a week. The stolen touches in the shop and easy banter that made the previous night's drama feel miles away. But school was waiting, and Ryan needed to know.

Ryan cleared his throat. "What are you doing on your day off? I happen to know that it's Sunday."

She smiled. "Who told you?"

"I've got a good in with the scheduler."

Jaime tasted her beer, enjoying the malty depth of the red. Her day off should probably be dedicated to tying up the loose ends with Jonathan. But thinking about that potential argument-maybe-fight, right on the coattails of wondering how she was going to tell Ryan about leaving Plant Life, made her want to spend the whole day either sleeping or golfing. She went with the latter option. "I might try and golf a full course."

"You golf?" Ryan straightened, his eyes widening and his mouth depressing momentarily before his expressions returned to neutral.

"Is that so surprising?"

He sat back, thumbing the edge of the table. "I guess I'm just trying to picture you in the sweet ass little visor.

I hope you've got one of those green reflective ones. Or are you a golfer like John Daly, getting drunk with the boys in the golf cart?"

She laughed. "No and no. I golf on my own, it's not a party."

"I don't believe it. You probably show up in your polka dot pants ready to start chain smoking your way from hole-to-hole."

"I didn't know you had such a thing for John Daly— you know him so well. Have you always been into older, bearded golfers?"

"Neither him, nor golf are my thing. But I'll be your caddy anytime you want. I'm going to complain about the waste of land and water under my breath the whole time, though."

"You're definitely not invited, then."

"Can I take you on a date after you get done scaring the fish in the lakes of whatever course you use? A real date."

Jaime's stomach tightened with desire and dread. This was the point where Ryan was laying his cards on the table and making what they had real. This was the point where he deserved the truth from her. She was still a teacher; she hadn't quit like she'd originally alluded. Plant Life was temporary.

"First—" She sipped her beer again, stalling. The fizz tickled the back of her throat, slipping down into her stomach where she could feel the alcohol warming her from the inside out, taking her back to the kisses in the backroom and now, the possibility of being with Ryan during hours that were theirs to control. "You haven't told me what you like to do away from the shop."

He lifted his glass and clinked it against hers. "I'm

a simple man, Ms. Krause. I like to work in my garden. And if you play your cards right on Sunday, maybe I'll show it to you."

"I'd like that," she said.

If Ryan had asked her something about her future plans, if he had asked her about what teaching had been like last year, if he'd said anything about the state of education in America, Jaime would have told him that she'd never quit her job. That she'd lied. But Ryan didn't ask. Instead, he had questioned her about golfing. How she'd first been introduced to the sport, whether she still played with her father. Then he shared the story of his first plant, a cactus that he had been given by his stepsister and that he'd killed by overwatering, a little kid who was overzealous in wanting to care for the small succulent.

That drove Ryan to begin paying attention to what grew in the garden, learning how to get his mom's hydrangea to bloom more fully year after year, starting the vegetable garden that would teach him the importance of nutrients in the soil and plant rotation.

Jaime listened, forgetting that this might only last as long as her secret. Awareness of it had been edged out by the growing sensation that this budding relationship that felt so right was a new chapter of her life slowly revealing itself. She didn't want to put the book down. Especially not if it meant that she might end it before she was ready.

✳✳✳✳

Later that evening, outside in the sticky humidity that the wind earlier had done nothing to dissuade, text messages from Talia and Bree pinged Jaime's phone rapid fire, making her back pocket buzz. All she'd told them was that she was going on a date with Ryan, that she may or may not have kissed him, and that Bree and Talia weren't, under any circumstances, allowed to read The Roam Rover until Jaime told them they could. GIFs and long text bubbles made up of emojis and exclamation marks flooded the chat.

Jaime was able to ignore the messages but avoiding Bree's calls felt wrong. When Bree called for a third time in a row, she answered.

"Which one are you at?"

"The usual."

"Be there in twenty. If you leave, you better text me."

Jaime looked around the green of the driving range that she typically frequented, courses a luxury for long weekends and saved for when she could golf a full day. The enclosed lawn extended forward like a lesson in perspectives amidst the fading light. Cicadas hummed in time with the buzz of the overhead lights, switched on early to avoid any period of darkness, and now, adding a reflective sheen to the gray-blue grass as evening wore on. The range would close before the sun was fully set. In the winter though, when Jaime really needed to hit a ball on a weekday, darkness was her only option.

Tonight, she'd splurged for the large bucket of balls, a fee she'd most likely be paying tomorrow evening as well, even though she'd once again only manage to play in the limited time left after a full day of work. It was worth it.

Bree called six swings later. "I'm in the parking lot. They won't let me bring beers in, and the guy warned that they were closing in fifteen minutes anyhow."

There were four balls left in the bucket. "Give me

five minutes." She hit them rapid succession, letting herself enjoy reckless swings instead of the methodical, focused approach of normal. It felt good, winding her to the point of breathlessness. Exhilarating to just attack with abandon. No thought to what might come next or how well she was doing. Whether she was accomplishing anything beyond release.

Out in the parking lot, Bree sat on the hood of her car, a six-pack sitting beside her. "I'm not risking more trouble. We're going to yours to drink these."

"Is this going to be a sleepover sort of situation? Should we grab more?"

Bree tsked. "Don't you know where I work? There's more in the car."

She followed Jaime back to the apartment where they both slumped onto the couch the second the lights were turned on, purses and beer set on the coffee table and shoes slipped off then thrown back toward the front door, landing scattered across the linoleum entryway.

"Not Kobe," Bree said, making a pouty face and shaking her head at where the shoes landed. Far apart from each other, and not at all near the small shoe rack.

"I still love you. Professional shoe tosser, or not." Jaime leaned forward and grabbed one of the beer cans. She offered one to Bree before popping the pull tab. "I wonder if Mom would be happy with an athlete for my sugar-daddy."

"Sounds like you already found a different one." Bree raised her eyebrows, pretending to get distracted as she looked away, forehead scrunched, drinking her beer.

"First I need to talk with the one that Mom did want."

"When did you become such a heart breaker?"

"This summer." Jaime sighed. "The moment I began living *the plant life*."

"Ooh, you bad." Bree laughed, stretching on the couch, and draping her legs over Jaime's thighs. She bent one, resting her knee against Jaime's chest, nudging her with her toes. "But that's part of why I'm here, and why I came bearing gifts."

Jaime raised an eyebrow and set her beer on top of Bree's foot.

"Hey! That's cold." Bree pulled her foot back. She sat up. "And now, even though you don't deserve it, I'm going to remind you of that day that you came to my office going on and on about some crazy lady who was warning you off Ryan. The Ryan who you swore you weren't into."

"Elise," Jaime said. She'd forgotten about Elise's threat, and the possibility of one more fight this summer.

"Right." Bree cracked another beer, but it must have been shaken, because froth spilled from the open tab, causing her to lean forward and begin slurping, probably to avoid staining her shirt or permeating the couch with a smell that would soon go from hoppy to foul.

To Jaime, the spill felt symbolic. She even considered texting Gretchen, just to give her sister the satisfaction of hearing that she was right. Jamie's life was a mess.

Bree put her hand up. "I see you getting all up inside your own head, probably plotting ways to wriggle out from this without needing to confront anybody, but I suggest you talk to Ryan. Most likely, this Elise lady was just trying to use corporate intimidation tactics, and never had any intention of telling him anything. She probably just used you for some sort of twisted stress release. But say she's decided to go full *Days of Our Lives*—" Bree intoned the name like she was on television introducing the soap. "Then you need to be one step ahead of her drama by telling him yourself. Plus, I doubt Ryan would even care that you're not sticking with the job."

"I think he will."

"Not if he hears the truth from you. He's an adult. Hell, we're all adults. And people move on from jobs and choose careers over part time shit every day."

"But he doesn't see his shop as part time."

"He will if whatever you two have becomes fulltime." Bree elbowed Jaime and wiggled her eyebrows. "Know what I mean?"

Jaime pretended to push Bree away.

"But seriously. You're going to make more trouble for yourself trying to avoid a fight. I mean, look at what happened with your sister. If you'd just called her out on her bullshit last Christmas, you'd have found out what her sleazy husband had said you'd done and been able to set the record straight then and there. It's going to be the same with this Ryan stuff, girl."

"I know," Jaime said. She breathed out through her nose. "First, I'm going to talk to Jonathan. I'll break things off with him—not that there is anything—but I'll make sure he knows that too. And then on Sunday, I'm going out with Ryan; I'll tell him then."

"Jesus, Jaime. I should have brought more beer."

"I tried to tell you."

****

The morning started off with the shop already open and a coffee waiting on the counter for Jaime when she walked through the hall door and out to the area where she normally liked to set up for the day. Ryan wasn't anywhere to be seen, but his scent lingered, an added note of woodiness on top of the soil and usual plant smells. The entire vibe of the place was clean without being off-putting or artificial, the coziness that came when everything was taken care of, and relaxation permitted. Jaime stretched, leaning into that feeling as she blew on her coffee and basked in the morning light streaming through the windows.

Soon, she'd have to text Jonathan and set up a time to meet. But not right away. Not in this perfect moment, a moment where she felt she was living out the best, most ideal version of the American summer vacation fantasy. Days filled with sandals and shorts, warm cheeks that no longer needed blush thanks to the extended sunlight, and the excitement of first kisses and somebody new. So new that Jaime's arm hairs still stood on end, just thinking about Ryan.

And, as if on cue, the back door opened, Ryan's smell becoming more than just a background note. Jaime swiveled on her stool, smiling. "Thank you for the coffee."

"If it's no good, you can blame Mom. I got the recommendation from her."

"You interrupted her Greek islands vacation to confirm that I love lavender lattes?"

"No, she somehow sent me her entire notes folder, and she'd made one entirely dedicated to you."

"Nu-uh." Jaime grinned. "What else did she write?"

"Not telling." Ryan trailed her arm with his thumb and then circled her shoulder. "But I'll say, some of it surprised me."

"Helen doesn't know anything about me that could

be considered surprising."

"That's what you think. But good to know that there's more you're not sharing."

"Not what I said."

"Don't worry." Ryan tapped his nose. "I'll put her on the case as soon as she's back."

"Siccing your mother on me is not fair."

"Well, you know what they say, all's fair in love and war."

Jaime's ears grew hot. She swallowed, avoiding the first part of what he said—*love*—and trying to pretend as if she'd only heard the second part. "I didn't realize we were at war."

"Oh we—"

The front doorbell tinkled, cutting off whatever Ryan was about to say. As soon as Jaime saw who had crossed the threshold, her stomach bottomed out and mouth went dry. After being so absorbed in the floral sweetness of her coffee, the home-like familiarity of the shop, her guard had slipped to nothing. She wasn't prepared.

"Jonathan," Jaime said, voice constricted.

Ryan looked from Jaime to Jonathan then back again, his expression blank.

Jonathan ran a hand through his hair, turning from one side to the other as he took in the shop. "It's a Saturday that I have off, and I was headed out with the guys but then decided that I should take an extra minute to stop and see you. Confirm that you're where you say you are every Saturday." He winked, his jaw ticking as he chewed his gum.

"Here I am." Jaime tried to catch Ryan's eyes before sidling out from behind the counter.

"It's a plant shop, isn't it?" Jonathan began walking toward her, looking from one end of the space to the other. "Don't flowers count?"

"What do you mean?" Jaime stopped by the table of ivies, twisting one of the long trailing vines around her finger.

"I want to buy you some flowers."

Jaime cleared her throat and took a deep breath. "It's not really a flower shop, Jonathan. We don't do bouquets. I told you, it's houseplants." She wavered on whether she should introduce Jonathan to Ryan, who still stood behind the counter, drinking his coffee, and so far, saying nothing.

A woman with pink hair walked into the shop, smiling broadly at Jaime before sensing that she was already tied up with Jonathan. She moved on to Ryan, who continued to watch Jaime and Jonathan from the back of the shop. Expression yet unreadable.

The woman with pink hair pulled out her phone and began to swipe through photos. "I'm having a problem with gnats. All of my plants seem to be bringing in bugs," she said to Ryan.

He edged out from behind the counter and guided her to the shelf with decorative pots and the sticky tape, bright yellow and cut into fun shapes on a popsicle stick, that they recommended to help with bugs. Jaime knew that Ryan would soon have some sort of snarky comment about how the woman must have used soil from one of the big lumber store's garden centers—*riddled with bugs and disease*—but Jonathan was now beside her, his hand resting on her shoulder.

"Do you want any of those? They're flowers of a sort," he said, pointing to the orchids in the corner.

Jaime gave a half smile. "Too high maintenance for me."

"My low-key girl." Jonathan beamed, pausing his gum chewing.

Now was the time. The first on her to-do list of hard conversations. Jaime reminded herself of what Bree had said the night before, that avoiding what felt like conflict had led to a long, drawn-out fight between Jaime and Gretchen that had kept them from talking for more than six months. Dragging this out could do the same. "Actually Jonathan, we really need to talk. Do you have a minute?"

Jonathan's jaw flexed and clicked again. He grinned. "This sounds serious."

"It is." Jaime looked to Ryan and found him still watching her, the woman he was helping busy comparing the designs of the sticky sheets.

"Can we step outside?" Jaime asked Jonathan.

The faint hint of crow's foot wrinkles appeared on either side of Jonathan's narrowed eyes, then quickly disappeared into tan smoothness. He gestured. "Lead the way."

Jaime walked in front of him, heading for the front door. She stopped a few paces from Ryan and said, in as professional a tone as she could muster. "I just need to have a quick chat with my friend." Emphasis on *friend*. "I'll be back in a couple minutes."

Ryan nodded, his poker face still strong, refusing Jamie any hint at what he thought was happening, and whether she'd have to do damage control with him once she was done with Jonathan outside.

Outside, the summer sun was at its peak in the middle of the sky. Cars rushed past the sidewalk.

Exhaust fumes contributing to Jaime's headiness as she stepped beyond the shade of the shop front and waited for Jonathan a few steps behind. The day was shaping up to be gorgeous from start to finish and a stab of jealousy snuck through Jaime's apprehension, knowing that Jonathan would be spending the rest of his afternoon out playing golf with his friends on one of the best courses in the state of Virginia. She knew she shouldn't begrudge him the escape if the news she gave was hard. But it was hard to want to offer him any generosity when she knew she'd be walking back into the shop with work and hard conversation number two to look forward to. Jonathan needed to know that there was no future for them as anything beyond friends. Ryan needed to know that she had never quit teaching.

Jaime put her hands in her pockets, slouching her shoulders as she tried to recall the words she'd practiced with Bree last night and in the car this morning. "I know that I did a lot to encourage you—about us. And I want you to know that I did mean what I said. I was willing to consider a fresh start."

Jonathan took a step back.

Jaime swallowed, taking note of the other people in the area. She knew Jonathan. He wasn't the sort to get violent. He was the sort to yell. Having other people around made her feel as though the chances of him shouting, like he had last time, might be lower with others in ear shot.

Though, Jonathan knew her well enough to know how much she hated a fight. He'd used it to his advantage how many times? Like taking her *I'll think about it* and telling his mother and hers that they were dating again. Jaime crossed her arms. "But I should have listened to that inner voice that kept insisting we weren't going to work. We want different things."

"Like what? What do you want that's so different?"

The pink-haired woman walked out of Plant Life and Jaime forced herself to smile and wave goodbye at the woman. It bought her a minute to think on what Jonathan was demanding from her, answers that were as of yet unanswerable because it was a feeling instead of a concrete list. How could Jaime explain that somehow, in just a few weeks, she'd felt more comfortable, more at ease, more herself around Ryan than she'd ever been with Jonathan? That answer wasn't easy, nor fair. She cleared her throat. "I'm sorry."

"This is how you ended it last time too. Sorry." His voice took on a high-pitched, mocking cadence. "*Sorry*. But nothing for me to actually work with. Nothing to help me understand you better or understand what I did wrong."

"You didn't do anything wrong."

"Obviously I did."

Jaime kicked at the ground with the toe of her sandal, catching the break in the sidewalk. "I don't think that I'll ever be able to make this as tidy as you want it to be. Maybe Gretchen's right, and I'm just a messy person, creating messy problems that don't have clear solutions. But I'm doing my best to clean this up before it gets too bad. If we continue to pretend that we belong together because the reasons that we don't work are hard to explain, then I don't think we're doing either of ourselves any favors. I want you to be with someone who never doubts the relationship. And that can't be me."

The summer sun was at its peak in the middle of the sky.

Jonathan's lips twisted. "Fuck it, then." He put his sunglasses on, blocking any expression of his eyes, took the gum out of his mouth and flicked it onto the sidewalk in the direction of Plant Life's front door. Then, he turned and walked away. Jaime took a step backward, her knees weak and the ground unsteady. She rallied her nerve before righting her posture and using an old receipt from her pocket to pick up the littered gum. That hadn't gone how she'd thought, and though she was glad to not be fighting on the street, the sudden silence felt equally terrible.

There wouldn't be any sense of resolution. Maybe not ever. But she'd done what needed doing. She'd been brave. Jaime dropped the gum into the garbage can a few paces from the shop and tried to envision what a pep talk from Bree would sound like now. *Resolution is for things that matter, walking away for the things that don't.*

The sting of Jonathan's abrupt parting would pass, and Jaime would eventually make peace with today's unresolved fight, same as she had with their previous, much sloppier breakup. Even so, tears clouded her vision and threatened to run her mascara. She sniffled, putting the edge of her hand to her nose and giving herself a minute to indulge her weariness.

When she walked into the shop, Ryan stood a few feet from the door.

"I wasn't eavesdropping. I just wanted to be close-by to make sure that you were okay." He looked at her in earnest. "Are you okay?"

Jaime nodded, but something about the question made it impossible not to begin fully crying. As she raised her palms to her eyes to keep him from seeing it happen, he closed the distance between them, pulling her into his arms.

"I've got you," he said. "We'll make it right, whatever's going on. It'll be okay."

And Jaime believed him. Here, with him, it would all be okay.

****

With most of her eye-makeup long gone, her eyelids slightly swollen and puffy, and a runny nose that hadn't quite stopped since she'd cried and cried into Ryan's chest earlier, Jaime looked up from her book to see who had walked into the shop.

Ryan had needed to make a quick run to the store, and without anyone there to help if needed, Jaime had the immediate, adrenaline-fueled response of every woman who feels cornered. A tightening of the muscles that worsened the sudden spark of anxiety. Unclear whether her body was frozen or ready to fight, Jaime edged herself forward on the stool, testing her ability to move if needed.

"Don't worry. I didn't come back to try and change your mind," Jonathan said. He crossed the length of the shop and set a small box on top of the counter. His voice was hard when he spoke again. "I can't keep holding onto this forever. It'll never be meant for anyone but you, though."

And without another word, with averted eyes and a set to his walk that indicated that this was his final departure, Jonathan left.

It wasn't until the bells on the door stopped chiming that she breathed again.

Jaime knew what was inside the box but looked anyway, if only as one last favor to Jonathan. Nestled between two velvet cushions was a large, square cut diamond on a white gold band studded with smaller diamonds. It caught the light, winking at her as she turned the box one-hundred and eighty degrees atop the counter. The ring should have caused her to feel sad, to feel something akin to regret. Instead, Jaime felt relief. She snapped a photo of it and sent it alongside a follow-up message about the day's events to the group chat with Bree and Talia.

Talia—*I'll take it*—

Bree—*Go on and leave that bad juju shit to T. But when she's got bad luck for seven years, don't say I didn't warn you both*—

Jaime closed the ring-box and the chat thread. Deciding what to do with the ring could wait. For now, she only needed to make sure it was well out of sight when Ryan returned.

Chapter Fourteen

Jaime had spent hours getting ready, shaving her
legs with actual shaving cream instead of the hair
conditioner that always outlasted her shampoo. She
dabbed her wrists, behind her ears, and her lower back
with perfume, and yo-yoed between the black lacy
underwear and bra-set or the navy tee-shirt-bra that felt
more like her. Less for show than functionality and
comfort. She went with the navy option. Paired with a
cotton thong that she reserved for certain skirts and
dresses that showed every single underwear line no
matter how thin the material.

When Ryan rang her doorbell, insisting on picking
her up as if she were a high school sweetheart that needed
the ride—*I want to do this right*, he'd said—Jaime nearly
ran back to the bedroom to change into the lacy option.
She had gone with the other, not wanting to be
presumptive, and afraid of looking too eager, too
desperate. Whatever she and Ryan shared had existed in
the shop alone. Bringing it beyond those walls made their
connection feel fragile, like something she'd possibly
made up, and something she could easily lose.

One glance at the clock above the stove confirmed
there was no time to change now. Jaime would just have
to trust the instinct that had guided her toward the more
everyday choice. She smoothed her hair one last time,
adjusted her boobs, and opened the door.

Ryan wore a Henley-style tee that hugged his shoulders and showed each of his pec muscles, making Jaime's vision tunnel and her heart begin to throb. If there had been any leftover tension over the finality of breaking from Jonathan for good, it was a long-buried thought now. Around Ryan, the past no longer mattered, the future too exciting to want to look back.

The present too. From the doorway, Jaime took Ryan in appreciatively. Everything about him was devastatingly manly. His beard that was the groomed product of someone long used to facial hair. His muscles that didn't speak to hours in the gym but instead, hours spent outside, shoulders flexed under the Virginian sun as he dug into the ground. Biceps built not by curls under halogen lights with dumbbells but instead, hauling pots heavy with trees and bushes. And his eyes. His eyes bored into her, intent, and clear. Ryan was a man, a man who knew himself, and who had no problems making what he wanted clear.

The intensity of his stare and the held breath quality of the moment made Jaime feel tight between her legs. She knew how to describe what was there, but the muscles contracting felt beyond her anatomy, like desire was reinventing her as blood rushed, leaving her hands shaky as her possessed body moved her closer to Ryan, still, nothing yet said aloud.

His eyes half-closed and he dipped his head. "You look so beautiful. And the way you're looking at me is making it hard to want to leave your apartment." He swallowed. "We're going on a date."

All Jaime would have to do would be to squeeze her thighs a little tighter. Dinner was the furthest thing from her mind. "Do we have to?"

"Date. You and me." Ryan's mouth twitched. "I'm not just a piece of meat, you know."

She reached out and pulled a small leaf from his shoulder. "Of course, I know that. You live the plant life, remember?"

He took the small green boomerang from her. "Maple seed."

They hovered on the threshold of her apartment and Jaime considered grabbing hold of him and pulling him to her bedroom, kissing him until he saw reason and skipped the unnecessary date. Wasn't sex what they were both here for? She felt the bubbling over inside of herself that had caused her to stand up at her parents' table the other night, defend her job choice and herself against what Gretchen believed, and finally, fully say no to Jonathan. It was a boil that made Jaime want to stand up to social customs that at this moment, with the pull at the base of her belly like a balloon that was near to popping, appeared so frivolous. Who needed a drink when Jaime already felt woozy, ready to fall into Ryan? Who needed dinner when she felt that she could go years without eating, sustained instead by him?

"We have to leave, or I'll lose all that's left of my willpower." Ryan flexed his hand at his side and cleared his throat. "Come on."

He offered his arm, and Jaime, with one last look at her bedroom door, the bed meticulously made with new sheets, the books from the unused side cleared away, she took it. His thumb caressed hers as they walked toward the stairs, circling her knuckles and squeezing as they started their descent.

****

The restaurant that Ryan chose was one that focused

on local foods, and the seasonal specials were written on an additional cardstock menu, leaf caricatures bordering the dark green text. Greens from farms that extended as far as Ashville, and meats from local butchers. Jaime held her silky black tee shirt dress down as she sat, aware that Ryan stood behind her, waiting until she was seated before helping her push her chair closer to the table. She reached back and brushed his forearm with the side of her hand. "Thank you."

After he was seated, after a minute passed, he set his menu down. "You typically order a beer, but would you rather get a bottle of wine?"

Jaime hedged, trying to decide if a bottle of wine was necessary to keep up with the atmosphere of a first date. A normal date. One where what might happen later was still up in the air. This was the part where he'd tell her what to order. Or somehow make her change her mind about what she wanted.

"This isn't a test." Ryan smiled and raised his eyebrows expectantly.

"Do we have to get wine?" she asked, breathing out hard.

His laughter was a quick bark. "We don't have to do a single thing you don't want, Jaime. Tonight is about you."

"I thought it was about us." She flushed as soon as she said it.

He didn't smile. Instead, his face smoothed into expansive planes. His eyes were completely open to her, and the gnawing inside Jaime became a pulse that she could barely settle by engaging her core and crossing, recrossing her legs.

"I want everything to be about us," he said.

"Can *us* not get wine?" Jaime asked, trying to lighten the mood. "I don't know about *us*, but wine always makes *me* headachey. I'll enjoy it for a bit and then regret it an hour later. Like clockwork."

"Us wants whatever makes *you* feel good."

Her insides were molten. "Is that right?" Her heart beat inside her ears. How long had it been since she'd last been with a man? Years. Decades, it seemed. Nothing compared to the way that she felt around Ryan.

"Mmm hmm. Us wants—"

"Do y'all know what you'd like to drink?" The waiter had a bored expression, apparently oblivious to the near ninety-degree angle that Jaime had fallen into, leaning toward Ryan, desperate to hear more. His words undoing her like the slow pop of buttons, releasing the pent-up lust and longing she'd been storing inside herself for years, waiting for him to come along.

Ryan smiled, biting into his bottom lip as he picked the drinks menu back up. "The sour gose, please."

Jaime didn't look away from him, focusing on his teeth and fantasizing about them grazing her skin, the way they had in the backroom of the shop. Ordering for herself only intensified the sense of power. She was crackling with the raw energy of all this potential between her and Ryan. "The hazy, please."

The waiter left and the air between her and Ryan continued to pulse with charge. She picked up her napkin and folded it into her lap, waiting for him to tell her what he'd been about to say.

He leaned forward, folding and refolding his own napkin. "If you had to choose between a beach vacation or some sort of mountainy-forest one, which would you choose?"

The sudden change in tone surprised Jaime enough that she relaxed, her muscles loosening and the electricity of the moments before fading into a gentle hum.

"Beach," she said, remembering each summer vacation on the South Carolinian coast. Searching for seashells and the pleasure of digging her toes into the sand that went from surface hot to cool and moist below where the water waited.

He nodded.

"You'd choose forest?" Jaime asked.

"I like both, at different times of year. Beach in the winter, forest in the summer."

"My turn," she said. "Phone in the bathroom, or no phone?"

"Getting to the nitty gritty right away, I see."

Their drinks arrived, glasses set on the table sweating and bubbling. The girl who brought them wasn't their waiter and left as soon as she'd made her delivery. Jaime was grateful that small talk had been unnecessary.

"I mean, I hate to ruin what we've got going but I'll admit it. Phone."

She shook her head. "Nasty."

He picked up his glass. "I bet you do it too."

Jaime sipped her beer. "No comment."

"Good morning texts or goodnight texts?"

The bubbles slid down Jaime's throat. She wanted all of it. Before she could question how much she was allowed, how much she could demand before being labelled *needy,* or *crazy,* or *over-the-top*, she blurted, "Both."

His foot nudged hers and settled alongside it,

pressing gently. "Your turn."

"Toilet paper over or under?"

"What's the purpose of the bathroom theme here?"

"Just getting all the ugly stuff out of the way, I guess. I don't want any surprises."

"When it comes to you, ugly isn't a word that exists."

The flush started at the base of her throat, the sides of her neck heating.

"You're beautiful," he said again. "And over, obviously. Under is for sociopaths and soon to be exes."

"That's not us," she said, trying to work through the blush that was still making her cheeks flame.

"Never."

The waiter who had taken their drink order came back and they paused to pick food for the night, both of them scrambling and pointing to the first thing that caught their eyes. Another blush stole its way back across her face when the waiter pointed to her glass already near empty and asked if she wanted another. She nodded, but resolved to go slower. She didn't want to miss any part of this night by dulling it with alcohol or other distractions.

Before Ryan could ask the next question, she jumped in again. "I've got one that's not bathroom centered. Wash dishes right away, or leave them in the sink?"

"Right away. Anything else is just stalling."

"I knew it." Jaime sat back, smiling. "Sink."

"Of course, you do." Ryan's foot pushed against hers, making their ankles touch. "Left or right side of the bed."

She scooted herself further into the table, lining their

calves more evenly, his leg hair soft but the muscles hard, the long shaft of shin bone like a brace that would only let her go so far. "I think I sleep on the left-hand side."

"Then I'll take right."

They stared at one another.

"Kids or no kids?" Jaime asked, embarrassed that she had asked such an assuming, expansive question, but desperate to know.

Ryan's eye contact didn't waver. "Kids." He leaned forward, and with his thumb, brushed her hair away from her face, tracing the curve of her cheek down to her jaw.

"Me too," she whispered, catching his hand with hers and holding him there, suspended halfway above the table, linked to her.

"Jaime?" A woman's voice interrupted them, and Jaime immediately leaned away from Ryan, his hand falling from her face. He responded in kind, repositioning so that even their feet lost contact beneath the table.

One of her co-teachers stood a few feet from them, gesturing for her husband to go on without her.

"Hi Amber," Jaime said, trying to make her voice sound like her school voice.

Amber tightened her ponytail and gestured to Jaime "I thought that was you. I'd ask how your summer's been, but—" She looked Ryan up and down. "Looks like you've had a great vacation."

Jaime's throat constricted. "It's been a very necessary change of pace." She needed to be the one to tell Ryan. Not Amber. Whatever happened afterward, it had to have been her who let him know. Jaime needed to maintain neutral language, capable of applying to both her as the ex-teacher, and her as the soon-to-return-to-school-teacher. She added, "I hope you're ready to go back."

Amber pulled a tortured expression and Jaime quickly interrupted whatever might follow. She blurted, "Well, it's been so good to see you. I'll see you soon, I'm sure."

"Yep," said Amber. "Three weeks." She pulled another face.

Jaime stood, gave Amber a hug and waved her off to her husband who was waiting by the front door of the restaurant.

"Three weeks from now is the start of the school year?" Ryan asked.

A fluttery nod. Diverted eyes. The sinking sensation that the night was about to get away from Jaime. That now was the time she was supposed to tell him everything. That she had never left teaching, that she would soon be leaving Plant Life. Him. "Summer always goes by so quick."

"When you're not in school, it's just another of the four seasons."

She licked her lips. "Yep."

"Jaime?"

Their food arrived, and if it weren't for the intensity of Jaime's awareness around Ryan, of his every word, his every gesture, each time he repositioned, and his proximity to her through all of it, the night would have felt like a strobe of starts and stops. Conversation flowing, conversation broken. Them alone, then surrounded.

Through it all, Ryan had remained in his seat, available and constant. And as much as Jaime wanted to end this secret that had gone from being a simple slip of the truth to a burning hole in her chest that was tunneling ever quicker, the truth felt like a drill that would eventually reach her heart and break it.

She should rally the courage to tell him everything now and be done with it. All it took was a handful of words to set things right. But what she and Ryan had was also burrowing into her, tracing lines around her heart, a pattern he continued to sketch out more fully each day. She didn't want to interrupt that before she knew exactly what the design looked like.

"Jaime?"

It was the barest tilt of her chin and then they were staring into one another again. All her courage replaced by yearning from so deep within her that it eradicated everything else.

"Ending the date here, or somewhere else?"

"Finally, the this or that I've been waiting for." She exhaled. "My place or yours?"

"Mine."

****

Inside his house, they were shy. He held the door, insisting that Jaime walk in first, and she began the process of figuring out his home in the dark. All the furniture a suggestion and the color scheme still something to be imagined. The lights switching on felt like one more interruption within the unfolding of their evening, as startling as the continuous questions and check-ins from the waiter, and the unexpected intrusion of her coworker.

But, as Jaime's eyes adjusted, as Ryan's home came into focus, the books became multicolored spines instead of dark rectangular patterns against the wall. They took up the bulk of the living room. A small television was wedged into the corner beyond the bookshelves. Ryan's house was surprising and yet exactly right. His physical space as self-assured as his attitude that made him appear standoffish at first, and then merely quiet. Comfortable and easy to relate to, once that reservation that was either shyness or a lack of willingness to participate in the social hamster wheel was acknowledged.

The kitchen was off to the left, barstools lining a long island. But it was the denim blue sectional, the coffee table beside it, the rows of books and the smattering of house plants that Jaime never would have been able to name even a month ago, yet knew now, that drew her. She wanted much more than just tonight in this room. She wanted to do a puzzle on the coffee table, to drift to sleep on that couch some lazy Saturday, head nestled in Ryan's lap as he read one of the books from the pile on the table beside the armrest.

"We don't have to have sex." Ryan's words came husky and gruff, like it was an effort speak.

She turned to face him and couldn't help but grin when she saw that he was blushing. He rubbed the back of his neck.

"I'm sorry to make it awkward. I just didn't want it to feel like it was an expectation. It's not. I just wanted to see you here. In my home." He looked to the ceiling. "Jesus, that was fucking awkward too."

She was happy to be here in his space. It felt like an extension of the shop that had become so familiar. And sex wasn't an expectation but a desperate, desperate need. Though in this moment, the desire to touch him had cooled, the desire to explore his house, to learn more about him, taking precedence. She wanted to know what the inside of his junk drawer looked like. Whether he was a solids or patterned towel sort of guy. If the lack of wallpaper was special to the main area or if the off-white walls were common throughout the house.

"There's less plants than I'd imagined," she said.

"They prefer to be outside."

"Like you?"

"Like me."

Jaime pointed to the stairs. "Am I allowed to go up?"

"You're allowed anything you want here. Except the garden—only for now. And not because of hidden bodies or anything creepy." He smiled. "I want you to see it first in daylight."

The refusal wasn't a real one, simply a delay, but it was enough of a stop to stall Jaime at the base of the stairs, making her self-conscious about continuing to snoop. The garden was so important to him, and he'd told her no.

"Come on." Ryan took her by the hand and began the procession upward. Holding her hand as they climbed made his shoulder blade tent the material of his shirt and Jaime couldn't help herself from staring at the flex of his muscles, the push of his spine in his neck, divots perfect for her fingers. Her eyes traveled from there down, where his jeans hugged his butt in that perfectly masculine way—pants not tight enough to reveal everything but enough to show what kind of butt he had. Square, narrowing when the muscles engaged.

"Only three rooms," Ryan said. "Which one do you want to see first?"

"Yours." The shyness from earlier, the overriding interest in the house, had both faded with her view of him from the stairs. She was less curious about what was likely an office and guest room, maybe some sort of plant dedicated space, though that was unlikely based on his comment downstairs, and more intent on giving in to that press in her abdomen that demanded she take off Ryan's shirt and kiss from his shoulder down his clavicle, along his chest that had beautifully molded his tee in the restaurant's low lighting, then down, down, down. Until he was out of his clothes and tearing at hers, fulfilling every single fantasy she'd had since that first kiss.

He squeezed her hand and pulled her onward, through a door to the right. This was better than any of the daydreams. Imagination was limitless, but this was real. His scent was in sharp focus, the brush of his hands passing across his beard while he watched her like the quiet opening of a window in the early morning, the anticipation of a cool breeze and airing out the house. She breathed deeply and took in the spindle bed, a large quilt topping it and giving it a timeless feel. A wooden dresser with plants atop and curling off the edges, and a Kennedy rocker that, had Jaime lived here, would have an extra blanket on it and a stack of books. His clothes hamper was half-full, and the bathroom door was partially opened, a slit of darkness inviting Jaime to end her explorations in a room where she could double check her breath and make sure her mascara was still intact.

"You're already fully aware, but, I'm not—I'm not good with words." Ryan's voice was tight. His thumb traced the path between the first knuckle of Jaime's pointer finger and the base of her thumb. "I have a thousand things I want to tell you right now, but I don't know how to say any of them."

Jaime closed the small space between them and pulled their joined hands to the small of her back, pressing them into her spine. "Try."

"I've wanted you in this room for a month now."

"A whole month?" Jaime let go of his hand and put her arms around his neck, bringing them nose to nose.

"Since the first time you used one of the plants' Latin names. Don't ask me which." He bent down, slid his mouth along her neck, then spoke into her skin. "I don't remember. But I remember the way that you looked, this mole on the side of your neck. The way that your forehead creases when you're thinking. You were wearing stripes that day."

Jaime unbuttoned the three buttons of his Henley collar and pressed her lips to his chest.

"I remember wanting to kiss you when you yelled at me that day. I was a jackass, but at least I wasn't such a dickhead that I did that."

"You *were* a jackass that day."

"Many days."

She tugged at his shirt. "That's what I have to look forward to, then?"

He covered her hands with his and looked into her eyes. "No. I told you. I'm not good with words. I'm not good at knowing how to say what I feel without it getting away from me. Yell at me when I'm an asshole. Like you did then."

Jaime's exhalations shallowed. Ryan was close enough that she could feel their breath mingling in the fraction of air separating their mouths. He angled his face until his nose pushed against her cheek, his lips resting on hers. Warm silk framed by the whiskers of his upper lip, tickling her enough to make her want to push into him and take control.

"Jesus, Jaime." His words were hot on her lips.

"You don't know what you do to me."

Her head tipped back and he cupped either side of her face, pulling her mouth to his. Initiating the kiss and deepening it all at once. Their tongues met as his hands roved over her thighs, sliding up her dress and onto the bare skin that her thong underwear left exposed to him, squeezing her until she was pressed all the way against him.

Under his shirt, Ryan's skin was warm and tight, the sudden jut of his ribcage pushing her hands inward and up, onto the softness of his chest hair. Then over his shoulders and squeezing as he began to massage her butt. Both refused to be the first who needed air. Instead, breathlessly maintaining the kiss. Searching the muscle avenues of each other's bodies for satiation.

Jaime stepped against him, cinching their bodies and forcing him backward toward the bed.

Ryan broke first, panting as his hands wove their way to her waist. He gripped her there, stalling them. "If you tell me no, we can stop here. At this."

"Don't stop," Jaime said. She bunched the material of his shirt then pulled it up and over his head. "I'll say yes every minute if you need. But don't stop."

"Say it then."

"Yes," Jaime whispered. Her dress came over her head.

"Again." He mouthed the word into her clavicle. Then the other. "Again."

"Yes. Yes. Oh please, yes."

His lips traced her cleavage and she put her hands into his hair, fanning her fingers through and tugging. Nothing felt like enough. She needed more. She ground herself into him, his skin smooth and hot against hers, and worked at her bra, struggling as if it wasn't her own. The last clasp undone, it fell to the floor, and though she tried to reclose the distance between them, he held her elbow and made space for them to see all of each other.

Jaime's chest heaved, her breath quivering. "Your turn." She pointed to his pants.

He unzipped his jeans and slid them down, revealing black briefs that made Jaime think of the black lacey underwear that she'd considered wearing. "Are these your sexy undies?" she asked.

"God, I hope so," he said. His eyes raked over her, and she leaned her head back, reaching out for him and trying to bite back the moan built from so much attention and so much waiting. He cupped her breast with one hand and pulled her into him with the other.

Jaime parted her legs, making space for his thighs and straddling until she could feel the hardness of him. Grinding her hips against him, she bit his shoulder. "Yes."

Ryan's touch moved from her breasts to her back, down to her butt, lifting her and then nudging her onto the bed. She scooted all the way to the headboard, until she'd reached the pillows. He kissed his way up the length of her, hovering. "Again," he said, lowering himself to her. Jaime's nipples pebbled, hard with urgency. He slowly took one into his mouth, sucking and tugging. Licking round the tip before pulling more of her into his mouth.

"Yes." Jaime moaned.

He kissed the expanse of her rib until he was at the center of her belly, trailing his mouth downward until his face was between her legs. With his thumb, he found the center of her pelvic bone and inched toward her most sensitive spot, pressing small circles until she could feel her clitoris somehow, impossibly, harden more. The pulse of it was like the drop of a roller coaster making her arch up and against his hand, grinding into him and riding. He slid her underwear down and used his feet to pull them away from her ankles. His beard tickled the insides of her leg as he ran his bottom teeth lightly along its length. Following the pressure with kisses.

"You're so fucking gorgeous," he said before lowering to trace the top of her thigh with his mouth, back to her vulva, which he outlined with his thumb again before repeating the same with his tongue. Again and again before finding her middle. Sucking hard on her soft, fleshy entry. Jaime gasped, unable to stop from rocking into him. Normally, she would have started to conjure some sort of fantasy. Something to make her want to participate in sex and to give her what she needed to finish. Every time she started to indulge the habit, Ryan brought her back to herself, tonguing the roof of her sex until Jaime thought that her mind would short out from the pleasure. From what was happening now.

Ryan sucked until she was in his mouth, using the flat of his teeth to grind against her harder, kneading her clitoris. There. He was right there. Jaime grabbed a handful of his hair and moaned.

Ryan purred against her. Slipping two fingers inside her and pumping as his mouth continued to work.

"I can't—" Jaime was breathless, so close.

"I've got you." His tongue continued to flick against her, his fingers creating counter pressure. Rubbing right where she needed him.

She sank back when she came, legs shaking and the rest of her body quivering. Ryan circled her vulva lightly with his tongue, easing her from her high. She grabbed his hand, breathing hard. Needing a minute. His eyes were dark, his face flushed.

"Please," she said. "Please, please, please, tell me you have a condom."

He smiled a wicked smile that Jaime immediately wiped off his face by kissing him with everything she had.

His *yes* traveled across her tongue and into her throat, reverberating there. She tried her best to say it back, their consent a shared hum.

****

Ryan finished first. "That wasn't meant to happen," he said, flushed and breathing hard, rubbing her clitoris with his thumb as he pulsed inside her. "I told you we needed to switch. You're just too fucking much. Beneath me like that."

"I wasn't ready." Jaime's voice caught. "I'm ready now. Here—" She tapped his shoulder.

The maneuver was clumsy, their chests sweaty as they slid against each other. They both laughed as he struggled to stay inside of her when they switched to her on top. Jaime repositioned and began slowly, luxuriously contracting herself around Ryan, pushing until she was able to find the same spot he'd found with his fingers earlier. Being able to be fully in control made her even hungrier with each release and she had to force herself to slow down. He massaged her boobs and started to flex his hips but Jaime stilled him. "No," she said. She grabbed his hands and flattened them against her breasts, trying to catch her breath as she rocked, contracting and letting go, contracting and letting go.

"Jaime, you fucking goddess," he said, his eyes

drifting closed.

"You mean yes?" she said in a breathy exhalation.

He growled. Eyes closed, lips folded inward, he leaned his head further into the pillow as she worked him.

This time, the orgasm wasn't sudden—not the explosion of sensations from before—but a slow unfurling, like the opening of a flower at daybreak, delicious warmth licking over every petal as the muscles of her pelvis relaxed into unbearable lightness, fully open to the sun that was Ryan's body inside of her. She clung to him, letting the sensation spread throughout her whole body until she couldn't contain it anymore. She collapsed on top of his chest, breathing into the flat expanse of her insides pushed open.

His fingers made lazy circles across her back.

"Still, yes?" he asked.

Sleepy, and arching into Ryan's touch, she smiled. "*Sí.*"

"No others?"

"*Oui. Ja.* God yes." She nipped at his ear. There weren't enough languages to account for the *yes* that every cell in her body was shouting. She was completely undone, and yet still—still—she wanted more. "Yes."

Chapter Fifteen

Twelve nights spent at Ryan's house instead of Jamie's small apartment meant twelve mornings of coffee being delivered to her in bed, flowers freshly cut from the garden and arranged in a pitcher vase that sat on the bedside table beside what had become her half of the bed. Jamie inched herself up on the mattress, unfolding the pillow and fluffing it to stand vertical so she could sit supported and fully upright in bed for her first sips from the steaming blue clay mug.

The window was cracked to let in the fresh air, and a cool breeze rustled the drapes, bringing the sounds of the birds from outside and the start of the morning for the neighborhood. Cars driving past and lawn mowers cranked to life. Jaime knew from the last full Sunday here that starting midmorning, children playing would punctuate the sounds of industry and nature. Competing with the drone of insects and air conditioning units. This was the sort of area where people moved wanting to settle and stay forever. And between the bouquet of sweet peas, candying the breeze as it pushed away any of the accumulated heat from last night, the cup of coffee in her hand, and the sounds of Ryan making breakfast downstairs, Jaime did not want to leave, either.

Every day that passed where she still hadn't told him the truth, the truth that she only had this weekend before her last two weeks at the shop and then school would restart and thus, her real life, Jaime became more desperate to cling to this image of what life could be like. It was hers to pursue fully if she did what her mother had been asking for years, what Jonathan had implied was the logical next step. If she gave up her career.

Jaime pulled one of the sweet pea tendrils from the pitcher vase and put the flower to her nose, breathing it in before looping the skinny, viny stem around her pointer finger. If she were to leave teaching, it would be as difficult as wondering which sub was taking over her classes the first few days. In the following weeks, whether the curriculum was being shifted to accommodate the new teacher's preferences. Whether the students were offered a letter box next to the teacher's desk the way she did, so that if it was needed, each of them had the option of private correspondence. Would her replacement know that for some of her kids that letter box had been the only way they'd felt safe sharing important, often traumatic details about their home lives? Some things were easier to write than to say. Would her replacement take the time to not only listen, but read when it was necessary?

Jaime repositioned herself as one of the headboard slats began to dig into her back, balancing the coffee so she didn't spill on the white sheets.

The door opened a little further and Ryan walked in, carrying the coffee pot. "Bed or garden for breakfast today?"

On that first Monday morning that she'd woken up in his room, she'd chosen the garden and he'd had to carry a kitchen chair out to sit on, refusing to let her use the straight-backed dining chair instead of the one outdoor Adirondack. The next day he'd bought a garden table set and fairy lights. They'd eaten dinner al fresco, watching the fireflies blink amongst the crepe myrtle trees. Then breakfasted every day after, listening to the bees flit from the round purple chive flowers in the vegetable beds before buzzing their way over to the patch of dahlias, showy in their heavily petaled reds and pinks.

"The garden," Jaime said. She tried to smile as she made her now usual choice, but it was tight, permeated by her growing melancholy. Her thoughts remained with her students, and the fear that she would have to choose between them and Ryan. The anxiety of no longer knowing which was the right choice.

It was unfair—everything else with Ryan felt so different, miles away from the claustrophobia of her last relationship. And yet, here she was again, being forced to choose between herself and the priorities of others. Yes, the shop was important to her—but it was Ryan's life, not hers. And she couldn't imagine spending hers at the cash register there until she was off the hook from her initial deception.

"Hey." Ryan sat down beside her and pushed a stray curl behind her ear. "Everything alright?"

Her nod was as false as the smile. No, things were not alright. She didn't want to give him up. But she didn't want to start another life that chafed. That insisted she wanted wine at dinner and to wear the form fitting blue dress instead of the loose, red one. That viewed teaching as a temporary box check, versus something that gave Jaime purpose.

"You look sad, Jaime."

She leaned into his hand, still resting against her cheek. "I don't want this to end."

"Doesn't have to. We'll leave the shop closed for the day. Claim that we're busy celebrating being front page news." Ryan ran his knuckles along her thigh.

Jaime's eyes widened at the reminder, and she found that despite knowing later, when she finally told him the truth, that she was leaving at the end of summer, potentially making this her last morning spent at Ryan's, she still had a reason to be genuinely excited for today. A reason for a real smile. "I'd completely forgotten about The Rover!"

"You haven't looked at it?"

She shook her head. "Have you?"

"I wanted to wait for you."

"Well, here I am. Quick." Jaime waved her hand in the direction of her phone still on the charger. "I want to see."

He leaned over and grabbed her phone from the table then held it out to her. Jaime shook her head.

"You do it," she said. "Ten-twelve for the passcode."

Ryan put his hand on his heart. "This is a whole new level for us."

"Oh yeah, I'm putting a lot of trust in you." A sourness followed her statement, the shame of knowing how little he should trust her in return. At least she had the article as a legacy for her time at Plant Life, a reminder that though she may have to leave, she'd made a small difference to the shop. It was now a feature in Roam's best businesses section.

"Well," she prompted, nudging Ryan. "What does it say?"

He climbed over and lay beside her on the bed, settling so that Jaime could drape her legs over his, and

233

holding the phone so they could both see the screen. The first photo was of the two of them, Ryan smiling as he watched her pour from the decorative watering can onto a blurred array of leaves. A sea of green that left the two of them the main focus.

"A pocket of Eden," Jaime read aloud. She snuggled into Ryan, resting her head on his chest. "They're calling Plant Life *the* Roam gardening stop."

Jaime tried to scroll down to keep reading but he toggled back up to their photo. "You look gorgeous here."

Her cheeks burned and she playfully tipped her head back, hitting him. "I want to see what else they say."

"None of that really matters. You're the best thing in this," he said.

The breeze from earlier had stopped, the birds silent as if they were holding their breath alongside Jaime, caught in the moment of deciding between revealing the truth about her role in the shop or letting herself simply live in these small blips of magic.

"The best thing that's happened to me as well," he said. He shifted in the bed and the noise of the outside—of the entire world—began to trickle back into place like the play button had been hit, the pause effectively over.

"Ryan." Jaime was going to tell him. She had to tell him now. If she didn't, then another day would slip by where everything that happened was too perfect to ruin, too wonderful to stop.

"It's okay," Ryan said. "You don't have to say anything back to that." He slid a hand up her night shirt, tugging her back down the bed and then folding her to him in the way that had become habit in days. Jaime's body hummed, vibrating with anticipation, chill bumps punctuating the exclamation of his kisses as he pushed himself further down her body.

He lowered himself until he was between her legs and Jaime moaned, pulled into the moment again. Pulled from the knowledge of what she was supposed to be doing. Nothing could be more important than continuing this. Ryan kissed the insides of each of her thighs, his hands finding each of her hip bones.

The kisses circled round and round until his words were hot against her. "Breakfast in bed, or the garden, then?"

Jaime shuddered, her voice melting into stutters. "Depends on the menu."

Ryan smiled. "I'll show you that part."

He nuzzled into her, nipping at her undies, and Jaime strained to get them off. He stilled her, intertwining their fingers and then pushing her hands up and above her head, kissing the top of her nose before traveling back down her body. "Every time I get to hold you, I wonder how I got so damn lucky," he said. "Look at you."

He licked from her jaw down her neck. "The way your pulse ticks. Right here." He took one of his hands back and traced the wet line his tongue had just tracked.

"Your collar bone." He dotted kisses along the expanse of her clavicle. "And your boobs kill me, Jaime. I could die happy sucking on these nipples." He took one into his mouth, taking turns circling the small pebble with his tongue and then sucking.

"Please don't die," Jaime said, leaning her head back into the pillow and tugging at his hair, encouraging him to keep going. "I need you too much right now."

His mouth worked her harder and her body loosened

beneath him. She could feel a mirror sensation of what he was doing to her breast between her legs, and she brought his hand to her clit, taking his palm and rubbing it against where she needed him. "Please," she said.

"How do you want me?" Ryan asked, pausing just long enough to make eye contact. His brown eyes were the darkest she'd ever seen them, pupils and irises barely distinguishable.

"Me on top," she said, voice gravelly.

He slid an arm underneath her butt and hoisted her atop him, flexing into Jaime as she ground against his hardness. "You're wearing way too many clothes," she said.

"Help me fix that."

Jaime rolled his sweatpants down and tugged them off, catching them on his feet. They both laughed, teeth bumping as they kissed. Jaime raised her hips, tracing his erection with her wetness. He moaned, low in his throat before pulling her to him. Kissing her harder. Sucking her lower lip until she groaned in kind. "Ryan."

Some women could put on a condom and make it sexy; Jaime was not one of them. When he leaned to the bedside table to grab one from the drawer, she inched down until she was facing his cock and kissed the tip before taking him in her mouth.

Ryan's inhale was sharp, and his erection pulsed against her tongue and palate. She sucked, taking more of him. As much of him as she could. Tracing him with her tongue as she rose, until only the head was between her lips.

"Oh Christ," Ryan's voice grated.

Jaime pumped him with her mouth.

"Jaime, beautiful, you gotta stop or I'm going to

come."

"Then, can we have sex now please?" She smiled, licking lazy circles around him.

"Whenever you want. However you want." He ripped the condom packing. "You know where to find me."

It was a stutter of a thought that soon, he wouldn't know where to find her unless she told him the truth. But then, he was pulling her into his lap, guiding himself into her. All Jaime's hesitation blinked out.

She rode him until her legs were trembling, trying to hold on, her center of gravity shifting to exactly where they joined. "I'm going to—" Her breath hitched. "I'm—"

"Together," Ryan said, voice straining. "Together."

They embraced the wave as it took them at the same time, Jaime's body collapsing into Ryan's and his arms circling around her, sliding up and down her back, slick with their efforts. As he leaned back, situating himself against the headboard and holding her tight, their breathing evened, inhales and exhales happening in tandem.

Love, Jaime wanted to say but knew she shouldn't. Not yet. It was too early. Yet, still, this felt like love.

****

Despite skipping a second cup of coffee and having ignored the buttered baguette that had grown as cold as the preserves it was sitting besides, Jaime and Ryan were still ten minutes late for the shop's regular opening. Unshowered and red-faced from having rushed from bed to the car and then through the back hall and to the shop's front door, she grabbed the closed sign and swung it to open.

And though it was Friday, the weather glorious, and the shop in spectacular shape, everything greener and lusher than Jaime had ever seen it, nobody had waited outside to be let in. The first customer arrived close to twenty minutes after they'd turned the lights on. Ryan had gone to buy breakfast to make up for the one they'd missed, and Jaime helped the customer choose between aloe plants.

A group of shoppers had replaced the lone woman by the time Ryan returned, balancing to-go cups with a bag containing a muffin and a scone for Jaime to choose between. He handed it over, gesturing for her to sit and eat, and began chatting with the customers, his communication easy, as it had seemed to be more often lately. It appeared small talk no longer caused his shoulders to hitch. The gentler tone he now maintained convincing people of his recommendations and bolstering business more and more each day.

He may have taught Jaime to identify every plant in this room, giving her the tools to care for them, and the appreciation of their inclusion into every type of space, but she had taught him to be more approachable. She had helped him to become a better salesman. Between that, and the glowing praise in The Roam Rover, Jaime felt that her job here was coming to a natural conclusion.

It was time for her to get back to school, where the changes she could make would only continue to expand and grow, rather than shrink and fade. She sipped her latte, steadying the growing shake in her hands—her body's prep work for the coming conflict—by gripping the cup tightly. These customers had to leave. They didn't seem the sort to buy anything anyhow, and Jaime needed to talk to Ryan before she lost her nerve.

One of the women in the group gestured for Ryan to show her the Shrimp begonias in the hanging baskets. She tapped his forearm as she pointed to where they lined the windows, happily growing in the brightest spot of the entire shop. The hand on Ryan's skin made a flash of jealousy run through Jaime hotter than her espresso. She'd wanted these people out before. Now, she felt the wild need to kick them out.

He shrugged away from the other woman's touch and took one of the baskets from the ceiling hook, slowly spinning it to make sure it was one that she wanted. The woman smiled and Jaime's irritation only grew. To avoid openly scowling, she got off the stool and rooted through her purse until she found her phone.

There were eleven notifications. Talia had screenshotted The Rover's first photo, Ryan staring at Jaime as she cared for the shop plants like a modern Snow White, happily doing the daintiest of all garden tasks.

Talia—*Please tell me you jumped his bones right after this was taken*—

Bree—*If you ever do decide to leave teaching, I highly suggest a career in modeling for dating websites*—

The thread continued until the messages were more emoji than text, eggplants and drooling faces making up the bulk of the content.

When Jaime clicked out of it, smiling, and no longer ready to chase the woman who liked the begonias out of the shop, she was surprised to see that the notifications beside her text app still indicated an unread message.

Bree had sent a separate, private text.

—*Please, dear sweet baby Jesus, tell me that you've*

come clean with this man and that you're not about to fuck things up with a guy who looks at you like you're the gorgeous, amazing woman that you are—

Jaime swallowed and responded.

—About to—

She took another sip of her latte and then typed quickly.

—Please keep your fingers crossed he won't hate me after—

Three dots appeared in the chat, doing the wave across the screen as Jaime waited for whatever Bree said next. A pep talk would be really nice right now. The group of customers by the windows followed Ryan over to the cash register where Jaime watched her phone. She scooted out of the way, turning her back to them after a quick smile and set her phone down on the counter that bordered the back wall behind the till counter.

Bree—*Just tell him the truth and he won't. Love you—*

It wasn't a pep talk but it was affirmation that even if Ryan did get mad, she wouldn't be alone, and she'd have one of her favorite shoulders to cry on later if things did go south. She texted Bree that she loved her too, then put her phone away, lightly brushing Ryan's upper arm as a silent *he's mine* to the woman laughing too loudly at whatever he had said as he printed the receipt. Jaime wound her way to the front of the store where she opened the door to see the large group out. As soon as they exited, she'd shut it and turn the sign to closed. The closure would only last as long as it took Jaime to say what she needed to say.

The group of customers filed out, thanking Jaime as they left. The woman who had flirted with Ryan went last, giving a head nod that felt as much like defeat as gratitude. Jaime used the concession as a reminder that she had power. She was capable of doing hard things.

Before the sliver of light from the door closing winked out, another person pushed it wide open, bumping Jaime backward. A floral, sparkling smell that transported Jaime to the morning's bouquet wafted in alongside the woman. It wasn't until said woman was inside, her large basket tote hiked higher onto a shoulder, tortoise shell sunglasses pulled on top of her head, that Jaime realized it was Elise. Elise, who had made it clear to Jaime that any indication of something beyond strictly professional with Ryan would be met with drama. And Elise, in those perfectly smooth green shorts that Jaime remembered from her first visit to the shop, looked more than ready for some drama.

"Ryan," Elise said. She turned to Jaime. "And Jaime." Her voice was crystalline, bright but hard-edged. "I just saw the article. Congratulations."

Ryan raised a hand in more salute than wave. "Thank you. It means a lot to get the feature."

"I'll bet it does. It's great for business. Good for the brand." Elise let her tote drop and she left it beside the succulent table, walking slowly down the main aisle toward the back counter.

Jaime had an urge to cover both the herb table that Elise had wrecked the last time they were in the shop together, and Ryan, protecting all of them in whatever way she could from this woman who was clearly too bored. Adults were just like children. The drive to make trouble significantly diminished as soon as they had positive outlets to focus their creativity and energy. Elise needed a new challenge. But Jaime wasn't her teacher, nor was this the moment to encourage Elise. Now was about mitigating whatever damage Elise intended.

"If I'd known that day that Jaime here was schmoozing with local media, not just ignoring me for the sake of a cute kid, I wouldn't have gotten so mad." She turned around to face Jaime.

After pulling a pouty face, Elise asked, "Can you forgive me?"

Jaime opened and closed her mouth. Now was the part where she asked Elise to leave the shop so that she could have a conversation with Ryan. Now was the part where Jaime didn't get scared of this woman who was acting like a nine-year-old, because Jaime was plenty used to those. But her tongue felt thick and useless. Elise might remind Jaime of her worst behaved student, but it didn't matter, she was an adult and nor was this Jaime's classroom.

Ryan intervened, shooting Jaime an expression of concern. "What can we do for you, Elise?"

Elise was slow to turn away from Jaime, yet with Ryan's attention on her, she seemed to become more herself again, her shoulders relaxing and the bristling energy that signaled trouble, settling into awkwardness. She looked around the shop. "I was just in the area and thought I might stop by. It's been a minute, hasn't it?"

"It has." Ryan stepped out from behind the counter and began to walk the corridor between plant tables opposite of Jaime. He didn't stop until he was beside her. His hand rested on the small of her back.

"You need her to leave?" he asked quietly.

Jaime shook her head and turned to Ryan. "I need to talk to you."

"I know what's eating her," interrupted Elise.

Ryan's eyes darted from Elise back to Jaime. "Elise, I think you should—"

"Go?" She laughed. "Don't worry, I will. I never meant to stay long. I really did come by just to congratulate you both. It's really too bad that Jaime has what, one week, two weeks left? That's what's making you look so blue, right?"

Ryan's hand pressed more firmly into the small of Jaime's back and she felt heartened by his continued presence at her side.

Elise crossed back to where her bag sat on the ground, pulling it up and over her shoulder in one fluid motion. With a hand on her sunglasses atop her head, she said, "See you later Ryan. And good luck with school this year, Jaime. It's so great that we have teachers as dedicated and steadfast as you."

She left the shop.

Ryan's hand on her lower back slid away, leaving Jamie to wilt as he followed the path Elise had just taken to lock the front door.

"Are you okay?" His expression was searching.

Jaime's cheeks flushed, her lip quivering. Her plan was to sound strong, to sound confident in this conversation. To find a voice that could convince him she had never meant to let the lie sit so long between them.

Instead, she stood crying, voice breaking as the speech she'd prepared in her head fell apart.

"What is going on?" Ryan asked, reaching for her. "What am I missing here?"

"She's in love with you," Jaime said, pushing herself back, stepping away from him as tears fell and she steeled herself for the conversation she'd been delaying all summer.

Ryan shook his head. "Not Elise." He sighed and grabbed the back of his neck. "But if I tell you the truth, you might not believe me."

The habit of delaying her admission was strong. Jaime wiped her cheek. "Try me."

"Elise wanted me to be her sperm donor. She first asked a year ago, and I told her I'd think about it after the divorce was all settled. Since the beginning of the summer, she's been... well. I think it's been tough for her. I shouldn't have strung her along."

If it weren't for the fact that her nose was running, her mascara clumping so that black dots edged the bottom of her vision, Jaime might have felt embarrassed about the sputtering noises that rose from the bottom of her throat. "What?" she finally managed. "Her what?"

He shuffled from side-to-side then reached out for Jaime's hand, curling it into his. "It's not something I think I could do. But last year, I didn't have the words to say no."

Jaime stared, wide-eyed. "She threatened me to back off. To leave you alone. Because you were hers."

"She only wanted me for a very—" He grinned, blushing. "Very, small part of me."

"Oh." Jaime couldn't think of anything more to say. All that she had thought of Elise was flipped on its head and the blankness that followed the perfect opportunity for Jaime to avoid what she was supposed to be saying. She shook herself. No more. It was time. She squared her shoulders. "Ryan."

He pulled her close, bringing their held hands to his chest. "I promise I'll explain everything. I know it sounds sketchy, like a movie pact where you're going to get pulled into something messy, but I promise, it's as simple as her asking me if I'd consider sperm donorship. I was surprised, and I didn't say no outright because it made me feel like I was denying someone their dream. But I don't think I could do it. And it's why I never mentioned it."

"No," Jaime interrupted. "I'm not upset. I'm surprised too." She breathed him in, allowing herself to soak in their closeness in case this was the end of it. "It's you who should be upset."

"Why?" Ryan pulled back a fraction, enough so that with his free hand, he could wipe the tears from her cheeks.

"Because what Elise said was true." Jaime looked down to where Ryan's thumb still rested against hers, the casual interlacing of their fingers. It felt so right, to have woken up that morning next to him, her face nestled into the groove between his shoulder blade and spine, as natural as touching him now. But knowing what she knew, what she'd been warned, she was likely giving all that up. Her throat felt swollen, giving her words a hoarse, hushed quality. She continued anyhow. "I'm going back to school in two weeks. I made you believe that I'd quit so that I could keep the job here through the summer, but I was always going to go back to teaching."

His palm slid from hers so that her hand was left open and alone in the space between them. "Why didn't you tell me?"

"I needed this job. And then, and then, because I didn't want you to hate me."

"Why would I hate you?"

"Because it turns out that I am the flake that you accused me of being when I first started here."

"Taking the time to learn every plant in this shop, being careful with the routines of this place, and putting up with me is anything but flakey."

"Because I'm just another person who has abandoned you in some way."

Ryan blew out through his cheeks, shaking his head. "What are you talking about, Jaime? Between Elise and now this, I'm trying hard to keep track of what's happening here. You're losing me. You couldn't tell me that you hadn't quit your job because I have abandonment issues?"

"Your mother—"

"My mother—" He interrupted, his voice raised and ratcheted by a disbelieving laugh that made Jaime's eyes well up again. "Of course." His leftover smile was an awful mockery of the real one, a stretch of his lips that looked more like a grimace.

"She warned me not to tell you," Jaime said, quiet. Her nose ran, and she dabbed at it with her wrist, struggling to keep herself upright. None of this was happening how she'd imagined, and somehow, it was worse than the yelling she'd expected, the shouting she'd prepared for, the accusations that she was just like everyone else. "But Ryan, I can work every single Saturday. I'll keep the shop open for you on Sundays if you like, I'll be here every weeknight evening. I can—"

"Just stop."

"Ryan, I—" She did what he asked and stopped. There wasn't anything else she could say. There was likely nothing that would make this better. She pushed into the fleshiest part of her palm, trying to find the pressure point. Her breathing coming in gasps. She pushed harder.

"Mom is obsessed with making me this victim of childhood trauma that I'm not. You heard her say that she's been with her boyfriend Gerald for years, yes? And that I still haven't met this guy who's apparently an important part of her life because she doesn't want to hurt me. Do you see how *that's* hurtful? That she has a partner I'm cut off from because I acknowledged that I was hurt when my father left while I was just a little kid. When the next family got broken up too? You even asked me about all this, going as far as to ask who I talked to about it all. Do you remember me telling you that I'm fine? That I've even gone to counseling for all this?"

"You did," Jaime said. Her whole body was stiff, her eyelids heavy as they grew more swollen with each passing minute. Everything he said was true. She should have trusted him, and beyond that, she should have believed in herself enough to recognize that the flakiness he was talking about wasn't whether she'd commit herself to the shop forever but commit in the time that she was here.

"Did I ever say that my mother is a person I confide in?"

"No."

"And I'd say that it was pretty clear that she's got a fairly out of proportion method of protecting me. One that cuts me off from getting to make new relationships and expand my family." Ryan sucked in both of his cheeks, setting his jaw. "I wouldn't have hated you, Jaime. You accused me of acting like a child before, but I'm adult enough to appreciate when a person has a passion for what they do. It didn't seem right to me that you'd quit teaching because of how much you love it. But I figured that was something that you were working through. Because of how much you love it, I knew your time at Plant Life wasn't forever. I'm only angry that you didn't just tell me. You should have told me. Especially after these last two weeks."

"You're right." She couldn't bring herself to make eye contact with him. She was nodding, trying to keep up with the sudden reversal of how she'd understood things to be with how they were. This perspective— where all her beliefs about why she had to keep her secret were upended into a tidy simple sentence—she'd done what she'd been told instead of doing what had felt right—was hard to bear. It put her so firmly in the wrong that all Jaime could imagine next was getting into her bed and never leaving it again.

"I think I need to leave now," she said. The desire to curl up under her covers and hide became a heavy fatigue that pulled on her, dragging her toward the door. "I'll be back tomorrow," she added, chancing a glance at Ryan.

His face was pale, splotches of redness dotting his cheekbones. He took a deep breath. "You don't have to."

His words thudded against her chest. "All I can say is that I'm sorry." Swallowing the sob that threatened to overtake her apology, Jaime turned, fetched her bag from its cubbyhole and left the shop, leaving the coffee that Ryan had bought for her sitting on the counter. She looked back one last time before closing the back hallway door. Ryan leaned against the herb table, his head between his shoulders. The shop bright, the mid-morning sun streaming through the windows and making the greenery come to life in a dazzling array of hues and varying textures. Jaime swallowed, pulling her lips inward as she said a silent goodbye to both the shop and to Ryan.

The door closed with a soft click, like the drop of a curtain.

Chapter Sixteen

A second pail of balls thumped onto the ground beside the first, rattling the contents like dozens of eggs all trying to hatch on top of each other. Jaime glanced toward the noise, and without looking to her new benefactor of golf balls, leaned over to grab one, balance it on the tee, line up her club, and take a deep breath.

"Hello Bree," said Bree in a breathy, falsetto voice. "So nice to see you again, bestie. Can't wait to finally fill you in after all those cryptic messages from the last three days."

Jaime swung, club connecting with the ball in a gratifying crack, watching it arc over the grass into obsolescence. She held her twisted position, waiting for the landing, remaining quiet.

Bree's falsetto voice picked back up, even breathier. "And I've spent the whole weekend processing what happened so I can finally explain it to you. I'm struggling because I was just really obsessed with this guy but then I lied to him about a few things, and he freaked out because I'm leaving his small plant business that he's way too prissy about."

Jaime righted her posture, balancing the now standing club with the palm of her hand as it waivered on the grass. "He wasn't upset that I was leaving Plant Life."

"Finally," Bree said in her normal voice. She sat on

the grass, spreading her legs wide in front of her. "So, what happened? Your texts literally told us nothing."

Another ball lined up on the tee. Another swing. "He was upset that I didn't trust him enough to just tell him the truth." She didn't add that he'd essentially, through their time together, given her every reason to trust him, and she didn't elaborate by telling Bree how the confession had finally occurred either. That it had been Elise that had forced her hand—that even once Jaime had made the decision, it still took an exterior push to mobilize her. She lined up another ball.

"I mean—" Bree slapped at a mosquito on her leg "—you know I'm on your side, but I think what he's saying makes sense."

Jaime drew her lips in, chewing on the top. She nodded.

"So, because everything that actually made him upset was legit versus some dumb reason about people leaving his shop, and because you are a thousand-percent into him, you've tried to call him again, yes?"

She balanced another ball on the tee. Swung. Too loose though, the landing far left of where she'd intended. Overhead, the sky was a mix of blue and orange, more golfers turning back to go home to dinner, to partners waiting for them. Mondays were usually the slowest day at the drive, and Jaime was grateful that she hadn't had to take turns with other golfers like the last two evenings. She could swing uninterrupted until she was out of balls. Jaime resettled the tee and reached into the basket again.

"You've tried to talk with him again?"

Once again, her swing was bad, and the ball flew far from her target, skittering to one of the netting's long sides. Jaime checked for a range picker or other golfers to give a saluting apology, but the place was empty save for a couple other diehards who were either still there to stress relieve like her, or practice, all of them unimpacted by the rookie angle of her last hit.

"Jaime?"

She exhaled hard and slumped her shoulders. "I blocked his number after he sent me a text saying not to come in for the next two weeks."

"What? Did he say anything else?"

"That I was still on the payroll, but that he didn't want my last two weeks to be spent miserably when I should be resting for school."

"Do we think that's nice? Not nice?" Bree slapped at another mosquito.

"I don't know," admitted Jaime. Ryan's texts could be read one of two ways. One, a man trying hard to keep his cool and give her space so that they could move on from the morning's fight and her bad communication, or two, and the more likely scenario, he was texting her from the position of wanting space that was meant to be permanent. If he had lied to her all summer, rejecting everything she'd told him about herself in favor of some story one of her parents had led with, would she want to give him another chance? Jaime didn't know. And not knowing made the possibility of having to suffer through a formal rejection too painful to consider. So, she'd blocked his number. She'd return the paycheck if it came, but she wasn't going to set herself up to hear something that would torment her for years to come.

It was easier to let these beautiful aspects of summer slip away in painful, miserable silence. Better that than ruining the memories with new ones that ate at the edges of those moments when it felt like what she and Ryan were sharing was the beginning of forever.

"You're running away from him then," Bree said, her tone brutal in its stiffness.

"How can I come back from months of lying, all because of something his mother said that contradicted something he later told me himself?" Jaime let the golf club fall and sat beside her friend. "And how am I going to get through this year at school, especially at the beginning when I need to be at my best, if I'm distracted and heartbroken."

"It seems to me like you're already heartbroken."

"Maybe I am. But it doesn't hurt as bad if I'm not positive that he wanted to end things."

Bree scoffed. "I love you, but that's stupid. You're essentially saying that you'd rather miss out on possibly making up with Ryan and getting back on track with the relationship that was making you crazy happy, than risk hearing someone vent because you screwed up."

"You know that I hate fighting." Jaime held up a finger. "And I've been doing lots of it. Look at how I stood up to Gretchen. To Mom and Dad. Even though it makes me feel sick. And that's how I've been feeling since Friday morning, like I want to throw up."

"Yeah. But look at how being brave has helped you. You and Gretchen are now *talking*—she's probably going to dump her shitty husband who abused not only her but you. And your parents are being more supportive than they ever have been because you finally forced it as their only option."

Jaime lifted her heels off the grass, hugging her knees to her chest and rocking on her butt. Her jeans would be covered in green stains, but that was a problem for a different day, a laundry day.

"Life's sometimes hard, Jaime. I've said it before, but you're going to have to face some fights for the things that matter. Or else they'll stop mattering."

"Is that the pep talk you give your employees?"

"Oh, hell yeah. Then I like to confuse them with the lecture about how the customer's always right and it's better to just let the old ladies have their hundred-year-old, expired coupons rather than go to war over it."

Jaime tucked her face against her thighs, laughing.

"Ryan's no coupon, girl. You going to go after your man, or what?"

"Maybe."

"Maybe?" Bree smacked her back. "I just gave the speech of a lifetime, and I get a maybe in return?"

Jaime inched closer to Bree until their shoulders touched. "Thank you for helping me to be brave."

It was true what Bree had said. Every time that Jaime had stood up for herself and faced a conflict that she'd been avoiding, things had turned out for the better. Her relationships more solid, and her understanding of the people she loved, and them of her, improved. How different would this summer had been if she'd listened to her gut in those first weeks and told Ryan the simple truth straight away?

And though her gut was currently confused and hurting, not giving any clear answers, that's what she had Bree for. Jaime was determined to begin listening to—no, trusting—her own intuition. Maybe she needed to also work at leaning on the people that she loved best. Jaime swallowed hard. "I'll talk to him if you promise to let me come over to your house immediately after."

"So, tomorrow?"

"We'll see." Jaime rubbed her swollen eyes as the hooded lights attached to the top of the range netting clicked on, illuminating circular patches of lawn. She nudged Bree's foot with her own. "Did I tell you that it turns out that CEO lady, Elise, wasn't even interested in dating him? She wanted him to be her sperm donor. And she thought I'd wreck her chance of that."

Bree snorted. "No way. Oh my god. Now you've got to get back together with him so we can have what's left of that story."

****

Jaime puttered around the kitchen. Pretending to cleanup when really, there wasn't much left to do. Unable to sleep the last week, she'd scrubbed the counters and reorganized the pantry—waited for the golf course to open each morning. Without the means of implementing a complete personality transplant, one where she sought out confrontation like a woman unleashed, where she raced to Ryan's house and demanded that he listen to her apology one more time, Jaime waited until Friday before deciding she was ready go back to Plant Life. She hadn't unblocked Ryan's number; she'd do that as soon as she got an answer from him in person. And she'd suffered Bree's daily text messages filled with hundreds of question marks and face smacking emojis because of her continued avoidance. Avoidance, yes. But avoidance that now felt less like hiding and more like Jaime taking a moment to breathe.

She'd needed these last four days to prepare herself for both possible outcomes. Either Ryan forgave her, or he wouldn't. Either way, in a matter of days, she'd be back at work, doing a job that she loved, with friends and family around to support her through whatever happened. Recognizing that privilege kept Jaime from spiraling into soap opera daydreams of worst-case scenario.

Either Ryan would forgive her, or he wouldn't. And no matter what, she would be okay.

The follow-up to that mantra was a cinching tightness across her abdomen that was part hope, part fear. Jaime wanted to go back to waking up to fresh flowers and coffee at Ryan's, their long talks over toast in the morning and pasta in the evenings on his back deck, surrounded by flowers and the spindly green tops of growing vegetables. Tracing each other's outlines at night as they laid together in bed. His side, her side already defined. In the last two weeks, Jaime had fallen in love with a routine that had felt as close to happily-ever-after as real life ever came.

She picked up her keys from the table beside her apartment front door, locked up, and got into her car for the trip downtown.

The humidity was hitting its summertime peak, and half brick, half siding-board houses gave way to the full-brick structures of downtown. Crepe myrtles lining the streets with their tufted crowns of pinks and purple unless they'd been given the brutal trimming that Ryan lamented. Jaime's heart began to beat harder. The world pressed into her with its massage of sticky heat, tunneling her thoughts and vision until the adrenaline coursed fast through her bloodstream. This was it. This was her braving the biggest confrontation of the summer yet. With the others, the outcome was mostly clear. With this one, she had to find the courage to face a future where what she wanted might not be possible.

Bypassing the alley entrance to the parking at the back of the building, Jaime found a metered spot out front and stopped the car. It was too bright outside to see clearly through the many-paned windows, and the brass lettering of Plant Life glowed like the scripted beacons in fantasy films where entry beyond the golden, shimmering words meant the start of a journey.

Either he forgave her, or he wouldn't. Jaime reached for the door handle and rested her hand atop it, trying to calm the rush of her heartbeat and the growing warmth in her cheeks.

Either way, she would be okay. She was a capable and more confident person every day. No matter what, this was something she'd recover from. She'd survived the breakup with Jonathan, hadn't she? Where he'd warned her that without him, she was nothing. In fact—she had braved him a second time, breaking up with him again. She pushed the door open, barely registering the familiar tinkle of the bells on the interior side.

The normalcy of Plant Life's smell, the stillness of the many living things housed in one small space immediately calmed Jaime, blanketing her in familiarity. So focused on how much she missed Ryan, how much she'd come to care for him, she hadn't realized that the same was true of his shop. This place had become a second home, one that she was happy to be back inside of.

She let her eyes adjust to the lighting inside before finally, looking up to the back counter.

It wasn't Ryan standing behind the till.

Instead, it was a young man with black hair and a matching black tee shirt, who smiled politely before saying, "Can I help you?"

Like a fish swimming toward its goal, only to be yanked out of the water by a hidden hook, Jaime sputtered. "I, well—I." She looked around the shop, losing all the momentum that had brought her this far.

"Are you looking for a plant, or something to help one that you already have?" The boy asked, voice kind. He seemed bolstered by her incoherence, as if her bad job of being the customer was somehow making him a better employee.

"New plant," Jaime lied, her cheeks hot as she looked around the shop one more time for Ryan.

"What size were you thinking? We just got a bunch of really good-looking *dracaena* plants. They work well in dim areas and are great filterers." The boy moved toward a line of new plants with long, cascading leaves that looked like a cross between a palm tree and a yucca.

Jaime's smile was tight, and she could feel herself turtling back into her shell after poking her head all the way out, prepared for hard, necessary conversations and the possibility of rejection. "I need something safe for a classroom." She was pretty sure that the Janet Craig variety of *dracaena* he was now holding up was nontoxic, but her trust in herself was wavering.

"Oh, super safe for kids. But not for pets. It'd be bad news if a dog or cat friend ate one of these." The boy held the plant higher and smiled. "No pets in the classroom, right?"

She shook her head. "I'll take it."

At the cash register, Jaime had to resist the urge to help him with the computer till's passcode after he typed it incorrectly the first two tries. She chewed on her cheeks, unclear whether she wanted the back door to open, revealing Ryan, or was anxious to escape before that happened. The door remained shut. No one else came into the shop.

"Do you need some help getting it out to your car?"

Jaime smiled, thanking him. She could do it by herself.

With the new *dracaena* under her arm and balanced on her hip, she crossed the space to leave, feeling like a failure. It wasn't until she started to open the front door, prompting the tinkle of the front door bells, like the chime of a clock reminding her that her time was almost up, that Jaime stopped indulging the lie that she was simply a regular customer.

She'd come here for Ryan, not a plant.

Jaime closed the door and turned around. "Do you know if Ryan is in today?"

"Ryan?" The boy brushed off his tee shirt and stood. "Yeah, definitely. He only left to run a couple errands. Should be back any minute." He gave a slight shimmy then pointed to the chair behind him. "You wanna wait for him? Or can I take a message?"

She rebalanced the plant and considered. Talking with Ryan when he came back meant giving the speech she'd rehearsed in front of this new kid. It was hard enough to say what she needed to say without an audience. "Maybe just tell him that I stopped by," she said.

He smiled. "Can I get a name?"

"Oh." Jaime flushed. "Jaime Krause." She nodded at the plants all around here. "I used to work here."

"Gotcha." The boy was busy fetching a pen and a sticky. "I'll let him know."

"Okay, thanks."

"Okay."

Silence made her lingering awkward and another minute ticked by without Ryan or anyone else to break the stagnating stretch of time.

"I'll just be off then," Jaime finally said. She turned, pushed through the door, and nearly smacked into someone on the sidewalk.

"Oh," she said, righting herself and checking on the person who had been about to enter Plant Life. "Are you okay?"

Helen brushed Jaime's upper arm reassuringly. "Fine, fine. But how are you?"

The blush that had started in the store intensified. Not only had Jamie endured embarrassing herself in front of what must be her replacement, but now she was going to have to force small talk with the mother of the man that she'd come to throw herself at. "I'm alright, and you?"

"You've met our new guy, Samson, then."

Jaime nodded, her ears superheating.

"Between you and me, he doesn't hold a candle to you, but with you leaving, Ryan finally dug through old applications and began reaching out to people. You really showed him how useful it is to have someone else around."

Jamie's throat felt slick, and she swallowed, unsure how much Ryan had told Helen about her departure. About them.

"I know he was really upset about you leaving, though. And you didn't hear it from me, but he's been pretty blue." Helen checked her smart watch and then looked to the shop. "I was actually headed in to see if our boy wanted to get some lunch. You should join. I know he'd love to see you." She smiled, winking behind her large-frame, red glasses.

Jaime's feet began to feel tingly with the need to leave. If Ryan showed up now, she'd have to grovel in front of the new guy Samson, and now, Ryan's mother too. There was bravery and then there was self-ruin. She didn't have the courage to beg for forgiveness in front of a whole group. And the longer Helen talked, the more it became clear that Ryan hadn't been very forthright in his story about her departure from Plant Life. "Helen, I'd love to, but I've really got to go. I told the bo—Samson, to give Ryan a message from me."

"Okay, dearie. I do hope you stay in touch throughout the school year."

"Of course." Jamie hiked the *dracaena* up and started to walk around Helen to get to her car. Though something deep inside her was screaming that she still had work to do, rooting her in place and making her call back out to Helen.

"Yes?" Helen responded, hand on the door of Plant Life.

"It's none of my business—" Jaime dug her toes into the pavement, shifting the pressure from one leg to the other. "But I really think you should introduce Ryan to Gerald."

Helen squinted, and Jaime resettled the pot against her side, bracing, needing to say this, needing to be bold for Ryan even if she never saw him again. "He'd really like to meet him. And Ryan's stronger than you think. Even if a goodbye was necessary, he could handle it."

Helen's eyes were shrewd, and she adjusted her glasses. "I take it that your goodbye went better than we expected?"

Jaime shook her head. "It's not about me. I just

know that he'd really like the chance to be a bigger part of your life."

Helen's nod was slow, deliberate. She looked to the shop and then back at Jaime. "You're probably right, sweetie. But if I'm allowed to make a suggestion too, I suggest you stay here and wait for Ryan. I think he'd like that even more than making old-Gerald's acquaintance."

"I wish I could," Jaime said, the energy rushing out of her. She'd maxed out her offensive reserves and was retreating to shield herself, back in the comfort of defensive language and communication. To be able to have the conversation she and Ryan needed, she needed some time to recover.

"I left a message," she said again, then waved, and got into her car.

****

The *dracaena* Janet Craig had been one of the first things Jaime unloaded into her new classroom. She'd considered bringing the begonia that Ryan had gifted her early in the summer as well, but ultimately decided to leave it at home on her bedside table. She hadn't heard back from him after that day at Plant Life but still considered it a win. At the very least, for the measure of peace from the effort and her conversation with Helen.

Jaime hadn't put everything right, but she'd done more than she'd planned on earlier in the week, enabling enough confidence that she was able to spend the rest of her time before school focusing on curriculums and hunting for cheap supplies. The driving range stayed busy in the evenings because of the collective knowledge that summer was winding down, but she'd been able to stake out a spot for herself each night, sending balls flying. A number of them landing on target. Her dad even joined her one of the days.

And Bree had been better than true to her word, seeing Jaime almost daily, no longer pushing her to engage Ryan again, now that Jaime had put herself out there and tried. Jaime walked back out to the car, pushing the cart that she was using to lug stuff across the school property and into her classroom. Next was the pile of books that had been donated for her reading corner. Books that she would be able to let her students take home and keep if they wanted.

Finding middle-grade books, books that bridged the space between picture dependent reading and novels, was harder. Lots of people bought their children board books and stacks of multi-colored hardbacks, but less people bought their children and then donated the stories for older kids. It was those that had made the biggest difference in young Jamie's life, though.

It was for the *Ramona* series, reading *The Boxcar Children*, and *The Babysitter's Club* that little Jaime had stayed up for, clicking her alarm clock to keep the snooze light lit, illuminating the words that kept her up at night. It was rarer for picture books to have the same lasting and memorable hold, and it was for those pivotal moments that Jaime taught. Moments where a book could make a child sit for hours in one spot, creating core memories and stirring empathy simply because the sentences were beautiful. Where a previous interpretation of the world was upended, readying the reader for a world like the one Jaime had lived in, her last two weeks at Plant Life.

She pushed the loaded cart through the main doors, shivering with anticipation of another school year as she headed down the hall. She'd learned that to get into her classroom, she had to, with one hand on the cart, prop the door and at the same time, nudge the cart into the opening as she leaned. Once the cart was wedged in the door, the angle had to be just right or risk toppling everything as soon as she applied some force.

She maneuvered herself back behind the cart, took a deep breath and then pushed. Yet there was no work to it at all. Expecting heavy resistance, the cart sailed smoothly into the classroom, forcing Jaime to take lunging steps to keep up. She almost fell from the surprise.

Inside the door, Jaime straightened, still unsure what had just happened.

Ryan stood on the other side of the cart. He put his hands in his pockets. "Hi."

The stumble from earlier gave way to a sense of free fall. Jaime couldn't seem to climb out of the sensation to find words. Her grip tightened around the cart handles as she opened and closed her mouth.

"Both Samson and Mom said you came by the shop, but I missed you. I've been trying to message and call you, but I can't get through."

She'd forgotten to unblock his number after she'd left the shop. Bree was going to give her hell.

"I'm sorry," Jaime said, instead of explaining that she'd been stupid, so terribly stupid, blocking him because she was afraid to hear him say that he was angry. That he didn't want to be with her the way that she still wanted to be with him. That she may have ruined everything with her cowardice. So, she said the one thing that had been the same throughout all her practiced speeches that summer. "I'm so sorry, Ryan."

His hands slid from his pockets, and he put them on

the cart, opposite from hers'. The tick of the giant analog clock on the classroom wall counted the seconds for them, screeches from down the hall signaling that fellow teachers were busy rearranging desks and other furniture, many of them here with their spouses to help with the process. "I tried to call you after that morning. Many times."

"I blocked your number," Jaime admitted. She took a deep breath, rocking back on her heels. "I was scared."

"Of what?"

"That I'd ruined everything."

Ryan shifted his weight from one foot to the other. "Isn't that why you refused to tell me about teaching before too?"

"Maybe." Jaime put one of her hands to her cheek, trying to stem what she was sure looked like a blotchy redness that only further highlighted how stupid she felt.

"I was scared too," Ryan said.

She dropped her hand. "You were?"

"Yeah." He gave a half laugh that finished as a cough. "At first, I was scared that I'd been too much of an asshole to you when I told you that you should have told me about—" He gestured around the classroom, "All this. But then I was scared that you were having second thoughts because of what I told you about Elise."

Jaime couldn't help herself; she smiled. "I mean, I'm definitely curious."

"And then I was just scared that you didn't feel the same as me after this summer. That going back to the classroom wasn't just an out from working at the shop." He put his hands back into his pockets, his face open, eyes unblinking.

The clocked ticked another second.

"I was scared to hear that was what you wanted," Jaime said, her voice a breath. Her hand slipped on the handle of the cart, and she grabbed it with the other, steadying the tremble that had developed.

"Never." He stepped out from behind the cart and closed the space between them by another foot. "When I couldn't get ahold of you, I was sure that's how it was."

"No." Jaime's lip quivered, a pressure behind her eyes threatening tears. She didn't want him to stop talking. It was supposed to be her, laying all her cards out on the table, and throwing herself at him, but his words sounded like chocolate tasted. And she was hungry for them.

"Then you came to the shop."

"I was looking for you. After—after, I forgot that I had blocked your number. I slept with it on loud, hoping you'd call."

"Oh." He grinned. "I tried. I even went full creep and came by your apartment."

"When?" Jaime hadn't known that he'd tried to visit. The thought of him waiting outside the door, no one answering, and leaving, thinking that she might have intentionally ignored his arrival made her want to throw her arms around him and repeat over and over that she'd wanted to see him every minute of the last few week. That each day had gone by mired in thoughts about him and plans on how to win him back.

"The night after you came to the shop."

"I was with Bree, then."

He took another step forward. "When you didn't answer then either, I really thought that was it. I decided to leave you alone until you came and found me again."

"But you didn't."

"No. Mom framed that damn magazine spread and put it all over the shop. I've been working, looking at your face since Friday, and this morning, I couldn't take it anymore."

Jaime grabbed one of her forearms. "Please tell me you forgive me. I know what I did was stupid and awful, but I swear, I only lied to you about the job because I didn't want to give you a reason to shut me out. I—"

"I'm glad you're teaching, Jaime." Ryan closed the rest of the space between them and put his hand on her cheek. "And I can see why you did what you did."

She leaned into him. "I've really missed you."

"I've missed you more."

Abruptly, he took a step back, his hand sliding off her and back to his side, where Jamie wanted nothing more than to scoop it up and wrap it around her, pulling him back. She narrowed her eyes.

"I messed up. I had this all planned out." He cleared his throat and intensified his eye contact, like he was trying to initiate the staring game from across a classroom.

She smiled, inching backward, waiting.

"Jaime." He corrected his posture, still maintaining the unflinching stare. "When I heard you came into my shop, even standing up to my terrifying mother, I learned to hope as I have never hoped before."

Jaime grabbed his arms, pulling him into her embrace. Into his chest, smiling, she said, "Are you trying to use a Mr. Darcy quote to win me over?"

"I've had nothing but time to research ways to win you back. I told you. I'm not good with words. I'm never going to win an award for a speech or a letter. But Jaime, I'll plagiarize the fuck out of some romances for you any day. Just to get you back. I thought about coming here in tights."

"You stole from one of my favorites," she said. Nestling into him, she added, "You in tights though, that might be an actual favorite."

"I'll bust them out tonight." He hugged her closer, kissing her forehead. "Did it work even without them?"

"You had me at hello."

"I don't know what movie that's from, but I guarantee it's not from one of my favorites."

"Actually—" Jaime rose onto tiptoes, centered her face in front of Ryan's, coming nose-to-nose with him. "I don't know which one it's from either."

"I'll teach you my favorites later."

"It's a date."

Their kiss was delicate, both of them still tender with the other, as if what they had was yet fragile and needed the gentlest of touches. But in it, Jaime felt a whirlwind of belonging and the knowledge that this man was worth fighting for, this man was worth braving difficult words and hard truths. She pulled him closer, kissing the corners of his mouth, up his jaw, then along his cheek over to his forehead, which she also dotted in kisses.

After, both of them grinning, Jaime put Ryan to work, helping her rearrange the classroom's new bookshelves and line them with early reader chapter books and hardcovers about adventure, bravery, and above all, love.

Epilogue

"I didn't get a party for my divorce," Ryan said, opening Jaime's car door for her. He loved the way she met his eyes every time he did this for her, the tug of her shirt as she leaned to get out, molding to each of her perfect boobs. Nine months later and he couldn't get enough of being the one to bring her a cup of coffee each morning, to rub her feet as she graded papers. Even if she did so, chewing on the end of her pen. He'd gone so stupid for her that it was equally gratifying to be the one to throw said pen out, before she swallowed any plastic.

"You wanted a divorce party? You were mad that we took you out for dinner."

Jaime's smile was that sly one, the one she used after a quiet joke during a movie, or in a crowd. Around that smile, it was hard to remember that it hadn't yet been a year since the paperwork on his divorce had finalized. This woman here and now had taken over his brain, making it impossible to think of what came before Jaime.

He cleared his throat and closed the space between them, nudging her against the back of the car, bending into her until his lips were on her neck. "Appetizers, not even a full dinner."

"You poor, poor man. How can I make it up to you?" Jaime put her palm against his chest, pushing him back a step as she spread her fingers and lifted her eyebrows, looking down, focusing on the crotch of his shorts. Shorts that felt way too short. Definitely too tight. The things he did for her.

"This is why I can't wear these," he complained. They were going to need to take the walk to the front door slowly. He rearranged himself then grabbed her hand, interlacing their fingers. "You stop remembering that my eyes are up here."

"But you look so good in them." Jaime laughed then slipped to the side, turning to the backseat door to grab the beer and wine they'd brought for Gretchen's party.

"Here, take this, will you?" She handed him two of the six packs and cradled the wine in her arm. Ryan took the beer, and then the bottle of wine as well.

Together, they walked to the front door where Jaime knocked once, then tried the door. Muffled music became loud as it gave way, throwing bright white light onto the porch step that was bathed in the yellow of the bulb beside the door, attracting moths and buzzing June-bugs. The foyer was a strip of parquet that opened onto a hallway and a staircase.

People hovered by the kitchen entry at the back of the hall, and Jaime slid her hand up Ryan's arm, holding onto him as she walked toward the loudest part of the house. Ryan was already tired. The noise was too much, everything too bright. But her skin on his was enough.

She wanted to be here, so here he was. Noise and all.

"Jaime, Ryan, you made it!" Gretchen's cheeks were already flushed, her smile wide, and one of her shirt straps drifting over toward her shoulder. Her red Solo cup sloshed over as she made her way around the kitchen island, eyes glazed.

"Happy divorce," Jaime said, in a sing-song voice. Ryan gave a two-finger salute. The Krause family seemed to prefer Ryan seen, not heard. That suited him just fine.

Gretchen bowed. "Thank you, thank you. Now, put those drinks on the back counter and help yourselves to whatever you'd like."

Ryan grabbed each of them a beer from the pack

they brought. If he was only going to have one drink tonight, he wanted it to be good. A group of doctors or nurses—exchanging hospital stories that made Ryan shudder—waved Jaime over, obviously recognizing her from one of Gretchen's parties that Ryan hadn't been to. Or, one that came before him.

He stood alone, appreciating the surround sound Lady Gaga, but not quite ready to be alone with the reverberation of her base beat, crowded by drunk people shouting and laughing. Gretchen began to yell, "Shots."

Pushed by people trying to get to the tequila, flowing from bottle to mini paper cups held high, Ryan scanned the room for Jaime. One more sweep and she was next to Gretchen, her face dewy and as beautiful as ever, hair curling at the ends and a little bit wild. That was his favorite. She leaned into her sister, presumably trying to hear Gretchen, and began laughing.

He took another sip of beer and, sure that Gretchen would keep Jaime close, so that she wouldn't be forced to try and socialize with strangers, he made his way to the back door.

Outside, the air hummed, the approach of summer obvious. The smell of the cooling, breaking humidity perfumed the air. At the start of spring when planting was meant to begin in earnest, Gretchen had asked Ryan for help in the garden. He'd brought over new hydrangea plants, a staple of any garden he tended thanks to his long history with the bushy flowers. But he'd also planted cosmos, cone flowers, peonies, and ground cover. Things that were generally low maintenance. That didn't mean no maintenance though. Weeds detracted from the beauty of the peonies. None of the cosmos had been dead-headed and thus, had been left to droop and brown.

A little care and there would have been twice the blooms. He needed a pair of clippers.

A few people walked outside to smoke, and Ryan straightened, trying to give them his best take-your-cigarette-and-get-the-fuck-out-of-here look. A doctor lived here for Christ's sake. And Gretchen had come to enough of the weekly family dinners that he knew she didn't need any extra job security.

The smokers stubbed out their cigarettes and slinked back to the house.

Ryan sighed, walked over, picked up the littered butts, then threw them into the metal trashcan Gretchen kept on the side of the house for yard waste.

Alone again, he began weeding. He didn't even notice when the back door slid open.

"You found your happy place then?"

Despite the slight fuzziness, probably from trying to keep pace with her sister's drinking, her voice was magic. Ryan turned on his heel to face Jaime. Her eyes sparkled in the low light and her cheeks flushed with that same grin from earlier. The one for him.

"Look at this mess." He pushed off the ground with his knuckles, wiping his brow, and gestured at the flower beds. "It's like she doesn't even care."

"I do," said Jaime.

He didn't know how she did it. Change her tone ever so slightly, enough to make him forget everything else he'd been doing, his focus shifting to her so fast that he could almost feel the tug of the zipline push she'd initiated. Jaime. His Jaime. Of course, he knew that she cared. She cared more than anybody he'd ever met.

He wiped his hands on his shorts and held out his arms. "It's why I love you."

Jaime walked into his open arms, pushing her face into his chest, and making him ache with how much he wanted to tell her all that he felt. He didn't have the words. She wrapped her arms around his neck. "I love you, too."

"Let's go home," he said. He kissed the top of her head. Then her neck, dotting her shoulders and arms with the brush of his lips. Her shirt was a problem. It was getting in the way and would need to go.

"Oh, Ryan."

His breathing quickened. He loved when she said his name, especially like that. "Was that a yes?" he asked.

She smiled. "You want me to say it?"

"It's my favorite word." He wanted her to choose him. He wanted to hear her accept him over and over. First thing in the morning. At the end of the quick phone calls about what else they needed from the grocery store. When they were both exhausted after work. Someday, when they were late to bed because they'd been up taking care of their babies. When they were old and gray. It was the best word in the whole world.

"Yes," she said. "Forever, yes."

A word about the author...

Rachel Cooper is a Johns Hopkins University writing program graduate who believes that banter is the spice of life, that the job of contemporary romance is to prove healthy relationships can be oh-so steamy, and that there's nothing better than a happily-ever-after. Her happily-ever-after includes moving all over the world with her husband, daughters, and her adorable dog. Keeping her Duolingo streak alive, and of course, writing romance. www.rachelcooperromance.com